HOPE FOR THE INNOCENT

Caroline Dunford

ACCENT

First published in 2020 by Headline Accent
An imprint of HEADLINE PUBLISHING GROUP

1

Cataloguing in Publication Data is available from the British Library

ISBN 978 1 7861 5 7560

Typeset in 10.5/13pt Bembo Std by Jouve (UK), Milton Keynes

Printed and bound in Great Britain by Clays Ltd, Elcograf S.p.A.

HEADLINE PUBLISHING GROUP
An Hachette UK Company
Carmelite House
50 Victoria Embankment
London EC4Y 0DZ

www.headline.co.uk
www.hachette.co.uk

For my boys
Wolf, Xander and Marcus

And my parents
Jean and Llewellyn
who, as children, lived through the Blitz

Chapter One

'I think, if you really must do this,' said my mother, 'that you would be far better off accepting Amaranth's offer to present you at court rather than letting your grandmother do it.'

She was arranging flowers in a tall Chinese vase with a certain abruptness at the time. We were in the drawing room and neither of my parents had yet lit the fire. Their many years of living out in the Fens had accustomed them to a level of cold that I had quite forgotten during my warmer years up at Oxford. Several red and golden petals had already scattered onto the polished marquetry table. My father brushed them off with the edge of his sleeve and edged his chair closer to the unlit fire.

At home, on their country estate of White Orchards, my parents, as ever, presented an extraordinary picture. My mother, though of average height, always seems tall. Her wavy chestnut hair has recently begun to grey. She wears it long, the complete opposite of the current fashion, so it tumbles around her shoulders. This bohemian look was at odds with her fitted straight line blue dress that reached to her calves and onto which she had insisted her dressmaker sew large pockets – pockets which are forever stuffed with everything from string to crumpled notes (once, when I was little, I was almost sure I saw the butt of a handgun protruding, but my mother has always denied this).

My father sat there sucking the stem of his empty pipe. My mother had forbidden him to light it as the smell 'got into everything'. He is very pleased with himself that he has finally been able to grow a beard – albeit a white and fluffy one, in striking contrast to his hair, which remains dark. It makes him look like an owl.

He wore an elegant velvet crimson smoking jacket complete with an embroidered yellow dragon. On his head he sported a fez with a golden tassel, which, when he thought we weren't watching, he liked to swish from side to side like an elderly cat would its tail. Being round-faced, on the short side, and definitely comfortable of body, the fez doesn't suit him in the least, but it is a recent present from my Uncle Hans and he loves it dearly.

Even as we spoke the large central pane in the main window of the drawing room rattled. Momentarily diverted, my mother said, 'Bertram, have you not got Andrews to attend to that yet?'

'Poor beggar's still working away on the window of the second guest bedroom. Said it was fit to bust. Can't have that happening to a guest, don't you know?'

My mother sniffed. 'Your language, darling! We have been socially isolated too long. We must have a party.'

My father's eyes widened in alarm. 'You don't mean you're going to take this bally thing on, do you, Euphemia?' He cleared his throat and turned to me. 'I say, Hope, why do you want to do this wretched thing? I mean . . . of course, you can, if you want to. But all those balls and parties and things. Not quite your style, hmm?'

He blinked at me, looking like a cross between a startled bird of prey and a fakir. I winced slightly. My father likes to keep up with things; things in the press, things in the world, and things young people say and do. However, he infinitely prefers the world to stay at arm's length. He might be up with the world, but it is not to be up with him.

'Nonsense, Bertram,' interrupted my mother. 'It will do the girl good. It's about time she started thinking about what her place in the world will be.'

'You mean marrying,' said my father gloomily. 'I suppose London might be the place to find a husband. As long as she doesn't get involved with Fitzroy. He's still working down there, isn't he?'

My mother ignored the latter half of my father's statement, instead latching on to the part that challenged her views on women's rights. 'That is not the only option open to a modern young woman,' she snapped.

'Yes. Yes. I know,' said my father, 'but it's not as if she did particularly well at university.' He glanced over at me. 'Sorry, Hope.'

'To allay your fears, Bertram,' said my mother, 'we will not be involved. A girl can't have her mother as a sponsor.'

'But you said Bernie's mother is presenting her,' objected my father.

My mother ignored him, as she always did when he made a point that contradicted hers. 'Besides,' she said. 'I was never presented.'

'Ah, now I see why your mother has stirred all this up,' said my father. 'She never got to do the circuit – or whatever they call it – so this is her hour to shine!'

'Did you not hear me suggest that Hope avoids her grandmother as her sponsor?' said my mother.

I felt the conversation was leaving my control and with it any hope of a resolution, so I broke in.

'You are quite correct, Father,' I said. 'My degree is acceptable, but not of the calibre to suggest my future is in academia.'

'Such a pity,' said my mother. 'When I think of the opportunities that could have been opened up for you . . .'

'Being a ruddy mathematician,' said my father with some force. 'Don't see much fun in that.'

'If you are going to speak of my friend, and your daughter's Oxford sponsor, with such disdain . . .'

'I never said a bally thing about her . . .'

'Will you stop using that idiotic word. It doesn't even mean anything!'

'What are you talking about, Euphemia?'

'You know exactly . . .'

3

I withdrew quietly from the room. I knew from long experience that an acerbic and passionate row was brewing. My parents adored each other, but they did so loudly, quarrelsomely, and with their total attention focused on each other. It is the reason they have been able to live in rural desolation for so long. It suits my father, but my mother prefers company. However, she makes do with the occasional party as long as my father indulges her with enough contradictions.

Their voices rose in happy disharmony. I doubted they would recall my presence again before supper. I hoped that I had made my wishes clear enough that next time we spoke it would be considered a 'done deal' that I was to be presented at court. How well I might fare on the marriage front I had no idea, being brunette rather than fashionably blonde, and while I am fit enough, I have never been as thin-as-a-rail as is de rigueur among the flowers of the *Beau Monde*. Quite unforgivably, in the eyes of any editors of the popular fashion magazines, I have curves. I had no qualms about having to fend off unwanted proposals.

My godfather, Uncle Eric, who has known both my parents for a long time, had been strongly advising me by letter to find a separate way to establish myself. What he actually wrote was, 'My dear girl, if you don't get away from the pair of them, you will disappear utterly.' Uncle Eric is one of the few people who are aware of the services my parents have rendered for the country in the past. It has been alluded to in my presence, but never explained. I have long suspected that they miss the excitement of that time – and that, in some small way, I was meant to make up for it. I haven't. I was born on the last day of the Great War. I once overheard my mother describe me to my father as 'disappointingly accommodating'. Then my father's health declined a little more and their activities were curtailed even further. My father writes for the newspapers now, although he uses a different name, and my mother . . . I'm not entirely sure what she does, but she is often in her study with papers, writing letters and talking on the telephone that she had specially installed there. I don't believe they are unhappy unless, of course, you count the problem of what to do with me.

The whole idea of being presented at court had been brought up by my grandmother, who had discovered, through some diabolical power, that my great friend Bernie Woodford was to be presented this year despite being, like me, in her early twenties and also an Oxford graduate. The idea that it wasn't too late for me had caused her to condescend to pay us a visit. She had even ventured beyond the safe confines of her second husband's residence, a Bishop's Palace, which she rarely left as the Bishop was now extremely old and rather forgetful.

'Hope Rose must be presented at Court,' she had declared in her formal way. She has always hated the name Hope, describing it as 'frivolously modern'. 'If those Germans are about to do the dirty on us again, this may be her last chance.'

Of course, the conversation had then devolved into politics and I had quietly withdrawn.

Bernie had been adamant that it would be a great lark to do the whole season together. She had raised the idea a few days before our finals. 'Think about it, Stapleford,' she'd said, 'parties, boys, adventures and maybe even meeting *the Right One*. Something to look forward to after all our hard work!' I gave her a stern look. 'Oh, all right, after all *your* hard work. Please!'

She was sitting on the end of my narrow bed in college, waving her arms about so wildly as she spoke that she knocked a whole sheaf of papers off my desk. Being Bernie, she ignored this completely. When I went to retrieve them, she said, 'When will you learn? That is what your maid is for. Sit down.'

Bernie has champagne blond hair that in the right lighting positively glows. She pins it up into haphazard curls and waves that results in a style that reminds me of my struggles with geometry, they are so full of curvy complexity. She looks fashionable, if not downright sultry. She is tall and thin and wears a signature bright red lipstick that clashes with her hair. This, coupled with her faintly American accent, ensures she stands out from the crowd. She gazed at me with her large violet-blue eyes. 'We get to meet the King,' she said.

'He's already married,' I said.

'I know,' said Bernie, sniffing, 'and, by all accounts, not the kind of man to take a mistress. Besides, he stammers.'

I couldn't help pressing my hand to my forehead. 'Woodford, you cannot talk like that. If anyone heard you . . .'

'Pooh!' said Bernie. 'It's only you I'm talking to. I know you'd never say anything. Mouth tighter than a clam.'

I sighed. 'Why on earth would I want to go through such a charade?'

'We'd get to spend more time together,' said Bernie.

'Tempting,' I said, 'but one sniff of a handsome man and you'll be off.'

'Perhaps,' said Bernie, 'but I'm more liable to behave if you're around.'

'Has your mother told you that you can only do the season if I do it too?' I asked.

Bernie went a little paler under her powder. 'I do think this ability of yours to leap ahead is a bit spooky. It won't make you popular, you know.'

'Who says I want to be,' I said. 'I'm right, aren't I?'

Bernie dropped her head. 'Yes,' she said. 'Stapleford, how else am I going to meet *the Right One*?'

'By kissing a lot of frogs?' I said.

Bernie reached out a hand to me. 'Please, Hope,' she said, breaking with college tradition, 'with the war coming this is liable to be the last chance for me to meet him. Mommy will only let me do this if you're there to keep me out of trouble.'

'I never keep you out of trouble,' I said. 'I only clear up the messes you make.'

'As long as Mommy never knows, that's good enough,' she said. Then she gave me her best tear-laden smile. 'I don't want her to send me across to the States. She'll demand I'm married off in a month.'

'Stop it,' I said. 'I'm not one of your lovelorn suitors.'

'No, you're my friend. My best friend. My one true friend. You're more like a sister to me.'

'Stop,' I begged, 'you're making me sick to my stomach.' I sighed. 'I'll think about it.'

But in the end, it was Uncle Eric who convinced me. 'You might as well,' he wrote. 'It's more than time you began to know the right people. As you doubtless realise, it's also liable to be a last waltz, if you follow me. I find there's something about being at these crucial little moments of history that can be quite enlivening.'

I took this to mean that Uncle Eric knew something interesting was going on. Uncle Eric always includes at least three levels of meaning in anything he says or writes. But I doubt even he could have foreseen what was to come.

I suppose, for posterity, I should record the actual presentation, though I have to say that for me the best bit was the Lyons' spread that was laid on afterwards. I wore a hideously expensive gown that Uncle Joe – my mother's younger brother, the Earl – had bought me. It was all white and lacy. With my pale skin and dark hair, I feared I looked as if I had been dead for a week or so. While I'm perfectly comfortable with my unfashionably curvy figure, it had been squeezed and moulded to appear socially acceptable and, as a consequence, I was deeply *un*comfortable. Bernie with her violet-blue eyes and champagne locks looked every bit a fairy princess.

A rather nervous princess, as it turned out. As the car drove up to the Palace she completely ignored the crowds who had come to watch the debutantes and wave at them. Although, considering the state of the economy, they would have been justified in throwing rotten fruit at us. But there you go, we of these lonesome isles do love our pageantry and tradition. One of my French friends believes this explains our national cuisine. (I doubt she meant this as a compliment.)

7

Bernie was repeating Miss Vacini's instructions over and over, as if they were some mantra. 'Approach the sovereign, two curtsies, and retreat.' We both had decent trains on our dresses, so we needed to take care when reversing, but honestly, one could instruct a dog to do it (provided one had enough biscuits). It was hardly a challenging manoeuvre, but all debutantes had to attend classes to practise curtsying.

When we arrived at the Palace it was all long marble staircases and red and gold corridors, lined with so many footmen that I wondered if it had been a reserved occupation during the war. I feared that seeing so many young men together in one place would be overly intoxicating for Bernie.

Buck House, as the younger set like to call it, is not to my taste. Decorated for Queen Victoria, it is very overdone in that showy Victorian way. And it was cold enough to rival White Orchards. I don't suppose one is meant to mention something like that, but we were all shivering in our thin dresses. I thought the whole place had a melancholy air and I didn't envy the princesses growing up here. There was a tedious preciseness about the furniture and ornaments that weighed down every surface and which shouted that everything had to be just so – though this was the ceremonial chambers. Perhaps the royals themselves have more cosy sitting rooms somewhere, with nicely stuffed settles and blazing fires. I will have to ask Uncle Eric. He has doubtless been in them. I know he was very tied up with the business of the last King's abdication. But I digress: the Palace was also, despite the huge windows, strangely dark, but that may just have been my mood.

We queued to be presented like lambs about to enter an abattoir, or rather fledgling young maidens about to be shoved out of the nest in the hope of finding a suitable match. The Season, on which we were all about to embark, was designed to train us to be good hostesses, demure wives of diplomats and the like, and to learn to observe and keep to the rules of our own set. It might be dressed up as parties and frolics, but there was a serious agenda

8

underneath. We were being made into the 'right sort'. Also, though no one would be so vulgar as to mention this, we were being auctioned off as breeding stock. It's rumoured the Queen is absolutely bonkers about bloodlines and, as always, whatever the sovereign favours filters down through the ranks to become imperative. And of course the season has to begin with us debs being presented to the King. No presentation, no entry to the season; that is the unbreakable rule. I doubt the poor King remembers any of our names or even welcomes his duty. He's had three years to enjoy his reign, and while his stutter is reduced, he never looks especially happy, poor man. No one ever imagined he would be the monarch, least of all he himself. The Queen, though, is a different matter: certainly from where I got occasional glimpses of her, I think she's rather enjoying it.

When it came to my turn to be presented, my grandmother's influence somehow overcame the court official who announced me as 'Rose Hope Stapleford' instead of 'Hope Rose'. But it all passed very quickly. The King looked kindly, if a little nervous, while the Queen watched over him like a hawkish mother hen. She also gave a slight smile to each girl, but it was accompanied with a piercing gaze that ran up and down each of us with an intelligent scrutiny that surprised me. The King was undoubtedly the milder of the two. Then came the Lyons' spread, with their particularly lovely lemon cake that I still remember. I've never tasted anything quite as good since.

Bernie was terribly excited. She barely ate a thing. I had not yet lost my interest in the buffet when she dragged me out to the garden, so she could show off her jade cigarette lighter and a pack of Abdullah's in a jewelled case that she had secreted in her little silver link bag.

'Oh my,' she said. 'That was heavenly.'

I was spared the necessity of thinking up something suitable to say – there were footmen everywhere – when I heard a small sob coming from the bushes. We had been very strictly warned against venturing off into the gardens on pain of ruining our reputations, and our shoes. So, of course, Bernie and I dove off in search of the curious noise.

'Do you think someone has been ruined?' whispered Bernie to me, as we ambled down some decidedly mossy steps. Despite it being a Royal Palace, we had been warned by our chaperones that unsuitable activity often happened in the shadows of the gardens.

'Only if they were surprisingly quick about it,' I said.

Bernie smothered a laugh. The muffled sobs continued. We traced them around the shrubbery and towards a small copse. A small, dark-looking copse.

'I wonder if we should get someone to escort us?' I said hesitantly. I'm not exactly the fearful sort, but the thought of having to explain a social faux pas to my grandmother can unsettle even the Bishop.

Bernie gave me what I felt, rather than saw, was a withering look. 'Buck up, Stapleford,' she said. 'For England and King George.' It sounded remarkably odd delivered with her American twang.

I sighed and stepped into the shadows. It was better if I went first. I didn't want Bernie to stub her toes through her delicate little slippers and scream the place down.

'Is there anyone there?' I called in a low voice.

At that moment a ray of moonlight broke through the parting clouds, revealing a startled female face surrounded by golden curls and with the biggest, deepest blue eyes I have ever seen. Her face was stained with tears and yet she looked heartbreakingly beautiful (I look more like a ravaged beetroot when I cry).

'Oh,' said the girl in sweet melodic voice, 'I am lost.'

Bernie, always the affectionate type, came forward and put her arm around the girl's shoulders. My eyes were now adequately adjusted to the dark and I could see the girl also wore a presentation dress. However, hers was not complete with all the trimmings and flounces my monstrosity bore, but took an elegant, figure-hugging form. It was an extraordinary match of demure and sexy.

She looked quite wonderful in it. I was already more than half way to disliking her.

'Do you mean that metaphorically or literally?' I said.

'I am afraid I do not understand you,' said the girl with the faintest French accent.

'That you are lost.'

'Both,' said the girl and burst once more into a flurry of tears that never once distracted from her innate beauty.

Damn her.

Chapter Two

If Charlotte Saulier could be said to have one fault (and I considered her to have many) it was that she had no sense of direction whatsoever. When she told us that she was lost, she meant exactly that. She had also been so well brought up that rather than try to work her way back to the Palace, she sat down on a stone bench and cried prettily, waiting for a rescuer to find her.

She seemed particularly wet to me, by which I mean she had as much backbone as the Ritz's best filleted Dover sole. However, Bernie took to her immediately and I could see she was in the process of adopting her, as one might do with a stray kitten. (Bernie was the only one who fed the pigeons at college, eventually tempting one into her room, with inevitable results. She'd had to pay her maid extra for the rest of the term.)

As Bernie and I were officially doing the season together, I foresaw that Miss Saulier would be much in our company and I resolved to try to like her, or at least show more tolerance, as I would to any of Bernie's pets.

'I tore my train retreating from their Majesties,' said Charlotte. 'It made such a horrific ripping noise I am sure the whole Palace heard. As soon as I could, I fled from the embarrassment with an intent to fix it. I carry a needle and thread with me always, as advised by Miss Vacini, but I have no idea how to use it. Then when I got outside I got quite turned around. And there was no light to see by.'

'It being night-time would account for that,' I said. Bernie frowned at me.

'Yes, of course. I have been quite stupid,' said Charlotte. Her golden head dipped, and she shed another tear in quite the most delicate fashion.

'You must come with us,' said Bernie bracingly. 'We'll find the ladies' cloakroom and help you sew up your train. At least Hope will. I'm useless at anything domestic.' She sighed. 'I'm going to have to find a husband who has a big staff.'

Charlotte dried her tears on a scrap of handkerchief that she produced from goodness knows where, and stood up, ready to accompany us. All trace of her weeping had miraculously subsided.

In the ladies' washroom – and I have to say the Palace's are ever so nice, even if they are extremely cold – I sewed up the tear in Charlotte's train. She stood there like a doll and let me do it.

'So,' said Bernie brightly, 'how come you're being presented on the diplomatic night? My mother is American, so it was thought best I came tonight, and Hope here – Hope Stapleford – is being sponsored by my mother. Though her uncle is an Earl.'

'Really?' said Charlotte, her eyes widening.

'No, he's not married, but he hates London,' I said pointedly. I knew most debs would never be happy with a man who didn't share their taste for the high life.

'Oh, poor man,' said Charlotte with feeling. 'Unless – is he very rich?'

I shrugged. 'Rich enough.'

'He bought Hope an automobile,' said Bernie, 'and it wasn't even her twenty-first birthday.'

'Gosh,' said Charlotte. 'He sounds very nice.'

'He's rather dishy too, if you like older men,' said Bernie. I had a momentary image of Bernie adjusting a Countess's coronet. I shook my head to dispel the image.

'He's not in town even for the season,' I said. Uncle Joe loved running his estates and hated the party scene, which was why finding a wife was proving so difficult for him. If he wasn't careful, Grandmother would take him in hand. I made a mental note to keep Bernie and Grandmother as far apart as possible.

13

'So, what do we do now?' asked Charlotte as she twirled and checked her train.

'Now the main event is over,' I said. 'I imagine we find our sponsors and go home.'

'Oh,' said Charlotte, 'my sponsor had to leave. I wonder if someone could call me a taxi cab?'

'You could try asking a footman,' I said, trying to keep a straight face as I imagined the driver trying to get past the sentries.

'Nonsense,' said Bernie, 'we're all going on to the Hillfords'. They're holding the biggest after-party. Mommy will join us for the first little bit, but she's a good sport and will leave after half an hour or so. Then we can let our hair down!'

'I'd love to do that,' said Charlotte. 'I have so many pins sticking in my scalp.'

I looked closely at her in the hope this was a sign of a subtle sense of humour, but she merely blinked her big eyes at me.

'It'll be a bit of a squish, but I'm sure we can all get in the Bentley,' said Bernie 'Come on, troops, let's find Mommy. She's going to love you, Charlotte. You're so the perfect English Rose. The kind of girl she utterly approves of.'

Bernie linked arms with Charlotte and led her out. I followed behind, feeling like a once favourite doll that's been ousted in the nursery by the arrival of a newer and shinier one. 'She has a funny accent for an English Rose,' I muttered under my breath. 'But then I suppose one European is like another to an American.' If Bernie heard me, she didn't respond.

As Bernie had predicted, her mother took to Charlotte at once and asked her a dozen questions about who her people were. I stopped listening and leant my head against the automobile's window. The cold against my forehead began to shift the headache I hadn't even known was building.

Amaranth, being an honorary American by marriage, had decided it would be delightful to sit up front with the chauffeur. (Usually it's the British going after American heiresses. How Amaranth turned it around and found a wealthy American I have

14

never been told. I suspect she has *an interesting past*. If so, she'd never tell Bernie, who would regard it as a challenge to do something worse.) She kept turning around to ask more and more questions of our new friend. However, she never gave Charlotte time to answer properly. Bernie and Charlotte were somehow sitting comfortably while I was squished against the door. It rattled alarmingly, so for several minutes I was more concerned with gripping the underside of my seat, in case I was suddenly ejected onto the pavement, than in paying attention to what promised to be a rather inane conversation.

Although the weather remained warm, a light summer drizzle was streaking across London's dark stony face. The lamps were all lit, fuzzy white moons littered among the sturdy monuments of our capital. As our chauffeur drove through the city streets the inside of the automobile was cast alternatively into light and shadow. Amaranth continued talking nineteen to the dozen, hardly letting Charlotte get a word in edgewise. I found myself fascinated by the older woman's mouth. She favoured the sort of bright red lipstick that, in shadow, becomes almost black. Her teeth flashed bright white as she talked and talked and talked. She is a kind woman, but somewhat besotted with how the English are all connected to one another. 'And do you know the Lipton-Smythes?' she asked Charlotte, who replied quietly, 'I think Mummy does,' to the majority of these enquiries.

I looked at Bernie. She was sitting back in her seat, an unlit cigarette in her holder held at a jaunty angle and watching her mother talk. A smile played around the corner of her lips and I realised she was laughing internally, not at Charlotte, but at her mother. There's a side to Bernie that I dislike seeing. She mentioned once that her childhood hadn't been the best. I knew she had been expelled on a couple of occasions from boarding schools whose rules had proved too confining for her. Now, I wondered for the first time if her home life had been the bad part. In a strong departure from her usual loquaciousness and open manner she always clammed up tight when I asked for any details of her childhood.

15

We joined a procession of automobiles that were crawling along. Amaranth's conversation deteriorated further, to 'How long does it take someone to get out of a vehicle?' and 'Are we even moving?' I saw no point in joining in and sat back in my corner, staring out of the window and wondering if my father had been right and I had made a great mistake in taking on the season. It was absolutely clear to me that Bernie, and even Charlotte, were the right type of 'gals' to do this. Uncle Eric had said it would be good for me to meet the right people, but if this group was a subset of those, my inclination to do so was quickly waning.

I chided myself mentally for being unkind. There was nothing wrong with any of the three women. I even counted Bernie as a friend – or was it that Bernie had counted me as a friend and I had got swept along? But I was bored to tears. I longed for a decent book. I had discovered early in life that you are never alone with a novel. In fact, it was my habit of indulging in reading that had made my mother insist I studied something practical like mathematics. I would rather have read English Literature – but then, as I had quite rightly assumed, it was all about being up at Oxford rather than what one was reading . . .

The vehicle finally stopped. I tried to get a good view of the house. Having spent a lot of my time in the Fens with Mama and Papa, and then at Oxford, I have not seen as much of the country as I would like. But a well-meaning umbrella thrust in my direction and the pop flash of a camera ensured I did not get to see the outside of our destination.

'Gosh,' squealed Bernie, 'how lovely. Our pictures in the papers.'

'Oh, I wonder which,' said Amaranth. 'We must buy copies.' She ventured away from us towards the photographers. 'Chaps, where are you from?' I heard her say. But Bernie and Charlotte were jostling me to get out of the rain and into the party. That was the last we saw of Bernie's mother. It's possible that Bernie even said, 'Tally-Ho' as her mother disappeared, but there are many things said by Bernie that it is better not to hear. Comparing her mother to a hunter after a fox did, I admit, adequately describe the startled look on the reporter's face that she had chosen to target. Rather than a tail, I wondered idly if she would bring back a notepad and pen as a trophy.

These thoughts were cut short by Bernie pushing me aside. 'Don't get between a girl and a set of dashing beaus!' she cried. She ploughed forward ahead of me. Charlotte gave me a quivering smile as she was towed past, Bernie's fingers wrapped in a steely vice-like grip around her wrist.

Before any more eager debs could assault me, I walked up the shallow steps and onto a serious amount of foyer acreage. Flagged with black and white tiles and with Ionic columns and Grecian statues dotted about, it was quite the largest entranceway I had ever seen. However, I soon discovered it was not completely unlike my own home; fierce draughts from the ever-opening doors gusted across its length unchecked. A huge fireplace, more than twice my height, stood temptingly a third of the way in, but before that was an official who took my card, whispered to the owner of the house, and presented me to a line of people whose hands I was supposed to shake. I had no idea who any of them were.

I observed the girl ahead of me dip a curtsy in front of certain ladies in the line and I copied her, hoping she had more of a clue than me. By the time I reached the end of the line I was shivering from cold. No one had said anything more meaningful than 'Welcome' or 'I hope you have a lovely evening'. To be fair, one of the ladies I curtsied to told me I had a lovely dress – but as she was looking all around her at the time, I didn't take it much to heart.

When the girl ahead of me had finished the line, a handsome young man had whisked her off on his arm. No one was waiting for me. I wondered if Bernie had thought to provide for herself. However, I am a Stapleford and, more importantly, my mother's daughter, so I held my head up so high it was perfectly clear that even if there had been a dozen young men awaiting my attention, I would have snubbed them all.

The problem with raising your chin that aloft is that it obscures your view of where you're walking. Still, fortune favours the brave, and so the waiter I collided with only had two empty glasses left on his tray. These performed balletic spirals in the air before succumbing to the effects of gravity.

'Oh, gosh, I am ever so sorry,' I said. I stood there helplessly. I wasn't sure of the etiquette of helping him retrieve the debris, but even if I was supposed to, I couldn't bend too well in that dress.

'No problem, miss,' said the waiter. He bent down and, with a practised air, flicked the shards from the floor onto his tray with the cloth he had had over his arm. 'These aren't the first and they certainly won't be the last.'

'Good,' I said not knowing what else to say.

'It is for the suppliers,' said the waiter. 'You wouldn't believe what they charge for a glass.'

'Oh dear, should I offer to pay?'

The waiter stood up and looked me in the eye. I noted he was reasonably handsome, having a certain affable flair and a twinkle in his eye. 'No, don't you be doing that, miss,' he said. 'Even if another waiter tells you different later in the evening.' He leant forward slightly. 'Some of them, believe it or not, try to take advantage of their betters as the evening wears on and the bottles pile higher, if you get my meaning.'

'Oh,' I said.

'Course, if you wanted to give anyone a small gratuity for steering you in the direction of the most eligible attendees, that's another matter entirely.'

'Where I'd really like to go is the library,' I said with sincerity.

'Really?' said my waiter, raising an eyebrow. Then he winked. 'Good choice. You and your beau are hardly likely to be disturbed there.' Raising his voice, he said, 'Of course, miss. I'll show you where you can clean up your dress. I'll have one of the housemaids brought to you in a jiffy. If you'll follow me.' He led me around the back of one of the columns and unhooked a rope that had been laid across a small staircase. 'We'd better hop to it, miss,' he said softly. 'If we're not to be caught.'

18

This was just the kind of situation my mother had feared I would get myself into. However, rather than feeling afraid, I felt my spirits lift. I was fairly certain this man was taking me to a library and not luring me away for salacious purposes. Besides, he seemed to think I already had an assignation awaiting me. I felt a little thrill that someone thought I looked like the kind of girl who had assignations. I scanned the waiter from behind. He was thin, but wiry. However, I was completely certain that should he try anything I could deal with him, so I moved quickly up the steps behind him.

We traversed the stairs past the first floor and onto a mezzanine level between the first and second. 'There's a bigger library further up and in,' he said, 'but it's a long way from the ballroom.'

'This one will do,' I said. I blushed. Something I don't often do. I gave a slight smile. 'I mean, I'm sure that's the one my, err, suitor meant.'

The waiter didn't exactly look me up and down, but he did frown. 'You sure about what you're doing, miss?'

'I do believe you've taken me under your wing,' I said. 'How much do I owe you?'

The waiter gave me a pained look. 'Why nothing at all, miss.'

I arched an eyebrow. 'Really? You're not some Earl in disguise looking for his true love, are you? Without your tray, you could pass for one of . . .' I tailed off. I had been about to say 'us' and that sounded all too rude. I dipped my head. I felt a fiery flush across my face. My blush had deepened so much I would have to take care not to get too near the drapes lest I set them aflame. Really, how could one waiter discommode me so easily? I thought I was made of sterner stuff.

'Ah now, miss,' said the waiter. 'No need to blush. You're quite right. This is that kind of event. Us and them.'

I raised my face bravely. 'I don't like those much,' I said.

The waiter frowned, but gave a slight nod. 'Each to his own,' he said. Then he pulled an odd expression. He pulled his lips back wide without opening his mouth. He looked like a cross between a cheerful duck and someone who had swallowed a difficult secret. I'm afraid I can't explain it any other way. Then he said, 'Would you mind if I gave you a spot of advice?' and I realised he had been deciding whether to keep his mouth shut. Immediately I was intrigued.

'On principle I never refuse to listen to advice,' I said. I could have added that I was all for an easy life and that listening to advice before doing exactly what I wanted was my default modus operandi, but as nice and oddly thoughtful as this waiter appeared, I felt that would be over-sharing.

'If you do decide to join the ball downstairs, don't stay past midnight,' said the man. 'And don't let anyone talk you into going anywhere else. No matter how respectable they seem.'

I knew exactly where my heart was in my chest, and I had attended enough biology lessons to know its position was a fixed one. And yet, I had the distinct impression that it tumbled suddenly into my shoes. 'Oh dear, is the whole season going to be like this?' I sighed. I knew I was unlikely to be persuaded otherwise. Oh, Bernie, how much trouble she could find!

'A first night ball tends to have quite a lot of bets placed on it.'

'Bets?' I said and this time it was the waiter who blushed. It took me a good thirty seconds before I understood his meaning. This is an enormous length of time when both you and your conversation partner are embarrassed. The waiter even resorted to rearranging the debris on his tray as he waited for me to catch up. 'Oh, men are disgusting,' I exclaimed when I did. The waiter muttered something that could have been, 'Not all of us', but I was already proceeding down the inevitable line of thought. 'Good heavens,' I said, 'I must warn Bernie.'

'If that was the girl who pushed you aside on the steps,' he said, 'I'd say she knows all too well what she's up to.'

'If only,' I said with feeling. 'She's a disaster on two legs trailing a cyclone of calamity in her wake—'

The waiter, who I suspected now regretted ever talking to me, interrupted. 'I have to have to get back, miss.'

'Wait a minute – you spotted me outside?' I asked. I leant in and I picked a small glass shard off his sleeve. He went rigid with embarrassment.

'Can't help but notice the real gems among the paste,' he said and, with that, hastily departed down the stairs. I watched him going, thinking he was an interesting sort and wondering if he would realise it was me that slipped a ten-bob note into his pocket while I distracted him by pulling at his sleeve.

The fire in the library had burnt low. I found a shawl someone had carelessly cast over the back of a settee and appropriated it. Checking the shelves, I deduced this was not one of those old libraries that had been bought by the yard, but that the owner was unfashionable enough to like novels. I picked a copy of *Gaudy Nights*, curled up in a wingback chair that stood close to the fire, and lost myself in rereading some of my favourite passages by Ms Sayers.

I could have happily stayed there for the rest of the night. I was warm, entertained, and away from that dreadful lot downstairs. But after a while I began to feel a trifle peckish. Bernie had dragged me away from the buffet, after all, and I supposed I ought to find her before she got into any real trouble. And if finding her took me past the buffet, it would be impolite not to show my appreciation for the hosts' attention to catering.

I was unwinding myself from the comforting confines of shawl when the library door flew open.

Chapter Three

'Oh, thank God, I've found you!' cried Bernie. Her tone of voice suggested she had barely escaped from a lion's den with her life. However, I was pleased to see there wasn't a hair out of place on her head and her lipstick was un-smudged. Whatever had happened, it appeared nothing physical had taken place. In all likelihood the champagne had run out, or she had spotted someone wearing the same frock. As she came closer and threw herself down on the settee that I had just abandoned, I saw her eyes were a little wild. Cocktails, I thought. Cocktails and overexcitement.

I dropped my shawl onto the arm of the settee and carefully placed the book back on the shelf. 'What's wrong, Bernie?'

'I've lost her!' She screwed up her face.

'Don't you dare wail at me,' I said. 'Whatever is wrong, an over-indulgence in emotion will not help the situation.'

Bernie relaxed her face and gave me her best wounded look.

'Who's lost?' I asked though I already knew the answer.

'Charlotte. Charlotte Saulier.'

'I wasn't aware she was our responsibility,' I said. 'Considering how we met her, it would appear she has a tendency to go wandering off. She's probably sitting crying prettily somewhere.'

'That's cold, even for you, Hope,' said Bernie, her eyes flashing.

I squirmed a little under her gaze. 'I only meant there was no arrangement for her to come with us. Perhaps she has been collected by someone?' I doubted this. Whoever was meant to be looking after Charlotte had, so far, shown a shocking lack of care.

'She's very biddable,' I said sharing some of my thoughts. 'Did anyone offer to show her a kitten, or a pony?'

The edges of Bernie's lips twitched. 'Don't be so cruel, Hope. I know she's not like us . . .' Exactly how she was not like us she didn't say but continued after a brief pause, 'She does seem very naive.'

'And not very clever,' I said under my breath.

'Isn't it our Christian duty to look after her?'

'Bernie,' I said. 'How delightful! You did read that Austen novel I lent you.'

Bernie stuck out her tongue at me. 'Be serious, Hope.'

'Are you sure she's not downstairs? It was crowded when I left, and there were hordes of cars queuing behind us.'

'Oh, what a crush,' said Bernie, batting her hand in the air as if she was waving a wasp away. 'A great success. But I tell you, no one's seen hide nor hair of her for some time, and it's far too early to even think of leaving, even if she had the strictest chaperone.'

'Really? It feels like we've been here for ages.'

Bernie stamped her foot. 'For goodness' sake, Hope, now is not the time for you to pull one of your misanthropic episodes.'

Truthfully, the more I scoffed at the idea of Charlotte getting herself into serious trouble, the more I began to feel uncomfortable. I don't believe in intuition. I know the brain picks up one thousand and one signals and sometimes those can bypass consciousness. This has led to what the uneducated call hunches. I was having one now – and it wasn't a good one. I tried to push the ideas the waiter had put in my head to the very back of my mind. 'Tell me how you got separated.'

'Well, Bobby Langton was explaining how he and Edgar Darling had been night climbing at Oxford. Edgar had ripped his trousers sliding on some tiles and was showing . . .' She gave a little giggle and I realised she was farther gone than I had thought.

'Night climbing! What an idiot! He could have broken his neck.'

Bernie waved her hand at me again as if she could bat my strictures away. 'Don't be so boring, Hope. It's quite a funny story. He didn't think they could identify him from what was showing, so when they were spotted by the beak, they dived in the nearest window, only to find . . .' At this point laughter overcame her to the extent she had to sit down. All I ascertained was the final words, 'he was in curlers, no less!'

I gave her a few more moments to compose herself while I silently counted to ten in my head. Bernie's bouts of philanthropy tend to be transient episodes. No unkindness is ever meant, but she has the concentration of a magpie in a jewellery store. 'So, in other words, two or more handsome young men were vying for your attention and you quite forgot Charlotte existed.'

Bernie paled as she recalled why she had come to me. I felt a twinge of guilt but, really, she was out of college now, loose upon the world, and for the sake of the latter she needed to buck up and not let herself be led so easily off course when talking about imbeciles in trousers.

'That's cruel,' she said, her violet-blue eyes brimming with tears. I hardened my heart. Bernie was already a terrible flirt and once her reputation was protected by marriage, goodness only knows what she would get up to if she wasn't pulled up on her behaviour now.

'But true,' I countered.

Bernie pouted. The tears vanished as easily as they appeared. Bernie wore her emotions on her sleeve, unlike I, who locked them away, saving them for a mid-life crisis. 'Oh, all right. Yes. I was having a topping time. I'm pretty sure one of the boys is heir to a barony or something . . .'

'Isn't that a little low in the pecking order for your standards?'

'He was German. It's more important over there. Besides, he had a winery – or was it a stud farm?'

'Oh, I imagine he told you that,' I said. 'Did he offer to show it to you as well?'

'Stop being a beast, Hope! You know what I'm like, but I didn't mean to lose Charlotte. Honestly, I didn't.'

I sighed for the thousandth time since I had embarked on this

24

season. 'Bernie, she's a grown woman. I'm sure she can take care of herself.' My friend frowned at me. 'Or, at least, you are not responsible for her. She may seem helpless, but she is no more a child than you or I.'

Our eyes met and we both knew I was overstating the case. 'Could she be with your mother?' I asked.

'No, Mommy's gone home, like we agreed.'

'What, we're here without our sponsor?' I said aghast. Bernie nodded. I blinked. 'Are you sure? I know you said she would, but I presumed she'd retire to a chaperones' room or something. I mean, she does know what you're like. And then there's me. I mean, I have my reputation to—'

'Oh, don't be so old-fashioned, Hope. It's 1939. No one takes that chaperoning thing seriously any more. Besides, Mommy knows you can look after us both.' There was more than a hint of truth in this. Amaranth bored easily.

'Do you honestly think something has happened to Charlotte?' I said. 'Something bad? This is London, not some backwater place.'

'Yes, but she's . . .' Bernie grasped for the proper description. 'Charlotte!'

I raised an eyebrow. 'We barely know her,' I said. 'I agree she seemed a bit wet, but as long as she's not gone off with anyone unsuitable, I'm sure she's fine. I really can't see her doing anything adventurous of her own accord. She's probably sitting somewhere quietly, reading poetry. She strikes me as the kind of girl who reads poetry.'

'I do hope so,' said Bernie. 'But I haven't told you the rest.'

'Which is?'

'Her sponsor turned up to collect her. That's when we realised Charlotte wasn't around. She's a right old battleaxe. One of those commanding types. She had all the young men searching.'

I felt a weight that I hadn't know I'd borne, lift from my shoulders. Trust Bernie to tell the whole story backwards. 'Well, I'm sure they will find her, and perhaps next time her sponsor will ensure she is more securely chaperoned. Lessons learned all around.'

'Wait. You haven't heard the worst bit. When she was gathering people to look for Charlotte we discovered that James Trask is missing too.'

I sat down in a nearby chair. 'Trask,' I said. 'I've heard of him! You don't think Charlotte would have gone off with someone like him, surely?'

Bernie nodded miserably. 'I do. I'd only known her five minutes, but even I could see she hasn't an ounce of worldliness about her.'

'I'm not that worldly myself,' I said. 'But even I know *his* reputation.'

'I don't think you realise, Hope, how many important people go to parties at your parents' house. You hear a lot more than most young girls.'

I was barely listening to her. 'You say they're still searching?'

'Yes.'

'Then we need to find my waiter. With luck, he'll know where she could have crawled away to hide, and at worst, he'll know if Trask was one of the ones laying bets, though I imagine he was. We need to find out what he was betting on. Or rather who. He won't want to tell us, but I've never met a man that you couldn't get information out of.'

'What?' said Bernie.

'Oh, come on,' I said, catching her wrist and dragging her out the door. I had no real idea of how to track down the waiter with my ten-bob note, but no sooner had we left than we ran into someone. It was not the waiter, but an old man in a velvet smoking jacket with a violently yellow cravat. 'Yikes,' he said. 'Girls!'

Bernie took one look at him, then she grabbed *my* hand and towed me away. 'Run,' she hissed at me.

'Don't go, lovely girls,' called the old man in a slightly slurred voice. 'Just want to have a little chat. Have the most fabulous collection to show you. Just upstairs . . .'

'I bet!' said Bernie, whisking us through a side door and down a set of servants' stairs. 'Worse than my Great-Uncle Bill,' she

26

muttered. She darted through another door, along a passageway and stopped in front of a large door.

'Do you have any idea where we are?' I asked.

'Oh, Lord, Hope! One of the first things one does at these events is find little hideaways. The ballroom's right through that door. Let's go find your waiter.' She opened the door. 'Anyway, why is he *your* waiter?'

I was spared the necessity of answering by the roar of noise that greeted us. Perhaps roar is a slight exaggeration, but the lovely silk-hung ballroom before us was filled with debutantes who had been remarkably refreshed by the sudden onset of a 'situation'. Everywhere I looked, girls stood in groups, whispering, their eyes wide with excitement at the possibility of a real scandal unfolding in front of them. The air was lightly fragranced with perspiration.

'Good grief,' I said, 'you'd think whoever her sponsor is would have had more discretion. Even if we find her hiding in a cupboard, her reputation is going to be in shreds.'

Bernie was turning on the spot. 'There's a load of waiters by the long table over there. Can you see him? Shall we go closer?'

I scanned the room. 'We should split up,' I said.

'But I don't know what he looks like,' said Bernie.

'Grab any waiter that knows the house and ask him to show you where the cupboards are. Try not to explain why. There's no point making this worse than it is.' I left Bernie goggling at me and took off at a tangent.

Then I spotted something that took me quite by surprise.

'Excuse me,' I said, approaching a group of young men in evening suits who had gathered by the secondary exit, 'but might I have a word?' I addressed one of them in particular.

'Certainly,' said the man, momentarily turning to the others. 'If you decide to comb the gardens, count me in.' Then he walked with me over to an empty corner and I confronted my so-called waiter.

'Look, I was just having a bit of a laugh. None of the toffs realised who I am. I didn't mean any harm by it,' he said.

27

I mentally reassessed him. In that moment I had taken him for one of us, but he was more interesting than that. He was pretending to be one of us. I pushed these thoughts aside for later consideration. If nothing else, he had talent. 'I don't care if you were pretending to be the King himself,' I snapped.

'Hey, I don't look that old . . .'

I held up my hand. 'No jokes. Look, the girl that's gone missing. She's a friend of mine – well, not exactly a friend . . . Oh, hell, do you have any idea where she might have gone?'

'I don't make a practice of seducing innocent young ladies.'

'Double hell,' I said. 'What's your name?'

'Harvey.'

'Well, Harvey, was James Trask one of the ones laying the sort of bets that you'd mentioned earlier on?'

'I should never have mentioned any of that to you.'

'No, probably not. But was he?'

'Yes,' said Harvey.

'On her?'

The tips of Harvey's ears turned pink. 'Do you think I'm the type to listen to that sort of thing?'

'Do you think he's the type to seduce her?'

'Look, lady, you know I'm just a waiter. How would I know what any of these toffs are liable to do? I don't know any of them.'

'Pah!' I said. 'You've got their measure.'

'I never said that,' said Harvey.

'Tell me what you know about Trask.'

Harvey sighed. 'Not much more than anyone else, I guess. Loads of money. Reputation as a playboy. He's exactly the kind that chaperones warn young girls about. But I never heard he was, well, the rotten type.'

'You mean he's the type to egg a girl on a bit further than he should, but not the kind to do anything about it by force?'

Harvey studied his shoes. 'Yeah, I guess so.' He raised his head. 'This isn't the kind of conversation someone like you should be having.'

'You know nothing about me,' I said.

'It's not something any nice young lady should know about.'

I snorted in as unladylike manner as I could manage. 'Have you seen the way the *ladies* in here are whispering to one another? They couldn't be more excited if the King had run through here naked.'

'Ooh, nasty mental image,' said Harvey, screwing up his face.

'Whatever's happened to Charlotte, they're getting ready to tear her to pieces when she turns up. From what you've told me, it doesn't seem all that likely that Trask has anything to do with her disappearance. I need you to show me all the cupboards and hidey-holes a place like this has that a wet-sop of a girl like her might go to for a cry.'

'That's an idea,' said Harvey. 'I had a scout around with some of the other chaps, but we didn't think about cupboards.'

'Good,' I said. 'Let's go.'

'Oh, no,' said Harvey. 'One reputation in shreds tonight is more than enough.'

'I don't care about my reputation,' I said.

'I'm talking about mine,' said Harvey. 'You go find your friends and trust me to do my best to find this Charlotte.'

'Why should I trust you?' I said.

'I might be a bit of a bounder,' said Harvey, 'but I'm not a cad.'

Three hours later, no sign had been found of Charlotte and reluctantly the hosts and her sponsor decided to call in the police. An extraordinary decision, as with police involvement would come a taint that make Charlotte a pariah for the remainder of this season at the very least. By the time we had all given our statements it was nearly four in the morning and even Bernie was eager for her bed.

'God,' she said as we finally collapsed into the car waiting for us, 'I hope the rest of the season is going to be less rough.'

I didn't answer. I leant my head against the window. My curls had given up all pretence of being bouncy and hung lankly around my face. Outside, London remained black, stony, and streaked with rain. The city endured, regardless of any personal crises of its citizens. As we crossed a bridge, I could not help imagining the dark water lapping below and hoping that Charlotte had not ended up swallowed by its depths. I mentally shook myself. I had no reason to think Charlotte been taken by Old Father Thames, but I could not rid myself of the feeling that something bad had happened and worse was on the horizon.

Chapter Four

'Wake up, Stapleford!' Bernie landed on the end of my bed with all the grace of a drunken baby elephant. 'We're in the papers!'

I struggled to pull myself up. The allure of the lovely warm covers far outweighed my interest in being in any newspaper. The maid must have drawn back my curtains earlier because painfully bright sunlight filled the room. I had missed this by virtue of sleeping face down. I buried my face back into the pillow, hoping Bernie would go away. Instead of taking the hint she bounced on my bed, sending shudders through the mattress. I lifted my head a quarter of an inch, mumbled something unintelligible, and dropped my face back down into the warm, snuggly softness.

I had not slept well. I never find it useful to check the clock, but I felt I had only been asleep an hour or two. Never one to be thwarted, Bernie battered me over the back of my head with a cushion until I gave in and sat up. She thrust a folded newspaper in my face. 'Us! Well, me. In the newspaper!'

I took the proffered object and blinked until my eyes focused. There, on the front page, was a large picture of Bernie, her locks flowing behind her and her dress pinned to her elegant figure either by a strong wind (which I did not remember) or by a risqué dampened petticoat. She pouted prettily at the camera. Behind her I could see the edge of Charlotte's dress. There was no sign of me. Underneath it read, 'Ambassador's daughter delightfully surprised to find herself centre of attention at post-presentation ball.'

'Oh, I'm sure,' I said quietly.

Bernie pretended not to hear. 'And this one,' she added producing another paper, seemingly out of thin air. It was almost exactly the same photograph. In this one you could see slightly more of Charlotte, but not much. Almost as though Bernie had stepped into the shot to obscure her at just the right moment. Underneath this one it read, 'Dixie Darling'.

'But you're not from Dixie,' I said thickly.

'Oh, who cares!' says Bernie. 'They got my name right in both stories. And they made sure everyone knows I'm American. Mommy says it gives me added cachet.'

'They've written a story on us?' I said. My brain seemed to be at full capacity. I reached out a hand for the tea the maid had left on the bedside table and took a big gulp. It was stone cold, but anyone who has ever stayed in a great house is quite used to this and I swallowed it stoically.

'It's either us or that dreary little German man with the silly moustache. What would you rather read about in your morning paper?'

'Is there anything about Charlotte?' I asked.

'Oh yes. I forgot. How dreadful of me,' said Bernie, not looking in the least contrite. She swiped one of the papers from me and turned a few pages. 'Here, page four. Mommy says someone must have pulled a loom's worth of strings to keep the details off the front page. So, it's not like she doesn't have protectors in significant places. Why, I doubt even Daddy could have kept it this quiet if I'd sneaked off with a beau during the party and not come back. That's the trick: not letting people know you've been away. You always have to come back.'

'Hmm,' I said, trying to ignore her prattling about how to liaise discreetly at a big function. She seemed to have thought about it far too much.

I read, ' "Miss Charlotte Saulier has sadly had to withdraw from the season after becoming unwell at the Hillfords' ball." Oh, they've found her,' I said with a cry of relief. I flopped back against the pillows. 'Thank goodness.'

'Oh, no,' said Bernie blithely, 'she's still missing. We had a police inspector here this morning. Mommy refused to wake you for him as you're the niece of an Earl. He said the family would appreciate if the investigation wasn't mentioned around town. But, he said, could we keep our eyes and ears open in case we heard anything.' Bernie stood up. 'Who'd have thought she had it in her. Running away with Trask. She had me fooled.' She said this in a tone that boded ill for the missing girl. 'I'd like to give her a piece of my mind. We all know Trask has money, but to think he's been caught by a wet blanket like her. Still, as you're always saying, Hope, I am far, far too susceptible to believing in people's goodness.'

I scratched my head, trying to piece together my thoughts. I was pretty sure I'd never said anything of the kind about Bernie. She was more than capable of empathy, but most of the time she chose to ignore this. At college balls she had been known as a good dance partner, witty, bubbly, and never overly serious. 'I suppose Trask is a catch,' I said slowly. 'Admittedly, he does have a reputation, and you said her chaperone was a battleaxe. I suppose she might have thought they wouldn't allow her to see him. But to be so sure? She'd only just met him.'

'Who's to say she hadn't already got her claws into him?' said Bernie.

'You really think they've eloped?' I asked. 'Trask hasn't shown up either? There's no question that he took her against her will?' I paused. 'No, that would have been too noisy. And why would he? I mean, I know some gentlemen have a type, but I can't imagine that Trask could have made a career out of abducting watering pots like Charlotte.'

Bernie pouted and sucked her cheeks in. It looked ghastly — quite far from the image of her picture in the press. I took this to mean she was genuinely thinking and not simply posing. 'I think it will be said they eloped. Probably announced in a few weeks' time. Trask might be a playboy, but he's the one being played this time. If Charlotte hasn't already dragged him to an altar, that battleaxe of a chaperone of hers will force him into marriage.'

'It's not that easy to get married quickly,' I said. 'It requires effort. Effort a man who is being forced into it simply would not go to.'

'Like what?' said Bernie. 'You can always get the rings later.'

I shook my head, dispelling the last of the sleepiness from my brain. 'No, licences, stuff like that. We have banns in England. People have to be able to object. And then you have to find a willing vicar.'

'Sounds very British, and very complicated,' said Bernie.

'I suppose,' I said. 'He doesn't have any family, does he? I have a memory of something I read once. Wasn't he a Great War orphan?'

'A rich Great War orphan. His father ran an arms company. He could have opted not to fight, but Mommy says he was very much made of the Englishman-must-do-his-duty sort of stuff. So, off he went to the trenches despite being right at the top of the age bracket, but he never made it back home. Trask's mother died around the same time, but I can't remember if she was dead before the father went to war. I would think not, wouldn't you? I wouldn't risk leaving behind an orphaned son. No, I imagine the stress of it all killed her. Poor thing.'

'You should be a novelist,' I said. 'You can't keep making things up and passing them off as true.'

'I thought it all sounded very likely,' said Bernie. 'If nothing else. I was giving his parents the benefit of the doubt. After all, I could have suggested his mother wasn't pregnant when her husband went away . . .'

'Oh, do shut up, Bernie,' I said. 'You're not giving me time to think.' I pushed back the bedclothes and rang the bell. 'I can see why he might join the bright young things. Being orphaned as a child would have left him feeling that nothing was permanent.' I

34

yawned. 'He'd be a little on the old side though. He looks as if he's in his thirties, but that may be his suits. So well-cut. Have you got the same maid as last time? She knew exactly how I liked my bath.'

Bernie shrugged. 'How should I know? And God, Hope. You're so unworldly! A man's age doesn't matter if he has money.'

There was a light tap on the door and the maid I remembered entered. 'Bath please, Enid,' I said. I could feel the tides of sleep trying to drag me back under. I stifled another larger yawn. My stomach rumbled audibly. 'I never said you were unworldly. Now, go away while I have my bath.' My stomach rumbled again. 'What time is it?' I said, 'I haven't missed . . .' I couldn't bring myself to say voice the hideous thought.

'Lunch is in half an hour,' said Bernie. I sighed with exaggerated relief and she laughed. I expect Bernie went away thinking of beaus and her photographs in the press. I went for my bath thinking about food. Poor Charlotte and her fate were all too easily forgotten by both of us.

In my defence I will say that a major advantage of staying at an ambassador's residence is the food. It is always excellent. The chef is constantly preparing for one major international event or another. If he likes the current ambassador in residence's family, he tries out his new recipes on them. If he doesn't, he palms them off with something quick. Amaranth can be beyond charming when she wishes. She treats her staff with such grace, and pays such hefty wages, that most of them would happily wrestle a crocodile for her no matter how dizzily American she can be when she wants. I was in high hopes for lunch.

I wasn't disappointed when it came to the meal, but the conversation was a terrible bore; all about dresses and dances and dinners and eligible suitors. I got my head down over an excellent plate of dressed lobster and let mother and daughter get on with it. I cracked the claws and pulled out the meat more or less intact. No one noticed my expertise. I decided I had had enough when Bernie embarked on a detailed comparison of her dress against all other blondes'. I cracked the next claw with a deliberately percussive viciousness. Both women started in a satisfying manner. The conversation lulled for a moment and Bernie's mother fiddled with her napkin. Then she gave me a blinding smile.

'You know what they're saying, don't you?' she said. 'Such a bitchy lot these English mothers – not yours, of course, darling.' She threw a scarlet-lipsticked kiss in my direction. 'Euphemia just right and up and says what she thinks. It's so refreshing.' I heard the slight quaver in her voice that suggested she had been on the wrong end of Mother's direct truths more than once. I broke my lobster's back. Amaranth faltered, her gaze flickered to my fingers, and she paled slightly.

'So, what are they saying?' Bernie leaned so far over the table, her beads dangled into her soup.

'Well, I shouldn't say to ones as young as you.' The Ambassador's wife waited a neatly timed moment, and then whispered, 'Trask.'

'Oh, is that all!' said Bernie, sitting back and splashing food on her dress. 'We knew that.'

'That he's missing too,' said her mother pouting.

'We didn't know that,' I said kindly. 'There was a suspicion they had gone off together, but it sounds as if they have eloped.'

'But why on earth would he marry her?' exclaimed Bernie. 'Why would he marry anyone?'

'At some time, he has to get an heir and perhaps he thought an amenable bride might let him carry on living the way he always has – more or less.'

'Goodness gracious me, Hope,' said Amaranth, fanning herself with her hand, 'the things you say. Where's the famous British reserve?'

Bernie blushed and giggled. Her mother turned on her. 'And you shouldn't know what we're talking about!'

'Hey,' said Bernie. 'Don't turn on me because Hope is a guest and you don't feel you can chastise her. I haven't done anything wrong.'

36

'The state of your dress,' said her mother. 'Can't you do anything nicely?'

There was a moment when I thought Bernie might flounce from the room, but I caught her eye and shook my head very slightly. It was enough for her to remember there was a multitude of parties and events on the horizon, any of which her mother could make difficult for her to attend. She said, 'Sorry, Mother' in a voice that anyone who didn't know might have thought was genuine contrition. This was the first time I had stayed for any appreciable length at the Embassy and I was starting to get the feeling that her relationship with her mother was much more complicated than I had realised. There appeared to be a resentment hidden beneath the layers of lipstick and scent they both wore.

Later, when Amaranth had gone out to do some 'terribly urgent shopping', I sat with Bernie in one of the reception rooms with a sneaky little jug of cocktails provided by their obliging butler. 'I don't know what the problem is,' I said. 'It sounds to me as if everyone has got a jolly good deal out of this. Charlotte was so disgustingly wet she'd never have found a good husband, and Trask is so wayward . . .'

'And old,' said Bernie.

'*Looks* so old,' I said, 'that getting a pretty young girl who will provide him with a son and heir and is unlikely to ever pluck up the gumption to complain about his errant ways – well, it sounds like a dream for both of them.'

'Yes,' admitted Bernie. 'But one doesn't say such things in polite company.'

'Only to you and your mother.'

Bernie pulled an olive off a cocktail stick and chewed it. 'I don't know whether I should be offended or not.'

I shook my head. 'No, it won't wash. I'm being a dope,' I said. 'Why didn't he wait until the end of the season? Why the first night? It's not logical at all. He's a man renowned for enjoying the single life, why willingly terminate it on the first night of the season? I know stranger things have happened, but I really

37

can't see that he'd think he needed to snap up Charlotte so quickly. All he had to do was signal a mild interest and he would have had the rest of the season to enjoy himself, as well as having a bit more time to assess whether or not she was malleable enough.'

Bernie poured herself another stiff one. 'Oh, really, Hope. You're the one who spelt it out so graphically.' She took a good gulp and gave a tiny shudder. 'The whole thing is becoming too, too boring.' She waved her hand airily around as if conjuring up an explanation from thin air. 'I expect, as you say, he saw a good deal and didn't want to risk blowing it. Girls like Charlotte do get offers, you know. What we find wet, gentlemen often find pleasing. Besides, no man would have wanted to wrestle with her chaperone.'

'Something's fishy,' I said. 'Charlotte might fit the requirements, but so would a lot of the other girls. She isn't due to come into lots of money, is she?'

Bernie set her glass down. 'Compared to Trask? Hardly! Now, Hope, why don't you go off and have a nice time in the library. Daddy ordered in some new books only the other day.'

'Why?'

'Don't look at me so suspiciously!'

I kept my gaze level and unblinking at Bernie and, as usual, she gave in. 'All right, so I might have given Johnny Willoughby one of the keys to the rose garden, and he might happen to be popping round this afternoon.'

'Bernie!'

'What? We'll be outside. It's not as if anything really naughty could happen.'

'I thought there had to be a reason why you didn't make your mother include us in her shopping. You love nothing more than getting elbow-deep into millinery.'

'You hate shopping! I was doing you a favour.'

I did, but Bernie rarely took anyone else's feelings into consideration when it was something she wanted to do. However, I knew from long experience that pressing her with questions would not help. In some ways she is as contrary as a cat.

I stood up. 'Fine. I don't want to know.'

And, of course Bernie knew me, and all my tricks, far too well. She immediately retaliated with too much information. 'He has the most divine lips . . .'

I held up my hand. 'I don't want to know,' I repeated sternly, attempting belatedly to take the high road. 'So that when your parents ask how you spent the afternoon I won't have to lie.'

'You can say I went for a little lie down,' said Bernie. 'The lawn was mown yesterday and it's—'

'Enough,' I said and walked out of the room. Behind me I heard Bernie laugh and I could only hope she had been teasing me about the extent of her intended activities. There was a restlessness in the air. I'd noticed it last night at both the Palace and the after-party. People were drinking too much. Women painted on bright smiles. Men strutted just a little too dashingly. This season had something hard and brittle about it. It was not at all as I had imagined. I didn't like the feeling this false brightness gave. I couldn't help but feel that nothing was real. Nothing was as it was meant to be. Over everything hung an unspoken acknowledgement that the world we knew would shortly crash around our ears as tension gave way to war. We all blindly went on dancing and drinking, as if by ignoring the world outside we could wash it away. This is the way things have always been done, said the debutantes, said the mothers, said the Queen, and nothing shall come between us and our British ways. But, in our hearts, all of us knew this was a lie. The shadow of the cost of the Great War haunted us forever through the loss of a generation of men. We united in an attempt to forget, to convince ourselves it could never happen again.

I diverted to the kitchen on my way to the library and got myself some milk and biscuits. Indigestion, I told myself. Last night's food and drink had been too rich for me. I found an excellent new novel and curled up in a window seat, prepared to abandon myself to fantasy. But I couldn't concentrate. I couldn't rid myself of the feeling that dark clouds hovered on the horizon. 'Nonsense,' I told myself severely, and ate a biscuit to put me in a better frame of mind. It tasted unpleasantly dry, all too like ashes in my mouth.

In such situations, there is only one thing to be done. I raided the kitchen for cake.

Chapter Five

Despite my dire forebodings, nothing more than slightly over-salted soup soured the next few days at the Embassy and on the social scene. The newspaper headlines oscillated between society photos and the growing concern over Germany's actions. The newspapers stopped appearing automatically with breakfast. It didn't take me more than a couple of days to realise that they were only presented when the headlines concerned the season. It was presumed that anything else had been rated bad for the digestion by Bernie's mother. If only the world was so easy to edit.

We attended a couple of brunches, where the debs somehow still found yet more to talk about regarding their dresses and who had the best figure. Bernie, who had discussed the state of the world with me late into the night when we were at college together, now threw all her interest in politics aside to concentrate solely on the season's gossip. I thought I would die of boredom. I was on the verge of asking to ring my parents to see if they could oblige me with a sudden illness, when Amaranth finally announced she had arranged an evening of genuine interest.

We were to take in one of Mrs Burgess' literary evenings, a prospect that almost reduced Bernie to tears. I scoured the Embassy library for the most recent acquisitions and set out for the night, hopeful I was up-to-date on the latest novels to attract the interest of the *Beau Monde*. When we arrived, the chaperones, including Mrs Burgess, gathered to discuss novels. The debs – as no boys were invited, everyone knowing it is a female pastime to read fiction – spent most of their time gossiping. I came home in as deep a gloom as I had previously experienced just before a mathematics examination. All that prevented me from making that phone call was that I had known full well what a season was all about when I accepted. And that, I thought, was exactly what my mother would say if I asked her to help me out with any minor subterfuge.

I was so bored I accepted Bernie's invitation to go shopping the next morning. Another grand ball hovered on the horizon and I needed new gloves – I had already covered several pairs with newsprint which, it seemed, nothing could shift. Due to the butler's intervention at the Embassy I had been driven to hunting down and reading newspapers in the houses of our hosts.

Amaranth was wanted by the Ambassador for wifely duties and so could not go with us. She apologised profusely and begged me to help Bernie, whose taste was somewhat brash, with her shopping. 'Gerry is so caught up with his duties that I simply must help him,' she said. 'Indeed, I don't believe he's dined with us once since your arrival, Hope.'

'I haven't seen him at all,' I said.

'Well, he sends his deepest apologies for that,' said Amaranth, making up an obvious lie on the spot without a blush. I was impressed. Every now and then I got true glimpses of Bernie's mother. I had even considered that her frankly vacuous and harmless air would encourage people to talk in her presence, and I imagined her feeding back titbits of vital information to the Ambassador. But Bernie had literally laughed herself sick when I suggested this to her and we had blamed it on the salty soup, which had sent the chef into a mood and made him incapable of serving anything but beige-coloured food for a tedious twenty-four hours.

'Darling, are you listening to me?' said Amaranth. 'Only you seem to be – what do you English say – herding sheep?'

'Wool gathering,' I said. 'No, I'm fine. I'll do my best to keep Bernie in line.'

'Oh, I'm not going to ask you to do anything as extreme as that,' said Amaranth, and gave a gale of high-pitched laughter that was essentially so childish, I lost all hope for her. Indeed, I wondered if I had a civic duty to save the very busy Ambassador from his wife's administrations. But then he is an American, and they look all set to sit back and let us get on with the business of sorting out Germany again, so I don't suppose it matters.

No sooner had we arrived in town than Bernie had dispensed with the car and chauffeur. 'Anywhere will send stuff on,' she said casually when I protested. 'Don't you think it will be fun, Hope, to get in the midst of things? You know, see the real people and shop among them.'

'Like getting a special entry to the zoological gardens,' I said cuttingly. 'You can be such a snob, Bernie.' She took my arm and we began to walk down the street. Luncheon hour was over, but the throngs hadn't yet returned from lingering over their post-prandial coffees. We wandered around rather aimlessly, stopping now and then to peer at the store displays. To my surprise I discovered some of these were really good. We stood outside one designed to evoke a feeling of the jolly seaside, and it was making me wistful for candyfloss, when a stream of words suddenly blurted out of Bernie.

'You might not think I pay attention to what goes on outside the society world, but I do. Sometimes, when Mommy is out, Daddy and I talk late into the night about world affairs.'

I turned to face her. This was certainly news to me and my face must have showed my surprise. 'Don't look like that. You know I'm not a total dimwit,' she hesitated a moment, 'don't you?' \

'Of course . . . idiot,' I said with a smile. 'I hadn't realised you were that close to your father. You've never mentioned it before.'

Bernie pouted, looked down, tracing out a half circle with the tip of a silver shoe. 'I don't know that you would say we are *close* exactly. Not like you and Uncle Bertie. I think he uses me to sound out ideas on.'

'Still, hearing an ambassador's thoughts,' I said. 'That's no small thing. He must trust you.'

Bernie gave a small nod. 'He did make me promise not to discuss the things he said. But . . .' She broke off.

'But?'

'But I think he would rather it was Mommy. The poor man needs someone to talk to about things. He's finding it awfully hard at the moment.' For a moment Bernie's cheery temperament faltered. Her expression reminded me of my mother's when my father has one of his attacks. She becomes frustrated, worried, and angry, because there is nothing she can do. Bernie appeared to be running through the same gauntlet of emotions. I knew there was something she wasn't telling me, but I didn't fancy taking a shot in the dark. For all her giddiness, I valued her friendship, and her unquestioning loyalty, a trait of friendship that Uncle Eric is forever telling me is hard to find.

My internal thoughts ceased as I realised Bernie was still talking. '. . . I mean, I've heard that the city is absolutely rife with foreign spies. Imagine if we ended up at the same counter as a White Russian?'

'I don't believe the White Russians are spying on us,' I said calmly. 'They came here for asylum. And should you be telling me this if your father told you in confidence?'

'Pooh, it's only you.' Bernie took a deep breath and opened her eyes wide. 'What a cover story!'

I cocked my head on one side. 'Have you been talking to that press baron's son again?'

'Oh no, Mommy would never allow me to mix with anyone whose papa had socialist leanings!' She gave a minxish smile as she said this.

'Cover stories. Honestly. That's exactly what they are. You can't believe a thing you read in modern newspapers,' I said.

Bernie pouted. 'I don't. But pressmen are good for the goss. They hear things we don't, like from the police.' I looked at her quizzically. She leant in closer to whisper, nearly taking out the eye of a passing gentleman with the edge of her hat. 'Apparently, they've found Trask's car. The police are trying to keep it quiet for now, but Peter says there's much more to it. He's going to try and find out more for me.'

I murmured something non-committal. 'Oh, I give up, Hope,' said Bernie. 'Why don't you wait for me in the Lyons over there while I go and buy some things that dear Mommy will definitely not approve of.'

She clearly wanted me to ask what these were so, rather pettily, I didn't. Instead I got myself an excellent pot of tea, a slice of lemon cake (which was nowhere near as good as the one served at Buckingham Palace) and a seat by an open window. It was blindingly hot today. A real egg-fryer, as my father would say. He once demonstrated the veracity of this by frying an egg on the tumbled-down stone wall near the orchard. I'd been six and wanted to eat it. Mother had not been amused.

Today I felt like the egg. Those of a wafer-thin disposition, like Bernie, might still wrap a shawl around their thin shoulders and mutter about going back to the Riviera, but I was of a curvier stature. We had been away from the automobile for less than half an hour and I had long progressed beyond the glowing stage. Perspiration clung under my arms and the small of my back felt like a tepid lake. I feared it would not be long before I sweated visibly through my clothing. A feat considered as unladylike as burping or, heaven forbid, passing wind in public.

I fanned myself with the menu and asked for a glass of iced water. I thought cool thoughts and tried hard to rid my mind of the image of Charlotte lying at the bottom of the Thames. I told myself I had as much reason to suspect this as Bernie had to suspect ordinary shoppers of being spies. Of course, this set off a train of thought about how spies were also people and would still have to shop wherever they were sent. Then, naturally, I went on to consider whether or not there were spy classes on how to shop inconspicuously, and whether I could take any. This led to me pondering the issue of how to not appear too much like your own national identity – change your accent, obviously. Then it's not just about what you wore, I thought, but how you wore it. I mean, take women's scarves, the difference between how a Frenchwoman and an Englishwoman tie theirs is like the difference between sherry and cider.

I was taken by surprise when, out of the corner of my eye, I spotted a familiar face. I am very prone to daydreaming so, when I was little, Uncle Eric used to play games with me to train me to be aware of my surroundings, even when my mind was occupied with chess puzzles, or imagining how my book would progress when I was finally allowed to get back to reading. So that's how I came to recognise Harvey, even without his waiter's suit or his tails. He wore a much more appropriate (for his station) dark blue suit and carried a medium-sized brown parcel. He appeared to be watching the crowds carefully. He was certainly making quite a palaver out of dodging people. I could only assume he was carrying something fragile and precious. Even so, his behaviour seemed a little over the top, like a bad mime act at the end of a pier.

Bernie trotted down the steps of the department store. She was fiddling with her gloves and carrying a small beribboned bag. Obviously, the shop had not been ready to forward something so small for someone who didn't appear especially important. She moved with the assuredness of a beautiful girl who knows people will get out of her way. The pit of my stomach lurched. I was out of my seat in a moment and flying across the road, but not before the inevitable collision happened. I heard the sound of shattering glass from across the other side of the road. When I arrived, I found Bernie apologising profusely and talking Harvey into showing her the receipt for the broken item. She paled a little as she read it.

'I know,' said Harvey, 'but it's my grandparents' diamond anniversary. You have to push the boat out at times like that.' He looked down at the parcel, which remained held together by string and brown paper. 'Not quite sure what I'll do though. Grandpa's pushing ninety. Not sure he'll see in another year, and I did want to do something special for them. What with them losing both their sons in the Great War.'

'Oh no!' said Bernie. 'Of course I will pay. I don't quite have this amount on me . . .'

'We could go to your bank, if you have an account?'

'We can,' said Bernie. 'I should have enough in this quarter's allowance to cover it.'

'What was it?' I asked.

Harvey noticed me for the first time. His eyebrows zoomed up and down in an amusing manner but, on the whole, he kept a straight face. 'A clock, miss,' he said. 'A very special timepiece. The lady has the receipt. I thought a clock was a suitable present to celebrate the time they had spent together.'

'Oh, how lovely.' said Bernie, blinking back a tear.

'What did it look like?' I asked.

'Look like?' said Harvey.

'Yes, what did this miraculous clock look like?'

'The usual – a face, two hands, a nice case.'

'A very nice case, if this receipt is to be believed,' I said, taking it from Bernie.

'It's got the name of the maker at the top,' said Harvey bristling slightly. 'I don't know what you're suggesting, miss, but—'

'Bernie,' I said interrupting him. 'I think considering your position, and your mother only wanting you in the newspapers for particular things, I should deal with this.'

'But Hope, it's so much . . . I mean . . . can you?'

I gave her the family look – the one with which my grandmother once made a young Duke cry.

'Of course,' said Bernie quickly. 'Shall I go and pick up those gloves for you?'

'Please,' I said, 'Pale lavender, but none of those silly pearl buttons. The gentleman and I will settle this over tea. You can come back and get me at the Lyons when you're finished. I expect it will take you at least twenty minutes.'

'Yes, Hope,' said Bernie obediently and walked off.

'Now, if you could pick up your parcel before a crowd gathers,' I said to Harvey.'

47

'And I thought you were a lady,' said Harvey. 'You're going to stiff me, aren't you? Maybe I should call a copper. How would that look?'

'By all means,' I said, with what I hoped was a thin and cruel smile but, with my luck, probably just made me look as though I had indigestion. 'Then, of course, you will need to open the package for both the constable and me to inspect.'

All the bluster seemed to go out of Harvey and he deflated before my eyes. 'All right, fair enough. Just give me the receipt and I'll be on my way.'

'And let you trick some other poor soul into paying for your broken – what is it? Beer bottles?'

'I'll have you know it's a fine crystal vase.'

I looked him straight in the eye.

'All right, it's a fine glass vase.' I waited. 'Oh, all right, it's just an old glass vase.'

'Chipped?' I asked.

'Maybe a tad,' said Harvey.

I didn't respond as had I spotted a policeman approaching behind his back.

'Yeah, with a few cogs and gears and whatnot. Most people have no idea what's inside a clock. Fools, most of 'em.'

'But not enough to fool me?' I said.

'No,' said Harvey mournfully. 'Not you.'

'Don't turn around, but there's a policeman coming up behind you – I said don't turn around.' I caught his wrist to stop him doing so. 'Now, you're going to pick up your parcel and we're going into the tea shop.'

Harvey's eyes widened. I felt his muscles tense under my hand as he got ready to run.

'Either you follow me, or I tell the nice policemen exactly what you've been up to.'

Harvey swore under his breath, but he picked up his box and glanced behind him, marking the policeman.

'Don't run,' I warned. 'It won't go well for you if you do.'

Harvey straightened his spine with the attitude of a man heading to the gallows. I took his other arm. 'Now, lead me across the road before he gets to us,' I said.

Obedient and defeated, Harvey escorted me into the Lyons tea room, leaving a confused member of the constabulary watching us from the other side of the street. I got Harvey to put the parcel down next to him and ordered a fresh pot of tea and some Empire biscuits. 'You strike me as the Empire biscuit type,' I said, pulling off my gloves. 'Now, down to business.'

'I didn't do anything illegal,' said Harvey.

I gave him my best Oxford blue-stocking look. It works best if I borrow Mama's spectacles, but a fierce frown is an adequate second-best. The family look only works well the first time you use it. 'Then what, exactly, would you call what you were doing with my friend?'

'I only showed her the receipt,' said Harvey defensively. 'I never asked for money.' His gaze dropped from mine. 'Or at least I didn't until you came over and started making things difficult. I had to hurry things along then, Or at least try to.'

He sounded so aggrieved I couldn't help laughing. 'So, I messed up an honest fraudster's day?'

'Man's got to make a living,' said Harvey.

'From what I've seen of you, you aren't doing too badly. Drinking till all hours with the debs and their beaus – when you're not serving the drinks, that is.'

The tea arrived, and I poured two cups. I positioned a plate in front of each of us but didn't help either myself or Harvey to the Empire biscuits that glittered luxuriously before us. It took some willpower on my part, but I was gratified to see that Harvey was unconsciously licking his lips. He reminded me of the exceptionally greedy whippet my father had had when I was very young. It used to salivate terribly whenever anyone rang the gong. I fear I teased it something awful.

'Sometimes needs must,' said Harvey. 'Besides, I never pick anyone who's obviously hard up.' A faint blush showed on his cheeks and I got the impression he was telling the truth.

'Who taught you the trick with the broken glass?' I asked.

Harvey said nothing, but merely stared stoically at the Empire biscuits. I slid one onto his plate. 'So, who are your usual marks? Gullible ambassadors' daughters?'

'She was . . . what?' Harvey now turned very pale.

'I think you can count it as a favour that I got you out of that.'

'Yeah,' said Harvey. He looked wary, but it didn't stop him attacking the biscuit with gusto. I waited until he had a mouth full of crumbs.

'I was thinking you might do me a little favour,' I said and smiled sweetly.

Harvey's eyebrows rose in alarm. They really were quite expressive. He began to chew faster and tried to swallow but the Empire biscuits were of a thick, buttery shortbread base and stuck to the inside of his mouth, just as I had hoped.

'Of course, it's nothing too major,' I said. 'It's not like breaking and entering.'

Harvey managed to choke out, 'I'd never do that.'

I pushed his cup of tea towards him and looked as sceptical as I could. I was pretty sure that he was a bit of a wide boy, running street cons, conceivably knowledgeable in the art of picking pockets, but I didn't have him down as a hard-bitten criminal type. He certainly wasn't the kind of person I'd choose to have at my side in a bar fight. I doubted he could dodge a punch let alone swing one. No, what Harvey had to offer was smarts. His observational skills were acute. He could read people, and their intentions, quickly. However, more than that, he'd acquired a sharp, analytical mind even without the benefit of a decent education. With instruction and encouragement, I believed he had a great deal more potential than he had ever realised. I wondered what had brought him to this. That he favoured rich marks suggested to me that he wasn't entirely a bad egg.

'Of course not,' I said scathingly. 'All I want you to do is have a little chat with the staff of the ball where we met. I want to know if they noticed anything unusual on the night.'

Harvey frowned. 'Your friend's still missing?'

'Along with Trask.'

Harvey sat back in his chair. 'That's a rum 'un,' he said. 'I mean, I know she was a bit of an heiress, but I can't see why Trask would do something as stupid as run off with her. I mean, she's got family.' He pronounced family with a capital F. 'He'll have to marry her and, well – no offence, but she didn't seem worth the loss of freedom.'

'Do you think they might already be married?'

'It's been too long to be anything else,' said Harvey. 'I mean, if she was a nobody there would other – err, options.' He coughed awkwardly. I poured him another cup of tea.

'You mean he might have shacked up with her?'

Harvey flushed pink. ''Ere, a nice girl like you can't go around talking like that!'

'Nice girls talk like that all the time,' I said. 'They just don't do outside of their little cliques. In fact, the prettier they are, the coarser they sound.'

Harvey looked at me as if I had slapped him in the face with a fish. He opened and closed his mouth and closed it a few times, continuing the fish impression in a most comical manner before he finally said, 'What's it to you anyway, whatever happened to her? She a close friend of yours?'

'No,' I said. 'I didn't even like her that much. But . . .'

'It happened on your watch,' said Harvey with more understanding than I had expected of him.

'Yes.'

'I can see how you might feel responsible.'

'Then you'll help?'

'Don't appear as if I have much of a choice,' said Harvey.

Chapter Six

I left the shell-shocked Harvey with instructions to meet in four days' time in Hyde Park. I thought that would give him ample opportunity to check out the matter with the staff. It was far longer than I wished to wait, but these things take time. And, if I was to think like Uncle Eric, Charlotte was either already dead, or she was not. The purpose and method of her disappearance remained unknown, but it seemed unlikely a kidnapper would kill his prize now. He might have panicked early on. One hears of such things. But if he had stayed the course so far, I felt reasonably confident that whatever state of being Charlotte was in, it was likely to continue so for the next few days unless something public happened. Hence my desire not to fluster Harvey into making a mess of his enquiries. I reckoned, in his own terms, that he would call himself 'a fly one'. I felt fairly confident that if I gave him his head, he would come up with the goods. Of course, I couldn't be sure, but nothing is certain in this life.

When I emerged from the café it was to learn that Bernie had indeed purchased gloves for me. However, according to the doorman, she had barely lingered before setting off up the street in the direction of the jewellery vendors. Bernie likes all things bright and shiny. I could only hope she had not caught a passing beau and prevailed upon him to buy her a trinket. I was beginning to appreciate how much trouble she could stir up during the season now that she had begun to see it a hunting ground. Besides, like other debutantes, we were only allowed to wear pearls and pale stones – but definitely not diamonds. The unspoken message being that one has to earn the diamonds from one's man. But, as we were both older than debs normally are, it was annoying. I have diamond earrings from my father who, like any true gentleman, strives to please a lady rather than expecting her to strive to please him.

I heard Bernie before I saw her. 'Oh, that would be darling, Timmykins. They would be just the thing to wear to the ball tonight.' She gave a happy laugh as I homed in on her. 'Of course you can have the first dance. We could be daring and make it the first two. We American gals are afraid of nothing.'

'Except,' I said taking her firmly by the arm, 'the retribution of their British friends.'

'Oh, rats,' said Bernie. She stood next to a tall, skinny youth, dressed in the most uncomfortable-looking tweeds. His prominent Adam's apple wobbled alarmingly under his recessed chin as he said, 'I say,' at my arrival.

'So sorry about this, Mr . . . ?' I said.

'Lord Dudley,' said the youth, attempting to square his thin shoulders. He looked every inch the product of his inbreeding and as if a mere gust of wind would snap him in two.

'Bernie isn't allowed inside jewellers any more. She has a little problem.' I leaned into whisper. 'Sticky fingers.'

Bernie opened her mouth, but I cut in, 'She always denies it, but being the Ambassador's daughter, it can cause quite a to-do.'

'Quite understand,' said Dudley, smiling in a doting and patronising manner at Bernie, 'my aunt the Duchess had the same problem. I don't know why the tradesmen get in such a strop about it. My uncle always pays. We all know women are weak, especially when it comes to the pretties, eh? I'll just pop in and . . .'

'Please, my Lord, don't encourage her,' I said. I trod heavily on Bernie's foot, so whatever she was about to say next changed to an 'ouch'. I had often seen my mother do this to my father and it had invariably brought him into line.

53

'Don't worry. I'll keep schtum, old thing,' he said to Bernie. 'See you at the ball. If you're a good girl, I'll give you a little something, what?'

I nodded curtly to him and wheeled Bernie away. Behind us we heard the tinkle of a shop bell. 'Really, Hope, you are the worst,' said Bernie as we walked off.

'I'm the worst? You keep taking trinkets off imbecilic young men.'

'Why not? I'm beautiful. I'm an heiress. I have exotic connections. He was only going to buy me a couple of pearl drops.'

'His tweeds had patches on the elbows, and the hems were fraying. Didn't you notice his suit shone slightly in the sun.'

'Did it? I was too busy watching his Adam's apple. How do you think he eats with such a large thing in his throat?'

'His clothes were not only inappropriate, they were clearly old. He's holding out for a rich wife.'

'Oh, I know that,' said Bernie. 'Most of the Brits are looking for American cash, one way or another. I'm quite used to being wooed. I think a couple of earrings for a first dance is nothing. It's not like I'm asking him to slay a dragon or anything.'

'You do realise your behaviour is only a class-based step up from that of a streetwalker?'

'I only said I was going to dance with him, Hope,' said Bernie in outraged tones.

'Grow up,' I said shortly. 'Pearl earrings are an investment for an impoverished peer. He'd expect a return.'

'I suppose if the earrings were good enough I could kiss him, if I closed my eyes,' said Bernie. 'It's not like that lump in his throat would actually touch me, is it? It wouldn't come up into his actual mouth, would it?'

'Did you go to any of the biology lectures I pointed you at?'

Bernie simpered. 'I always thought biology should be learned in an experiential manner.'

'Good God, Bernie. What would your mother think if she could hear you now?'

Bernie pouted. 'As if she would even notice. Besides, I'm getting bored. I haven't met anyone even remotely dashing.'

'Maybe you will tonight,' I said, trying to steer her thoughts in another direction. 'Are you going to wear the dress with the ribbons?'

'Will your Uncle Joe really not be coming down for the season?'

'No,' I said shortly. 'Besides, he's allergic to jewellery. Can't even have it in the house.'

'Oh,' said Bernie, looking confused. 'I suppose you did go to those chemistry seminars by whatshisname, so you should know.' She bit her lip. 'Poor man, no wonder he can't get a wife – even with his assets.'

For the remainder of the journey I felt like I was towing Bernie along the street. Finally, we reached the Embassy, where I relieved her of my new gloves. We retired to our separate chambers, but once Bernie was safely in hers, I went in search of her mother. I found her in her boudoir, a selection of purchases spread out around her – on the bed, over chairs, and even on the floor. 'I don't think I like any of it now,' she was saying to her maid, as I tentatively opened the door after knocking and being commanded to enter.

'Hope, darling, what do you think of this saffron blue? I thought it matched my eyes, but now that I see it in this light, it's not the same.' She held up a silk blouse of a startling turquoise shade.

'It does seem a bit vibrant,' I said cautiously.

Amaranth held it closer to her face. 'Vibrant is good. The Ambassador likes me being vivacious. He says I'm an excellent distraction.' She sighed. 'So much of my time is spent distracting men from their silly little talks about politics. Honestly, why can't they save it for the port and cigars?'

'Amaranth,' I said carefully. 'There is something I would like to talk about. It's a bit delicate.' I cast a look at the stony-faced maid.

'Oh, darling, darling, do come in and tell.' She swept a number of items off a pouffe and indicated to me to sit. 'All this shopping is so boring.' She turned to the maid. 'I'll keep the pink silk lingerie, the ivory lace nightgown, and the peach blouse. Send the rest back. Tell them that on examining the items more closely I found the quality lacking.' She made shooing motions with her hand. The maid began to carefully pick up and fold the various items. Amaranth sighed loudly, swept up a whole lot of clothes, and bundled them into the maid's arms. 'Out, dear,' she said curtly.

When the door had closed behind the maid, she turned her attention to me. 'So, Hope darling, dare I say it's about a boy? Your mother would be so pleased.'

I bit my tongue and didn't say my mother would be horrified. 'Actually, it's about Bernie.'

Amaranth's mood turned, as her fellow countrymen are so fond of saying, on a dime. 'Oh, what has that frightful child done now?' she said. She sank into a chair. 'Pray tell me I don't need to find her a clinic.'

'Good God, no,' I said, taken aback. It seemed a day both mother and daughter were out to shock me. 'Nothing like that, I promise you. It's a crush, you see. She seems quite keen on my Uncle Joe. Or, at least, the idea of him. I think she's only met him once, but I expect she likes the idea of being related to me . . .' I gabbled on, thrown by her suggestion that Bernie had already lost her virginity. I mean, I'd never actually asked her, but I'd always assumed she was saving it for the marital bed.

Amaranth waved her hand airily. 'Is that all?' She said. 'She fancies the idea of being a countess and living in a great house. His is one of the greatest houses in Britain, isn't it?'

'Well, it is large,' I said, 'but . . .'

She leaned forward, smiling. 'Darling, don't worry. Your Uncle Joseph is a lovely man. Very handsome, and quite the favourite among the more discreet ladies of the – do you still call it the "ton", "the upper five hundred", or is that too passé? Anyway, Joe is not at all right for my daughter. Or, more accurately, she'd be bored to tears with his country lifestyle and flinging herself into affairs left, right, and centre. It would be so embarrassing for the Ambassador.' She patted my hand. 'I do hope I haven't shocked you, but I know all too well how the world works. While I'm sure you play by the rules, my dear, my daughter is a law unto herself. We colonials are the absolute worst.' She laughed. 'Joe's quite safe.' She gave a sly little smile. 'Believe me, it would be completely inappropriate for my daughter to show an interest in him. He's already a close family friend.'

Amaranth was clearly hinting at something which I didn't care to delve into, not least because if I knew certain things, I would feel duty bound to tell my mother and it would all go downhill from there. Joe was almost twenty years older than me, but the bold and brash Amaranth seemed an odd choice for him, even for a brief affair. Besides, how, when, why?

Amaranth was still speaking. 'By the way, darling, your mother wants you back for a few days. I've sent a maid to pack for you. An automobile will take you to the station after an early dinner. I'm afraid you'll miss the ball tonight. I hope you don't mind too much. You'll be back for the Dunlops' grand affair next week, I should think. Unless, of course, it's you who have done something frightfully naughty.' She laughed and leaned over to pat my knee. 'Not that you ever would, dear, sweet, reserved little Hope.'

I made my excuses as soon as I could and left. After all, one is not meant to slap one's hostess in the face, is one? Reserved I could accept, but sweet? Sweet? I was not an Empire biscuit!

I returned to my room to find Enid had everything well in hand. There was little for me to do except wait for dinner. I claimed to have a headache, so I could lie on my bed and think. Being summoned by Mother is never a joyous occasion. I do my best not to live at home. Since leaving for Oxford, I have visited friends as much as possible, but obviously that situation can't continue for ever. Naturally, I return home frequently, and intend to continue to do so. I'm very fond of both of my parents, but I don't want to live with them as an adult woman – and, if they were honest, I don't think they'd want that either. They have always been very much – almost *too* much – in love with one another to want anyone else around for any significant length of time. As I grew older, I noticed Mother was called away on business more frequently. What business was never explained, but my father always pined terribly. If he hasn't had to keep up appearances for the staff, I dread to think how morose he would have become.

However, a summoning is another matter. It usually means 'something has happened'. This can be anything from my parents being convinced London is about to suffer an enemy attack to a potential new suitor being found for me. I'm not entirely sure which of these prospects is worse, though, of course, I would never wish for anyone to suffer. But imminent peril is often preferable to me than the men my mother has attempted to set me up with. She thinks I'd like a well-educated gentleman of decent stock. As a great many of those poor men were lost in the Great War, the ones she tends to unearth all too often resemble some of my more decrepit university lecturers. She often speaks to me of a 'marriage of minds' being the most important thing, but honestly, when you've seen a middle-aged scholar lose half his soup into the depths of his beard, I can assure you, you are not thinking of marriage one bit.

The Ambassador, once again, did not join us for the family dinner. Amaranth only picked at her food. 'Are you feeling unwell?' I asked. 'This heat can give one the most awful head.'

Amaranth gave me a wide smile that entirely failed to light up her face. 'No, dear, but I am expected at a reception today and there will be canapés. You know how Chef gets if I don't give him a full report. So very tiresome.' She looked down at her trim figure. 'I may even need to start exercising.'

'Mother!' said Bernie, her eyes wide.

'Don't worry, dear, I won't turn into one of those fitness and healthy air freaks. But I do need to find a way to ensure I don't put on extra pounds. After all, I'm not as young as I used to be . . .'

She waited a few moments. We both dutifully protested.

'Delightful girls,' she murmured. 'I'm sure we can find you both a decent match before the end of the season. If the Ambassador is right about what is coming, you need to snap up the best of them now. Otherwise, you, missy,' she said, nodding at Bernie, 'will have to marry an American. And I can tell you, your fortune doesn't mean much among the Vanderbilts and the Astors back home.'

'You mean you'll be going back to America?' I said.

'No, Mommy!' said Bernie. 'I like living here. I went to Oxford! Why, I'm practically English.'

'I'm afraid, dear, that if it comes to war, the Ambassador feels it's not safe to stay here – and he'll certainly not want to leave you behind.' She looked at me. 'I'm sure Hope will be perfectly safe up in the Fens. It's not like it'll go on for very long and then we can come back. Although I suppose one might have to learn German.'

'I'm sorry?' I said. 'Are you suggesting that Britain would lose a war with Germany?'

'Well, it would likely be England against Germany *and* Italy, if the Ambassador is right – and he usually is.'

'But France, Switzerland, Poland – all the countries in between! They would be our allies.'

'The Ambassador says that the German war machine is quite something. He also says there's a lot of sympathy for Germany among the aristocracy. Fascism appears to many as a return to the old ways. Besides, no one wants a war with Germany. Not after last time. And the Germans certainly don't want to fight you.'

'Just everyone else,' I said.

'Oh well, Europeans,' said Amaranth. 'It's not like they're British, is it? No great loss.'

I heard my spoon fall with a clatter. 'Excuse me,' I said. 'I feel quite unwell.' Then I did something I don't remember ever doing before and left a half-eaten tarte tatin on my plate. I heard Bernie call after me, but I couldn't bear to sit at the table with her mother and pretended not to hear.

★

I stepped off the train at our home station into a glorious sunset. The wide-open vista of the Fens provides the perfect canvas for nature to paint its glories on. Anyone who thinks a sunset is a dull shade of predictable boring orange should visit the Fens. There, every night, you will see a heavenly mix of gold, azure, vermillion, crimson, and, yes, even orange. The colours are so much brighter there than in the city. In London it has always looked to me as if the sky needs a wash. But here was a Fens sunset, welcoming me home, as marvellous as I remembered. I felt a weight lift from my shoulders. As much I might claim to be a sophisticate, my heart would always belong in the country.

Merrit, our long-time chauffeur, was waiting for me. He had acquired a limp during the Great War, and a certain sardonic sense of humour my mother said he'd previously lacked. She finds him greatly improved by it. He's married to my mother's oldest friend, which of itself is another story.

'Evening, Miss Hope,' he said holding out a hand for my case. I handed it over, despite his infirmity. I knew better than to hurt his pride. 'How are you this fine day? Must be good to be away from that awful London air. All dirt and fumes, so I hear. Surprised you're not as black as a chimney sweep. How's the Ambassador's wife? She were a right 'un when she was young. Can't imagine that she's changed much. Wouldn't let my daughter go and stay with her.' With that extraordinary statement he opened the automobile door for me. I got in murmuring something about Amaranth's hospitality.

Merrit rambled on as we drove home. I paid little attention to him. If I listened, I'd have to tell Mother when she asked me what he'd had been saying. Then I'd have to listen to her lecture me on how never to let a friendship and service mix as it turned everything upside down. Moreover, Merrit, despite his humorous aspect, was now a law unto himself – and my father would do nothing!

Instead, I did my best to imagine what Amaranth might have done in her youth. Could it be history repeating itself? Had Amaranth and my mother been out on the town seeking beaus in their youth? My mother never spoke of how they'd met. I shuddered. I had great respect for my mother, but I had no desire to tread in her footsteps. My father has always described her as much a woman of action as of intellect. I didn't particularly like action. Uncle Eric might have made me learn how to defend myself, but I infinitely preferred being in the background to taking a front and centre role in any great adventure.

My mother was waiting on the steps to greet me. She had wrapped a peacock shawl around her. Her hair tumbled in burnished chestnut locks over her shoulders. That told me that whatever else was happening, we didn't have guests. My mother is most particular about dressing for dinner even when it's only her and Father at home. She would never allow herself to be seen by guests *of an evening* with her hair down.

'You look well, Mother,' I said, getting out of the car and dutifully kissing her on the cheek. My mother caught my upper arms in the slightly painful clinch that's her version of an embrace.

'Eric's here,' she said. 'He has brought the most alarming news.'

'Oh,' I said. Uncle Eric, obviously, didn't qualify as a guest. He had been a frequent visitor throughout my lifetime, but had rarely, if ever, been the solo guest.

'Is that all you can say, Hope?' My mother pushed me forward into the house. 'Go and change into a proper gown. We are in the library. He will want to talk to you.'

Poor Father, he hated people eating and drinking in his sanctum. I hastened up to my chamber. My mother had filled it with roses and baby's breath, my favourite flowers. She doesn't often speak of her affection for me, but she shows it in a myriad of ways. I changed into a reasonable blue dress that could be taken as an evening gown. I took the pins out of my hair, brushed it out, and left it down. In the mirror I could see the strong resemblance I bore to my mother. This likeness often bewildered people because we were of such different temperaments. Thus, casually but smartly dressed, I made my way downstairs. If Mother could wear her hair down in my godfather's presence, then I need not

61

make a grand effort either. Which, frankly, after my first experience of the season, was a relief. My state of dress was not missed by my mother as she waited for me outside the library. She sighed and frowned.

Mother picked and preened at me, but I escaped into the library. I knew Uncle Eric wouldn't be the least bit interested in the dress I was wearing. As he always told me, *appearance is important at certain times and for certain functions. Outwith that, dress to please yourself. You will have few enough opportunities.*

I found my father sitting in his favourite wingback chair, the fire beside him blazing and his pipe, unlit, fixed firmly in the centre of his mouth. He still wore Uncle Hans' gift and the fez was sat at a rakish angle that suggested my godfather had been plying him with alcohol. He went to rise, but I bent over, preventing him from doing do. I saw his face was pale, waxy, and slightly clammy. I smelt whisky on his breath. I felt myself flushing with irritation at Uncle Eric. I kissed my father on the cheek and he patted me on the arm as I embraced him. He was not having a good day. Uncle Eric, on the other hand, seated across from him in a wider armchair, was the very image of health and vitality. He's older than my mother, in his fifties, I should guess. His hair is still thick and his face mostly unlined. He has a touch of grey at his temples and a few lines around his eyes when he smiles, otherwise he could pass for at least a decade or so younger.

I took a harder chair – nothing in my father's library matches. It's part of its charm. Or so he would convince my mother.

'No kiss for me?' said Uncle Eric.

'She's far too old to go kissing some man-about-town like you!' said my father. He looked at me. 'Keep wondering if the chap has a painting in an attic somewhere,' he said. 'Hardly looks a damn day older than when I met him.'

'She's cross with me,' said Uncle Eric.

'Nonsense,' said my mother.

Uncle Eric eyed me askance. 'She thinks I convinced Bertie to have that extra dram. But, my dear girl, I didn't.'

'Quite true,' said Father, nodding like an old hound, and making his fez slip further forward. 'Not feeling quite right tonight. Needed an extra tot or two for medicinal purposes.'

'I believe modern medicine offers some viable alternatives,' I said, giving my godfather a cold look, but blast the man, all he did was smile in amusement.

My mother poured two glasses of whisky and handed one to Uncle Eric and, to my surprise, one to me. 'Don't tell me you didn't learn how to drink at Oxford?' she said.

'I'm not that fond of whisky,' I returned.

'Good Lord,' said my father. 'Are you unwell?'

'She prefers champagne,' said Uncle Eric. 'While it might be loved of the bright young things these days, it started out life as a peasant's drink. I think that says it all.'

My mother sat down in a straight-backed chair. She perched on the edge as she had been taught by my grandmother. I would never have managed it. 'Stop it,' said my mother. 'We called Hope here to discuss something serious.'

'Which is?' I asked. I was tempted to say that I hadn't done anything, but the presence of my three childhood authority figures always makes me feel unaccountably guilty. Uncle Eric winked at me as if he knew what I was thinking.

'Eric,' said my mother, who rarely misses anything. 'Be serious for once.'

'I'm always serious,' he said, pulling a forlorn face that made my father laugh.

My mother turned to me with a huge sigh that showed what she thought of the men in the room. 'Hope, a debutante has died.'

'Oh no,' I said. 'Charlotte's dead?'

Uncle Eric's attention switched so intently to me it was like being under a hot light. 'You knew her?'

'Barely,' I said. 'We found her crying in the gardens of Buck House—' I got no further.

'Buck House?' cried my father. 'The disrespect!'

'You were in the gardens?' said my mother.

63

'Why was she crying?' said Uncle Eric.

'In order,' I said. 'It's the popular name for Buckingham Palace. Supposedly even the princesses use it.'

'That Margaret is going to be trouble,' muttered Uncle Eric.

I cleared my throat and continued. 'Bernie and I ventured into the gardens because she wanted to smoke.'

'Hope!' cried my mother.

'I don't smoke!' I said. 'But when we were out there we heard crying and Bernie looked for the source of it.'

'That girl,' said both my parents.

'Why was she crying?' asked Uncle Eric.

'She said she was crying because she was lost,' I said. 'I hate to speak ill of the dead, but I think she was rather a timid little thing.'

'She was unharmed?'

'She had torn her train slightly during the presentation, but otherwise she seemed perfect. Rather too perfect if you ask me.'

'Fairy Princess waiting for her white knight to rescue her?' said Uncle Eric.

I blinked at this level of whimsy. 'I meant how she might see herself,' he said.

'Oh, yes . . .' I said. 'And she cleared up in a jiffy when she met us. There was nothing seriously wrong – I mean, nothing had happened to her.'

My father coughed in alarm. I moved on quickly. 'Bernie took her under her wing. Got me to sew up the train and then offered her a lift in the Embassy vehicle to the after-party.'

'And she went with you? What happened then?' said Uncle Eric.

'We got separated in the throng. I went to the library to read.'

'Oh, Hope,' said my mother and Uncle Eric.

'Anything good?' said my father.

'Dorothy L. Sayers,' I told him. '*Gaudy Nights*.'

My father removed his pipe from his mouth and gestured enthusiastically. 'Some people think it's too long, but I think it one of the very best. Much more observation and much less of that little fellow trying to be witty.'

'So, you weren't with Charlotte?' said Uncle Eric.

'I didn't see her after we got out of the vehicle.'

'You mean Bernadette went off with her and left you alone? I shall telephone her mother!' said my mother.

'It's fine,' I said. 'If nothing else, it means whatever happened with Charlotte, I was nowhere near it.'

'Good,' said my mother and my father together.

'Shame,' said Uncle Eric.

'Eric!' snapped my mother.

He shrugged and spread his hands in a gesture of surrender. 'Do you have any idea what happened to her, Hope?'

'She just said she wasn't there,' said my father. 'Don't go trying to involve Hope in your schemes.'

I didn't get a chance to ask him what he meant by this as Uncle Eric broke in, 'I was merely wondering what the *Beau Monde*, of which lesser mortals such as I are not a part, think of the affair.'

My mother threw him a filthy look and pursed her lips.

'At the time the rumour was she had gone off with that play-boy James Trask,' I said

'Why?' said Uncle Eric. 'Did someone see them together?'

'Not that I know of,' I said, wondering how Harvey was getting on. 'Do you know the policeman in charge of the case, Uncle Eric?'

'Something like that. Did she seem the kind of young lady to go skinny-dipping?'

'I beg your pardon,' said my father. 'Skinny what?'

'She was found in water?' I asked.

'Both of them drowned,' said Uncle Eric.

'How perfectly awful,' I said. 'Poor Charlotte.'

'So, was she?' asked Uncle Eric.

'No,' I said. 'If Trask wanted a woman to skinny-dip with' – seeing my father's continuing consternation, I could feel myself getting hotter as I said this, but ploughed on – 'he could have had his pick of females who weren't heiresses, or who had relatives of less influence.'

'Or even simply paid someone,' said Uncle Eric mildly.

'It makes no sense to run off with this Charlotte at the beginning of the season. No one proposes for at least a month,' said my mother.

'I take it Trask was the kind of man you would not imagine cutting short his season, and its entertainments, merely because he had lost his heart to Charlotte Saulier?' Uncle Eric stated.

I swallowed. 'Yes, by reputation he was the sort of man who would intrigue himself with other women and only propose when he felt it was necessary to – err – secure her.'

'"Intrigue himself,"' said Uncle Eric. 'How archaic. Don't go all prudish on me, Hope. Do you think she was of the type to interest him?'

'I only know Trask by repute,' I said, 'but Charlotte, who I admit I didn't much take to, was a soft, sweet soul.'

'Gullible?'

'Certainly. If Trask offered her a lift home if she felt unwell, or tired, I expect she would have asked if she could trust him – she knew that much.'

'But when he said yes, she would have believed him?'

'I think so,' I said. 'I find it hard to imagine being that trusting of anyone.'

'That's because you have had the privilege of having me as a godfather,' said Uncle Eric without a hint of amusement.

'But I don't think he would have got her to go skinny-dipping or – or damage her virtue. He didn't have the reputation of someone who would coerce a girl to do . . . something.'

'You *can* say sleep with him, you know.'

'Damn it, you know exactly what I mean,' I snapped. 'She wasn't the kind of girl to be seduced into giving up her virginity.'

'Good heavens, Hope,' said my father, blushing beetroot. 'The things you modern girls talk about!'

'I'd lay odds that she'd have collapsed into tears long before he got to remove an article of her clothing. I've heard some bad things about Trask, but no suggestion that he'd rape a woman.

Besides, isn't – wasn't – he a bit old to go skinny-dipping? More of a college prank, that.'

'Hope!' said Father, 'Don't tell me you ever . . . ?' The hue of his face intensified.

'Certainly, Father, *I won't tell you then*,' I said.

'He very much liked to use cocaine,' said Uncle Eric quickly. 'If he got her to take some too she might well have become more malleable. That's the problem with users, they think that what they enjoy, everyone else will as well. They were signs on the bodies they had both been indulging in cocaine and alcohol.'

'Good grief!' I said, bemused. 'I can't imagine her . . . I mean, I just can't see her reacting without floods of tears to being anywhere on her own with him. As soon as he didn't take her all the way home, she'd have turned on the waterworks.'

'Anything else?' said Uncle Eric.

'I really knew her for no time at all . . .'

'But?'

'It feels wrong.'

'With that I agree,' said Uncle Eric. 'Let's try not to upset your parents further. We shouldn't have discussed this before supper. Talk about Amaranth and Bernadette – and how very well protected the Ambassador's daughter is.'

With that he got up. He leaned over me and kissed me swiftly on the cheek, taking me quite by surprise. But before I could react he'd left the room. I followed him into the dining room, but it was clear the subject of Charlotte was now closed. Instead Uncle Eric had us all laughing at his stories of the antics of senior Members of Parliament, which he told with a biting and irreverent humour. I noticed my father slowed his intake of wine to listen, even tossing in the odd comment between the serious business of eating supper. By the time the table broke up my father had much better colour. I caught my mother more than once looking gratefully at Uncle Eric. It was a pleasant evening during which the four of us shut out the rest of the world and merely enjoyed each other's company. My godfather can be tremendously entertaining when he wishes.

When I woke up the next morning Uncle Eric was already gone.

'He said he's very busy at the moment,' said my mother. 'You know, with the global situation as it is.' It says something for our relationship that despite my doing the season she assumed I had kept up with current affairs. What puzzles me is why she should think I know what Uncle Eric does. He's never told me, and any questions I've raised about his career, his past, or his family, my godfather has been very adept at brushing aside.

'It's a long way to come for such a short trip,' I said when we seated for breakfast. The sun flooded in through the large window, giving the room a light and fresh feeling. This was enhanced by the breeze that squirrelled in between the sash and the jambs of said window. But all of us had taken precautions. My mother and I thought nothing of wearing shawls at breakfast, and my father now seemed to be living in the smoking jacket Uncle Hans had sent him, though he had removed his fez for breakfast. However, he kept it protectively on the seat beside him, like a dowager with her favourite Pekingese. He already sensed my mother's dislike of it.

My mother patted my arm. This, for her, was a great outward sign of affection. 'He takes being your godfather very seriously. He's always shown an interest. I admit, I had some qualms when I suggested him to your father, but he's done very well by you.'

'Probably leave her something in his will,' said my father, appearing from behind the morning paper. 'Got a lot of cash, and no one to spend it on, old Eric.'

'Don't be so vulgar,' said my mother. 'As the heiress to White Orchards, Hope need not think of such things.'

'Do you hear yourself, wife? You know the upkeep on this bally place is sky high.'

'Then you should never have bought it,' said my mother.

'It was your idea!'

68

I crept quietly from the room. I suspected it would be some time before they missed me.

I stayed with my parents three days. I don't know if Uncle Eric spoke to my parents privately before he left, but they didn't suggest that I should curtail my season. However, when my mother saw me off at the front door, she kissed me, something she hardly ever does, and made me promise not to take any unnecessary risks. I was very glad she had included the word 'unnecessary' as I felt I could wholeheartedly promise that. Only a fool takes unnecessary risks and, unlike Bernie, I try hard not to be foolish.

I was seated on the train when I realised that the previous day was the day I should have met Harvey in Hyde Park. I decided the only thing I could do was to go there today and hope that Harvey would return again at the appointed time. The whole investigation thing would be new to him, but he might suspect I had many calls on my time and might not manage the first meeting. Besides, he would doubtless hold out hope of remuneration. He struck me as the optimistic type.

During our chat at the Lyons' Tea House, I had done my best to be both intimidating and enigmatic. At least as much as my height and gender allows. I tried to recall what I had threatened him with. For the present, I could not remember. It had been a weak threat. I had pinned my hopes on the fact that beneath his shady façade, as he put it, Harvey was 'a bit of a bounder' but not 'a cad'. I also had an intuitive sense that he might enjoy an adventure. His intellect was wasted on paltry con tricks. But where could he go from his current position? Only further downwards into criminality. Really, if you thought about it, I was doing the man a favour. All I needed to do was pop across to the park on the way to the Embassy and no one would be any the wiser. Things were working out so well I ordered another round of tea and cake from the guard.

The train arrived well on time and I disembarked into a bright and lively London. It's always a bit of a shock to return from the quiet of the countryside to the bustling metropolis. The station was crowded, with more people on one platform than you might see in the Fens in a week. Guards called out warnings of trains about to depart. Doors slammed. People swarmed in groups around porters all demanding their luggage be taken first. Children with sticky faces from eating bags of sweets, used to keep them quiet on the journey, now howled with sore stomachs. Businessmen in long swinging coats, with neatly folded newspapers under their arms, hurried past asking loudly, if with some politeness, to make way. Under the brims of their rakishly titled hats, furrowed brows and intent stares called on the masses to part as they had 'important business to be about'. Nursemaids chased their charges and herded them away from the perilous edge of the platform. Smart women, up for the day, hurried past in a fog of perfume. The platform clock struck the hour. Whistles blew, and engines let off hearty chuffs of steam as they readied for departure.

Fortunately, I had not called Amaranth, so she would not have sent anyone to meet me. Despite her outwardly frenetic attitude, I had noted that when she was required to achieve an end, she did so. Whether the Ambassador needed new handmade boots by the evening or she was required to throw supper for thirty with only an hour's warning, Amaranth rose to the occasion. I thought my unexpected arrival would occasion no real disturbance.

But as I got off the train into the waiting melee I realised I had not taken my luggage into account. Or, more honestly, as maids had both packed and unpacked for me, I had paid little attention to its size and weight. Amaranth's maid had originally packed my things in a large carpet bag, with a fanciful tapestried exterior of unicorns amid unlikely red trees, when I left the Embassy. It had a sturdy handle, but as I lifted it from the porter's trolley, the uniformed man looked at me with some concern.

'I can carry it to your vehicle, miss,' he said. 'All part of the service.'

I wrapped my fingers more tightly around the leather strap and lifted the piece, attempting to use my own weight as leverage. 'It's

70

perfectly fine,' I said, feeling somewhat breathless. 'I have arranged to meet my friend in a local coffee house. I can manage.'

'If you're sure, miss,' said the porter, who I could see was trying very hard to resist looking up and down my small frame, in case I decided not to tip him. I gave him a bright smile and a shilling and walked off, head held high. I was barely outside the station before I had to stop and adjust my grip. It would be a long walk. I thought I might take a bus. I had never been on a London one before, but my dress and coat were plain enough that I could just about be taken for a lady's maid. I stepped off the pavement, placed the bag indelicately between my legs, and searched my purse for change.

The bus turned out to be quite a jolly ride. If I hadn't had the wretched bag I would very much have liked to ride on the open deck above, but one look at the winding staircase told me it was impossible. The conductor was extremely polite and helpfully gave me change from the neat little till that hung around his neck. I marvelled at his dextrous use of it, especially when the dials were upside down, and he appeared to appreciate the compliment. At least, when I accidentally knocked the hat off a terribly officious bank clerk, he took my side, telling the man he should have helped a lady like me.

The woman three to my left did smell unpleasantly of fish, and the wooden seat pressed unforgivingly into my posterior, but between stops the bus took a reasonable turn of speed. Nothing like one might manage on an open road, but most certainly faster than walking. Although the frequency of stopping to collect more passengers I am sure would become tedious if one had to make the same journey every day. But for me, seeing working London up close was fascinating. It gave me a glimpse into the lives of shop girls, clerks, ordinary people who'd been touched by the glamour of the metropolis, who were all so unlike those I had known in the Fens and so much more plentiful than I had found in Oxford. Other women, both young and old, united in plain clothes, faces lined with care and exuding weariness, huddled at the back of the bus. I recognised them: cleaners, overworked and

71

underpaid. The woman nearest to me gave off a scent of carbolic soap and sweat. I remembered my maid at college and hoped I had tipped her adequately. It is so easy to undervalue those who serve. One tiny girl, who I could scarcely believe was of working age, fell asleep in her seat, her mouth open as she gave surprisingly loud snores. Among the stopping, the getting on and the getting off, there was the rhythmic voice of the conductor, 'Hold tight', and then the pressing twice of a little bell.

All in all, I was so rapt by the sights and sounds I almost missed Hyde Park. I managed to leap to my feet at the last minute, knocking off three hats this time as I fled for the exit. I landed on the pavement with a thump as the vehicle moved off. I headed into the Park and, to my delight, found Harvey pacing backwards and forwards.

'I thought we were meeting yesterday,' he said in lieu of a greeting.

'I was detained,' I said.

'No wonder you lot never do a proper bleedin' job. Timekeeping is important to those of us who have to earn our living.'

'Charlotte is dead,' I said. The words were out before I could check them. Uncle Eric had particularly asked me to be cautious and discreet and I had blurted the details out in a public park.

Harvey's face grew ashen. 'How?' he asked.

Now was the time to say it was a joke in exceptionally bad taste or attempt to tell him to forget what I had just said. I really must put some time aside to learn hypnotism. 'I shouldn't have told you,' I said, continuing to be devastatingly honest and surprising myself yet again. 'I was told in confidence.'

'By who? The murderer?' Harvey looked angry now and his voice had a sharp tone.

'Of course not.'

'Only, I know how you nobs are. Keeping it all under wraps, sweeping it under the carpet.'

'Let's find a bench to sit on,' I suggested. 'I see I will have to tell you everything.'

'I don't want to be an accessory after the fact.'

I took him by the arm. My touch startled him, and he actually jumped.

'Here. We can sit here,' I said, steering him to the cleanest-looking bench around. At least this one didn't have pigeon droppings on it. I was panting quite heavily from lugging the bag and Harvey took it, almost without thinking. Definitely someone in his upbringing had taught him manners. It only made me more curious about him. Also, it tethered him nicely to my side.

I spoke calmly and quietly. 'I do not know who the murderer is, and if I did I would immediately go to the police. I spoke without thinking. I betrayed a confidence.'

'I suppose it's over then,' said Harvey. 'You won't even need to know what I learned. Not that it was much.'

'You did what I asked, and I will still pay you.'

'That's not what I meant,' said Harvey, the sharp tone returning. He paused and sighed. 'Though, fair's fair, I'm not earning enough to stand on my pride. I'll take what we agreed.'

Questions vied in my head. What did Harvey do for regular employment? Why did he need money so badly? But most of all, why I had I told him? Could it be I somehow found this con man trustworthy? The thought was ridiculous, and I shook my head to banish it. Harvey misunderstood.

'Right, well, if you're going back on our bargain, there's no more to be said.'

He half rose. I caught his arm, causing him to jump once again. 'That wasn't what I meant. I was thinking out loud.'

Harvey frowned. 'I didn't hear anything,' he said.

'I meant . . . well, never mind. The thing is, poor Charlotte's body was found washed up on a beach in Brighton.'

'How the hell did it get there?'

'Trask's car was discovered in Brighton – damn, I didn't ask where.'

'Ask who?' said Harvey.

I ignored him. 'Charlotte's silver link bag from the ball was discovered in the back seat.'

'What was in it?'

'I don't know.'

Harvey raised his eyebrows at me. 'Your informant doesn't seem to be that well informed.'

'Or didn't choose to tell me,' I snapped. 'I get your point.' I paused. 'It gets worse.'

'Worse than being dead?'

'Her corpse was found alongside Trask's. Both had been washed up on the beach. Both were unclothed.'

Harvey shrugged. 'The sea rips away clothes.'

'It is not thought so. The clothes were found on the beach. It appears they had gone skinny-dipping.'

Harvey took off his hat and scratched his head. He gave a low whistle. 'Ain't it always the quiet ones,' he said.

'What did you learn from the household?'

'Oh, not a lot. Staff were rather close-mouthed.'

'More than normal? Like they had been paid off?'

'Maybe,' said Harvey. 'Although I imagine when they hear she's dead they might start talking. 'Ere, maybe one of your well-connected pals could get me a press badge. I could sell the story on—'

'Before you recast yourself as an ace reporter, can we finish our conversation? There will be an inquest, but at the moment I am told it is likely to be ruled as death by misadventure.'

'Who, exactly, is telling you this?'

'That's not important. What did you learn?'

'There was some kind of altercation at the ball. Charlotte was at the centre of it. And Trask was also involved. The stories I did manage to get out of the servants didn't match up. No one saw – or heard – Trask trying to drag the girl off. Some of them claim they heard shouting – multiple voices – before Trask even stepped back-stairs. That's where it happened. On the back stairs, and out in the backyard. The servants were all busy with their duties and were doing their best to ignore what their so-called betters were up to, in case it cost them their positions. And the lighting back there isn't good either. I had a look. Dark walls and even old-fashioned gas lamps in places. Would you believe it? All fancy on the outside, but back there, it's a bit of a deathtrap.'

'A most thorough piece of work,' I said.

Harvey flashed me a grin. It faded quickly. 'Can't believe she's dead. Such a tiny timid thing. Never have imagined she was the skinny-dipping type.'

I mused silently on what that type might be. 'It is believed drugs and alcohol were involved,' I said.

Harvey gave a low whistle. 'Well, if it's the snow powder, we're well out of it. Nasty people behind that stuff.'

'I need to get back to the Embassy,' I said, reaching for my bag.

'She really is the Ambassador's daughter?' said Harvey. 'I thought you were having me on.'

'Bernie? Yes, she is.'

'Gawd, I could have landed myself in a right mess. I owe you.'

I shook my head. I retrieved my purse from my pocket and paid him what we had agreed.

'I'm only sorry there wasn't a better ending,' said Harvey.

'I also,' I said and attempted to take my bag.

'Where is the American Embassy?' he asked.

'Grosvenor Square,' I said, 'about seven minutes' walk from here. No distance. I will not be in any danger.'

Harvey gave me an odd look. 'I wasn't so much thinking about the perils of London in broad daylight as you carrying that heavy bag. What you got in there? The Crown Jewels?'

'I have no idea. Maid packed and unpacked it for me. It is rather heavy.'

''Ow the other 'alf lives, eh? Give it 'ere, your ladyship. I'll carry it for you. You can tell 'em you're giving a poor bloke a shilling for helping you out.'

I thought about it. I didn't particularly wish to arrive on Amaranth's doorstep lugging my own baggage and sweating profusely. She would doubtless call up Mother if I did. 'I agree,' I said. 'And I will give you a shilling.'

'No, you bleedin' well won't,' said Harvey. 'I 'ave *some* pride.'

75

As we exited the park, I was about to point out his earlier con-travening argument, when I caught sight of the news-stand opposite. The ink had to be wet on the latest newspaper. The newsboy was engaged in putting the finishing touches to the fresh news sheet to be clipped onto the stand. It read, 'Debutante Dies in Disreputable Disaster'.

'Bleedin' hell,' said Harvey. 'Who writes that tosh? Even I could do better. 'Ere, what I said about a press card earlier, I was only joking, but now I come to think of it . . .'

'Oh, no,' I said, doing my best to ignore him. 'Bernie!'

Chapter Seven

Once through the doors of the Embassy, people descended on us from all sides. Two particularly large gentlemen stood either side of Harvey. 'Hey, I only helped the lady with her bag,' he said, throwing a worried look at me.

'Is there a problem?' I asked in my coldest voice. None of the (now eight) large men surrounding us moved. However, before I needed to take further action, a side door burst open and Amaranth burst in.

'Oh, thank goodness,' she said loudly, sounding more American than ever. She flung open her arms as she ran towards me. I steadied myself for the embrace but was not prepared for the cloud of scent and loose powder that accompanied it. I tried and failed to suppress a coughing fit. This only served to alarm Amaranth more. 'My darling girl, what has happened to you?' she cried. I could sense she was throwing poor Harvey the most evil stares over my shoulder. 'We were so worried about you!'

I managed to disentangle myself and my coughing subsided. 'Why? How?' I asked. 'I didn't even tell you I was returning today . . . No, wait. Mother. She telephoned you, didn't she?'

Amaranth didn't even bother to answer. 'Who is that person with you?' she demanded.

'This kind gentleman carried my case. I had taken a fancy to stop in Hyde Park, but I quickly realised my luggage was too heavy for me and he offered to help.' I turned and took the carpet bag from Harvey. I set it down and retrieved my purse. 'Thank you so much for your assistance,' I said and gave him two shillings. Shielding my face from everyone but him, I also winked.

'No problem at all, miss,' said Harvey, doffing his hat. He looked around at the guards in the foyer. 'If it's all right with you chaps, I'll be on my way.' When no one moved, Harvey turned on his heel and walked with dignity to the exit – although the skin between his shoulder blades must have itched from the looks the men were giving him. Once out the door, I saw him quicken his walk. I reckoned by the time he was out of sight he would be running full pelt.

'What an extraordinary man,' said Amaranth. 'You are so lucky, Hope. After the news today, the Ambassador doesn't wish either of you two girls to go leave the Embassy without a guard.' I sighed inwardly. This would be problematic. Moreover, it felt decidedly rude. The Ambassador had yet to join us at any meal, but he was dictating how I should behave.

'I quite understand you may have kidnap fears for Bernie,' I said as calmly as I could. 'But I am of no significance.'

'You are our guest,' said Amaranth firmly. She didn't need to add, 'and could be used as leverage'. I understood from her look alone. She signalled to the guards, most of whom slid back into whatever shadows they had emerged from, leaving only two, plus a middle-aged, overly made-up woman in horn-rimmed glasses, to man the Embassy entrance. Amaranth swept me off behind closed doors to the inner sanctum of the family apartments.

We had to transverse a number of panelled corridors. These were generally dim, lit only by the overhead lamps that shone onto seemingly never-ending lines of patriotic watercolours. The thick carpet beneath our feet muffled all sound of our footsteps. We passed several doors with slots for name cards. Even approaching the family area, the slender-necked lamps and ornately expensive vases on occasional tables continued. It reminded me of the state rooms at Uncle Joe's: the rooms none of the family particularly liked, except Grandmother.

'Bernie is so upset,' she said. 'She blames herself for what happened to that dreadful girl.' She shook her head and her earrings jingled. 'I cannot think why. Drink, drugs, going off alone with a single man: she doubtless got what she deserved. That's not even touching on the subject of how her clothes and her person got separated from each other.' She tossed her hair. 'And Bernie told me she knew all the right people. When did debutantes start lying? It's disgraceful. I told the Ambassador he should do something about it, or at least say something to the right people.'

My natural inclination was to object strongly to this description of Charlotte, but I merely said. 'It is most surprising. She did not strike me as that kind of a girl.'

'It's always the quiet ones,' said Amaranth, opening the door to the family lounge. I bit my tongue at the wildly inaccurate old trope. Besides, if that were true she would never have to worry about Bernie.

A tear-ravaged Bernie awaited us. She sat in an overly large chair, her shoes discarded and her legs curled up beneath her. Her face shone from recent washing and bore no signs of make-up. Dressed in a simple, high-necked dress, she looked half her age. She stood up the moment I entered and ran towards me. This time I stepped voluntarily into the embrace.

'I can't believe it,' she said, her voice cracking with tears. 'She wasn't like that.'

'Right,' said Amaranth behind me. 'I need to go and look over menus for the function tonight. It's going to be deathly dull, so I must ensure the Ambassador at least has decent food he enjoys. Men only, thank goodness, so we can go off to . . .' she waved her hand around, 'that soirée. Who is the hostess?' She shook her head. 'It'll come back to me. The invites are on the mantel. Perhaps, Hope, you can instil some of that famous British backbone in my daughter. She's talking about withdrawing from the season, which is impossible! What would people say?'

I felt rather than saw the door shut behind Amaranth.

'She's awfully cross with me,' said Bernie.

'Why?'

'For befriending Charlotte. For not believing what the papers have written. For wanting out of this dreaded marriage-mart you Brits call the season. For everything!' She gave a little hiccupping sob.

'Let's sit down,' I said. 'And maybe ring for some tea?'

'The famous British pick-me-up. I'd rather have bourbon!'

I rang the bell and requested tea and some light refreshment from the maid. I suggested cucumber sandwiches and lady fingers, but only received a polite but puzzled nod.

'I haven't read the newspaper report yet. It is very bad?' Bernie passed me the much-crumpled paper. It said much as Uncle Eric had told me, but in more salacious language.

'Goodness, the press is headed straight for the gutter,' I said in disgust.

The maid reappeared with coffee, and sandwiches filled with something cheesy and something fishy, along with piles of cream cakes. 'High tea,' she announced proudly. I duly thanked her and even forbade myself from mentioning that high tea was meant to be served at teatime. It was on the tip of my tongue to comment on how ridiculous it was that Americans had to be so over-the-top all the time, but Bernie was hardly in a mood to be teased. Honestly, though, they are so showy.

Bernie picked up the largest cake, a cream horn, and wrapped herself around it. It appeared to help her mood.

'I don't believe it either,' I said.

Bernie stopped eating, a cream moustache above her lips. 'Do you think she could still be alive?' she said thickly.

'No, I'm afraid that's too much to hope for,' I said. 'But I think this is what your police would call a "fit-up". You're absolutely right. We knew the girl for hardly any time at all, but both of us are certain she wasn't the fast and loose type. And it makes no sense for Trask to risk the scandal in whisking her off.'

'Do you think he might have mistaken her for a waitress or a maid?'

'In that dress? I'd bet it cost twice what yours and mine added together did. If Trask was half the connoisseur of women he was meant to be, he'd never have mistaken her station nor missed the money her family clearly had. Even if her chaperone wasn't around, they'd clearly decked her out to be spotted for what she was.'

'You make her sound like a commodity of some sort.'

'You're the one who called it a marriage-mart,' I said.

'It's all so horrible.'

'It will certainly be the last season for some time. If not the last ever.'

'What?' said Bernie, looking up at me and frowning. 'How do you mean?'

'War,' I said succinctly.

'Oh, that won't happen, Hope,' said Bernie. 'People like Daddy make a career out of ensuring those silly politicians get sorted out. I don't say it won't go right to the wire or that other countries might not get eaten up by that horrid man, but you'll be safe on your island. No one could ever challenge Britain. Daddy said if we were anywhere else he'd send Mommy and me back to the States. Europe is far too dangerous, but we're safe here . . .' She broke off, biting her lip. Her eyes brimmed with tears. 'Not that poor Charlotte was,' she said.

'No,' I said calmly. 'I am almost certain she was murdered.'

Bernie wiped the rest of the cake from her face and stood up. 'Then we have to find out who did it,' she said defiantly.

I picked up a sandwich and examined its contents closely. I didn't think the Embassy's kitchen would deliberately poison us, but this did not seem to be something produced by the normal chef. I assumed he was too busy preparing for the function tonight. Bernie was still talking.

'Don't try and talk me out of it,' she finished.

'Oh, indeed not,' I said. I nibbled on the edge of the sandwich. It was quite a pleasant taste, but annoyingly I could not work out what was in it. Pink, with little bits. 'No one else is liable to look into this. So we must.'

Bernie, who had adopted what I assumed she thought was a heroic pose, flopped back into her chair. 'Honestly, Hope,' she said, 'you do know how to kill a moment.'

'I have been considering the problem of how we might go about this,' I said. 'I suspect the first thing we need to do is make enquiries down at Brighton. Do you think this is salmon?'

'No idea. You mean the police?'

I shook my head. 'I think we can disabuse ourselves from the start of the idea that the police will be at all interested in our help. Indeed, even if we do uncover an alternative chronology for what happened to Charlotte, I doubt any of them would listen to us.'

'But if we had enough evidence we could go to the press,' said Bernie.

'My thoughts exactly,' I said. 'Preferably, I would wish to hand over a file of all our evidence and then remove our names from the whole business.'

'To hell with that,' said Bernie.

'Really?' I said. 'You want your mother, your father, my mother, and my *grandmother* to know we have been investigating such matters? You're a braver soul than I.'

'You're always so pragmatic,' said Bernie in a tone that I interpreted was not a compliment. 'I suppose you've thought about how we will get to Brighton.'

'Certainly,' I said. 'We will take my car. It's been sitting in its London garage doing nothing for far too long. It needs a run.'

'You have your automobile in London and you didn't tell!' said Bernie. 'Can I drive?'

'No. And we will also need a male escort.'

'Why?'

'There may be some places such as public bars that it would not be appropriate for us to enter.'

'I don't care about my reputation,' declared Bernie. 'We're seeking the truth.'

'Indeed,' I said in as deflating a fashion as I could manage. 'But

I imagine the customers of those establishments are unused to being questioned by young women.'

'Oh, I see,' said Bernie. She might be melodramatic, but she was smart. 'I could ask Timmy, I suppose. I think he'd do pretty much anything for me.'

'The one overburdened with an Adam's apple? No, I don't think so. Besides, he'd try and compromise you in the politest way possible, so you'd have to marry him.'

'You think I made that much of an impression?'

'Your anticipated inheritance did.'

'Blow it! Who do you suggest?'

'The man who tried to con you at the shopping emporium last week.'

'A con man?'

'Con men are excellent at manipulating people, and as whoever is behind this is trying to manipulate the entire British press and police forces, I can't think of a type better suited.'

'But he could con us! He might,' she cast around for something unacceptable Harvey might do, 'plant a bomb in the Embassy.'

'I can just see him sneaking in with a parcel under his coat, in his cheap blue suit, tipping his hat at one of your larger guards and saying, "'Scuse me, governor. Is there a convenient place to leave this here bomb?"' I laughed for the first time in days. 'Honestly, Bernie, he's harmless. There's a world of difference between your friendly London con artist and a bloodthirsty terrorist. He's only trying to make the best of the cards he's been dealt.'

'He's a card sharp as well?'

'No,' I said, this time with a sigh. 'Don't worry. I can take care of him.'

Bernie screwed up her mouth to one side, indicating she was truly thinking. She looked, I think the expression is, like a bull-dog chewing a wasp. Posing Bernie only ever looks pretty. 'But how will you find him again.'

'I had him downstairs before your mother's goons scared him

off. I'm hoping he picked up on my signals to meet him in the park. Shall we go for a walk?'

'You're quite the dark horse, aren't you, Hope?' said Bernie, putting on her shoes. I thought I detected a note of admiration in her voice.

'Indeed? And I thought I had escaped the equine facial tendency so many of our fellow debutantes suffer.'

Bernie giggled. 'I'm so glad you are back,' she said.

My luggage had been taken to my room, so I only paused to wash my face and hands and attend to necessities before we set out. It was now mid-afternoon; unaccountably no one had brought us lunch, but the high tea would do until we could find a nice little café. Outside the intense sunlight caused the world to look brighter. Looking around it seemed impossible that Mr Hitler and his horrible cohorts could exist in such a beautiful world. It also meant Amaranth could hardly object to the pair of us strolling in the nearby Hyde Park. Bernie even took great care to tell one of her security men where we were going, so there was no need for them to follow us, and even that we would be back for an early supper. 'I absolutely promise and cross my heart that we will only be in the park,' she'd said, batting her eyelashes.

'Will they fall for that?' I'd said. I decided not to mention my café plan, as it would only complicate matters. Bernie is always best telling the truth. When we were out a short diversion would cause no harm. We may be close, but I will never understand her ability to forget to eat for an entire meal.

Bernie shrugged. 'After we've made them stare at daffodils and tulips for long enough I hope they'll disappear.'

I found Harvey by the bench he and I had sat on earlier. 'You took your bleedin' time,' he said. 'I ain't had no lunch and I'm starving. I was beginning to think I'd misunderstood that funny face you pulled at me. Either that or those Americans had taken you hostage.' I felt an instant connection with Harvey when he mentioned lunch.

'I'm sorry about that. I'm hoping we might get a chance to

have a little something but have a shilling in case things don't work out.'

Harvey straightened. 'I ain't a beggar,' he said. Then even from a distance I heard his stomach rumble.

'It's expenses,' I said, holding out the coin. 'You missed lunch on account of working for me, so I should pay.' Harvey grumbled, but took the coin. I smiled brightly as if he had done me a favour.

'Where's the other one?' he asked.

'Catching up,' I said. 'She met an acquaintance that had a horrid little dog with them and stayed to coo over it.' I shivered. Harvey, I noticed, also flinched.

'I hate them things,' he said. 'Ankle-biters, the lot of them, and as bad-tempered as . . .' He broke off as Bernie caught up with us. She glanced at her wristwatch and I could see my café trip vanishing. Bernie took an awful long time to get ready for an event.

'We will sit down and await you on this bench. Why don't you go and get yourself a hot pie? It is always much better to discuss matters on a full stomach.' I desperately wanted to add, could you get me one too, but I knew that if I did Bernie would hold it over me later. No one, except perhaps my father, would approve of eating cheap pies, no matter how delicious their brown gravy was.

'What matters?' asked Harvey.

I stood heavily on Bernie's foot before she could speak. 'Matters to both our advantage,' I said.

'All right,' said Harvey and headed off.

'He's quite the catch,' drawled Bernie. She watched him walk away. 'He's certainly in no hurry. Do you believe he will come back?'

'I believe he has an inquisitive nature,' I said. 'I have also found him to be most trustworthy when he gives his word.'

Bernie gave me an odd look. 'Sometimes, Hope, you are so on top of things, and other times you're as gullible as a maiden aunt.'

I shrugged. 'I hope we even each other out,' I said.

Harvey returned within a reasonable time, still munching his pie. It smelt amazing. My stomach growled so loudly I had to cough to cover it. He did have the grace to wipe the gravy off his face and hands with a handkerchief, which from my quick glimpse appeared well-laundered. 'What's this all about?' he said. 'More to do with your dead friend?'

I explained that Harvey had already uncovered some information for me and told Bernie about the fracas at the ball below stairs.

'That doesn't tell us what happened,' said Bernie.

'I did me best,' protested Harvey.

'It tells us the important information that whatever happened to Charlotte, there was a scuffle around it. Whether Trask was dragging her off, or someone tried to prevent her leaving with him or even something we have yet to consider was happening. We know her exit was not smooth and easy.'

'I see what you mean,' said Harvey. 'You don't believe what they're saying in the press, do you?'

'I think there is more to it,' I said. 'And we would therefore like to travel to Brighton and ask some of the locals, possibly men in bars, if anything untoward was seen. For which we will need a man.'

'Me?' said Harvey catching on quickly but with a singular lack of enthusiasm. 'And 'ow exactly are we going to get there without the police deciding I've kidnapped two debutantes? They're crawling all over the place now like the head copper's got a squid up his arse.'

I paused while I interpreted this mental image. Bernie giggled. 'You're a card,' she told him. Then to me. 'You're right. He's OK. I like him. He's what my aunt would call a colourful character. Tell me, Mr Harvey, do you consider yourself typical of working-class men? Are they all so amusing?'

I could tell Bernie was entering flirt mode. Not seriously, but it might be enough to scare him off. The tips of his ears were already red. I tilted my head on one side, 'I'm not entirely sure one can describe Harvey as a "working" person.'

Harvey, as I'd hoped, forgot any embarrassment as he put up a feisty self-defence. 'Oi, I'll have you know I've done more work in my life than you pair have had hot dinners.'

I touched him lightly on the arm, making him jump. 'I apologise for my levity,' I said. 'I have a vehicle and will drive us to Brighton. I received the automobile from my uncle for my eighteenth birthday and have even driven as far as Scotland, so you need have no fear you will end up in a ditch. I will further arrange that Bernadette and I have a legitimate reason for being away from the Embassy. I will, of course, pay you for your time and ensure we return before nightfall. And if that doesn't entice you, I shall throw in a picnic meal on the way there and back.'

'You're going to dog me until I say yes, aren't you?' said Harvey.

'Of course not. I would prefer to go with a male escort, but if not, we are both intrepid women.'

Harvey gave me a long, hard look. 'You would go on your own, wouldn't you?' he said.

I nodded.

'Bugger. I'll 'ave to go with you.'

'Ooh, he's gallant too,' said Bernie, adopting a mock damsel-in-distress pose.

'Now you can just stop that,' said Harvey. 'I'm only doing what any decent gent would.'

'Though why he should take us under his wing I have no idea,' said Bernie, giving me a hard stare as we walked back to the Embassy.

'I have no idea either,' I said, and bent down to smell a flower. Out of the corner of my eye I caught sight of a park warden checking I wasn't about to pick it. I inhaled obviously and stuck my nose into another clump. By the time I had straightened my face felt completely cool.

'How are you going to explain our absence from the Embassy? You won't tell Mommy where we really are, will you? I mean, Harvey might be a pleasant chap but he's hardly the thing.'

'I won't. That's your task,' I said. 'I'm providing the transport and the escort. You can't expect me to do everything, Bernie. You're the one with the most society contacts. Call in some favours. And don't try the silly feeling ill stunt. It never works.'

The colour leached from Bernie's face. She said a most unlady-like word. I walked on ahead, contemplating whether or not the head chef would be preparing our supper or if whoever made those strange little pink sandwiches would be doing it. Really, I had no more idea what was in those than I did a hot pie, yet society endorsed me eating one — the less tasty option — and not the other. I feared I would never get used to London living.

Chapter Eight

Bernie and I took a cab to my garage early the next morning. 'I managed to persuade that awful Tessa Lloyds-Bowe to say we were spending the day at her "outdoor event". Then I had to convince my mother it wasn't an al fresco orgy.'

'Yes, I suppose it does sound somewhat risqué. What are we meant to be doing?' I asked, only mildly interested.

'Riding horses, eating a meal, playing games,' this last word she said with a visible shudder. 'And generally being young ladies of quality in the countryside. Apparently, the trip out alone takes an hour. They're going in charabancs.'

'Are you sure you have that quite right?'

'Some kind of multi-person vehicle that isn't an actual bus. The working class use them when they take outings to the seaside. Tessa promises it will be such fun. We will all sing songs, eat egg sandwiches from paper bags, and drink lemonade.'

'Sounds dreadful,' I said.

'I agree. But hordes of people are going, so we won't be missed. Or, rather, no one will be able to positively say we weren't there.'

'Perfect,' I said with a smile. 'You have done excellently, Bernie.'

'I didn't manage to do anything about food,' she said.

When Harvey arrived at the garage, he remarked upon the lack of food in evidence and not my nice little automobile. My MG TA tourer is actually a four-seater. Uncle Joe told me, when he gifted it to me, that there was nothing so annoying as not having space for one's dogs and luggage. I didn't have to answer their questions because the nice man from Fortnum and Mason's turned up that very minute with my delivery. I'd had to order everything for two meals al fresco, so the boxes were rather large. I suspected Harvey would be both windswept (from the elevated seat, which Uncle Joe pointed out his dogs preferred) and somewhat squashed. But then the two of them had made food a priority.

Bernie bagged the front seat. 'If I watch you closely, Hope, do you think I could drive on the way back?'

'No,' said Harvey and I together as one.

With this happy accord, we took our positions and drove off. As it was a lovely day I had kept the leather top down, but it did prevent casual conversation. However, not being distracted by the others' comments or complaints, I was able to make good time. I had checked the maps beforehand and picked an excellent spot for our first meal. Harvey and Bernie were too busy arguing about the relevant merits of two extremely popular champagnes to notice when I turned off the main road into a tree-lined lane.

'You certainly have aspirations,' said Bernie. 'I shouldn't imagine if you worked for a whole year you would be able to afford a vintage bottle of that!'

'You can stick that little snub nose as high as you like in the air, but,' said Harvey, 'I can assure you, I've drunk that and better!'

'I do not have a snub nose!' said Bernie, turning back around to face forward. This was quickly followed by 'Look out, Harvey!' I was too busy ensuring the vehicle stayed out of the deeper ruts to notice how low the overhanging branches had become. To be fair to me, this is not the kind of hazard you can spot on a map.

'Bleedin' 'ell,' exclaimed Harvey, making Bernie snigger. I felt the seat behind us judder as he threw himself out of the way. 'Where the flaming heck are you taking us, Hope? Are you lost? When I was last in Brighton it wasn't in the middle of a ruddy jungle!'

'We are making a slight detour,' I said.

'What are you up to now, girl?' he growled.

'Luncheon,' I said, forestalling further comment as I pulled up next to a low wall. 'There's a stile marked on the map. Ah, there it is. If you could help with the blanket, Bernie, we can hop over the wall and have a picnic.'

The meadow's grass was slightly overgrown, but nothing that the tartan blanket I had brought could not smooth out. The glistening yellow of buttercups mingled with the sky-blue of speedwell and the purple of overgrown thistle. A low hum of bees flitting from flower to flower made a restful change from the throbbing of the engine. The wind whispered in the leaves and butterflies flitted about the meadow creating intricate dancing patterns of red, yellow, and blue. I could feel my shoulders slumping down after the strain of controlling the wheel. 'After luncheon, I am going to lay back and bask like a shark on a reef,' I said. 'It'll be up to you two not to let me fall asleep for hours.'

'That's going to depend on whether you've brought any of Harvey's favourite tipple,' said Bernie, curling her legs under her as she sat down neatly on the blanket. 'Now, who's serving up?' She looked pointedly at Harvey.

'I'm not your bleedin' servant,' snapped the ex-waiter.

'I'll do it,' I said. 'It's fair shares for all, and no champagne.' The grumbling that accompanied this make me think what it might have been like if I had gone away to school and indulged in midnight picnics. I had to smother a giggle as I realised that I had accepted Harvey as an honorary girl.

We started with quail's eggs. I had to assure Harvey that the store had not 'stiffed' me and they were meant to be this size. Fortunately, there is something about sitting on the ground on a blanket, sharing a meal, that produces a natural camaraderie. The day had stayed warm, but a breeze ruffled our hair. Clouds so perfect a child might have drawn them puffed across the sky. In the nearby hedgerow, we could hear the chittering of blackbirds in their nest. The smell of fresh apple blossom clung to the air – I knew there was a large orchard nearby, and only hoped Harvey would not figure out they would sell him cider, but he made no suggestion that the lemon cordial and fresh coffee were not enough. The blanket Fortnum's had included was tartan in an eye-blistering way that no Scot would ever have claimed, but it was thick enough to keep the grass from pricking at our legs. They had even included two small cushions, which Harvey had gallantly given over to Bernie and me. If it wasn't for our errand it would have been a supremely pleasant outing. Albeit we were a most mixed company, as much by class as gender. But I like to think, for all her innate brashness, Bernie had the open-mindedness of a scholar. In fact, she was treating Harvey more like an annoying brother.

It was clear that Harvey looked to me as the leader of the little group – but then I was paying him. He and Bernie were beginning to develop a sort of teasing banter in the way only American girls can. Harvey even apologised for almost tricking her. Her face darkened when she remembered the incident, but Harvey assured her that becoming indebted to me was a grave enough punishment. Bernie laughed, and I felt quite uncomfortable. Yet again my dearest friend was proving more popular than I. I know it is unworthy of me, but Bernie has the ability to charm everyone and anyone. I might have been talking in knowledgeable depth with an Oxford scholar about some philosophical theory, hoping to impress him with my learning and intelligence. It would all go swimmingly, and then Bernie would turn up, and that would be it. My erudite comments were forgotten as soon as Bernie posed, smiled, and giggled. But I have always tried to lay the blame at the weakness of the opposite sex rather than at Bernie's door. She can no more help flirting than a fish can help swimming.

When we had almost exhausted the first hamper, Harvey raised the subject of what we might actually accomplish in Brighton. 'I was thinking, I could take a wander around the boarding houses and see if I could get any news from them. I don't think I can pretend not to be asking after Miss Saulier and

Trask, not after everything that's been in the press, but I thought I could say, if someone was getting really niggly, that I was working for the family.'

I nodded. 'If you say you're working for the papers they are liable to make things up and even ask for money for their story.'

Harvey nodded. 'I thought I could also drop into some of the public houses, as you suggested.'

'But what will we do?' asked Bernie.

'We cannot make too public a show of ourselves as we are supposed to be elsewhere,' I said. 'I thought we could visit the site where the bodies were found.'

'Oh God, will they still be there?' asked Bernie.

'Of course not,' I said. 'But I think getting a sight of that part of the beach, and where the car was found, might be able to tell us something.'

'Like what?' asked Bernie.

'I have no idea,' I said. 'But unlike the police, we at least have some acquaintance of one of the victims that might help us spot something they did not.'

Bernie pouted. 'It sounds as if Harvey is going to have all the fun,' she said.

'We're investigating a murder,' said Harvey. 'Not going to a bleedin' gymkhana!'

Bernie muttered something in a poisonous tone and flounced back to the MG. Harvey and I began to pack up the remains of the picnic.

'She's a bit of drama queen, isn't she?' said Harvey.

'You reminded her about Charlotte. She's trying to hide her feelings.'

'She's doing a pretty good job from where I'm standing,' said Harvey. I noticed he packed up the crockery and cutlery with considerable care. Most men of my acquaintance would have simply bundled it all into the hamper. I added this little foible to the growing list. Time and time again, for a con man, he was proving to be both loyal and honourable. There was most definitely a mystery about him and I was confident I would, in time, discover all.

We closed the hamper on the detritus of our picnic and I looked back over the field. I had an impulse to throw it all in and spend the rest of the day lying in the sun. I knew there was a chocolate cake packed for later in the boot. We could put the blanket back down and attack the dessert. We could send Harvey for that cider and have a blissful afternoon.

I became aware Harvey was hovering beside me.

'Is there a problem?' I asked.

'Er, just to say I'm going to pop off for a moment, but I'll be back. Didn't want you thinking I'd run out on you.'

'Where are you going?' I said perplexed.

Harvey made some odd noises, but eventually managed to say, 'Call of nature!' before he walked quickly away. Understanding, I blushed furiously and nodded, unable to either speak or look him in the eye. My notion of an idyllic afternoon picnic disappeared. If it had been only Bernie and I . . . but the mixture of Harvey's company and the natural side-effect of drinking cider did not bear thinking about.

'What's up?' asked Bernie.

I mumbled something incoherent.

'Oh,' said Bernie brightly. 'He's off for a widdle.' She said this just as Harvey returned. He too blushed. Bernie, however, was unabashed. 'You men have everything so easy. If I was to risk it, I've probably end up with a nettle up—'

'Bernie!' I said sharply. 'Enough.'

Bernie half shrugged in an offended manner. 'I wasn't going to say anything terrible.'

'That would make a change,' said Harvey. After that they began squabbling again like cat and dog.

The wind picked up, so that with Bernie half-turned around in her seat I could not hear what the two of them were saying. I was very glad I had brought my slightly old-fashioned cloche hat. It not only suited me but kept my hair under control. Bernie, who had attempted to do something stylish with a scarf, fared less well. It kept flipping her in the face, which made Harvey laugh. Although Bernie had the last laugh as before long Harvey literally had to hang on to his hat to keep it.

I saw the sign for Brighton before the others. Originally Brighthelmstone, since the days of the Prince Regent it had traditionally been the place people went to do naughty things. I decided to pull over beside a nice little tea shop. We had all eaten more than enough, but a quiet corner equipped with some calming tea would be just the place to arrange exactly where each of us would be going, and how we would reconvene. There was also a slim chance it might stop the other two fighting. And if they also happened to have cream cakes . . .

I knew Bernie well enough to know it was perfectly true that she was trying to hold Charlotte's death at the back of her mind, lest she give way to her emotions, but also, like all Oxford women, she was highly competitive – especially if that competition was with a man. It was de rigueur for any of us scholars to challenge masculine superiority. However, I felt it was most unsportsmanlike to do it with Harvey, who obviously had so few advantages in life. I would have to remember to point this out to her.

'Tea,' I said brightly, pulling on the brake. 'Everyone out.'

'Loos!' cried Bernie in a mock British accent and leapt out.

'You can't just leave the stuff in the back,' said Harvey. 'Someone will nick it.'

'I shall pay a waitress in the tea room to keep an eye on it,' I reassured him. 'Although I believe, in the normal course of things, Brighton is thought to be well-policed.'

'Tell that to Charlotte,' muttered Bernie. I pretended not to hear her and got out of the car. Bernie hurried inside the shop. I scanned the vehicle for any obvious issues and managed to roll my shoulders at the same time. I wanted nothing more than to stretch from the tips of my fingers to my toes, but that is not something a lady does in public. The fact that my muscles ached like billy-o was no excuse for unladylike behaviour.

95

'Bernie is right about blokes having it easier,' I said to Harvey, who was hesitating at my side.

'It's a man's world,' said Harvey. 'Except there aren't so many of us around after the Great War. There are some reasons why you should feel ruddy lucky you're a girl. No one's going to ask you to fight the Germans.'

'Yes,' I said quietly. 'That's true. But I do wonder if waiting at home and wondering about whether Germany will overrun us would be almost as bad as being in action.'

'Will?' said Harvey. 'I thought we were talking about the past, not the present?'

'Both,' I said, walking over to the tea-room door and opening it. A silvery tinkle heralded our arrival. The tea room stretched over a significant space, but the tables, mostly set for four, were situated quite close together. I saw a sea of hats, mostly of the large and dowager variety, with an occasional neat little one that sported a single feather rather than an entire bird.

'Here's your jungle,' I murmured to Harvey.

A fuggy warmth filled and room and clouded the windows. Two younger tea-takers had dared to light cigarettes and the taint from their smoke mixed with the smell of rich, perfumed, and slightly sweaty females. Either the place didn't have a cloakroom – why take up valuable retail space? – or in Brighton it simply wasn't done for women to take off more than a tippet or stole when taking tea. I spotted one woman with a fox fur, who appeared to be trying to feed a cream bun to her furry neckwear.

The tables were set with dainty lace cloths and a small white vase, with a strawberry painted on it and a wilted daffodil in it, stood on each one. The crockery I could see also all had a strawberry theme, which was doubtless why this tea shop had been called The Little Strawberry. Dotted around the edges of the room, on shelves that appeared to have been placed with no particular thought, were cats – pictures of cats, cat ornaments, cat tea cosies and plates painted with cats. I have nothing against cats, I find them intelligent and elegant. However, I do not like the hair of any animal in my cream tea. I resisted the impulse to bend down and check there were no actual cats weaving their way between the tables. I heard Harvey audibly swallow at my side, but then I suppose being faced with so many formidable women in close proximity would be most unlike attending a debutantes' ball. I turned to reassure him, but the swell of noise overwhelmed me. It seemed there had been a momentary lull in the conversation due to curiosity over our arrival, because now the level of chatter rose to an almost unbearable level. I took Harvey's wrist, to the tutting of the ladies nearby, and towed him towards an empty table. Within moments a young girl in a white uniform dotted with strawberries appeared and bobbed a quick curtsy. 'What would ma'am like?' she said.

'A cream tea for three, please,' I said. 'Does that include a pot of tea?'

'Yes ma'am, Indian or Chinese?'

'Indian, please.'

She bobbed another curtsy. 'Be with you in a jiffy, ma'am'.

'You might try not to make a man feel bleedin' useless,' said Harvey.

Bernie slipped into the chair beside me looking a great deal more relaxed. 'You'll have to forgive her,' said Bernie, throwing a teasing glance at me. 'She doesn't quite know what to do with men.'

At this moment the little waitress arrived back, pushing a small gilt trolley. From this she disgorged what even I felt was a great many cakes and sandwiches, as well as an enormous pot of tea and a large milk jug decorated with the inevitable strawberries. Only when she had left did I notice Harvey staring at me the way I generally stare at American daywear.

'You mean . . . ?' He goggled at me. Then his eyes began to dart between my face and Bernie's. At the same time his Adam's apple was bobbing in a peculiar manner and his face became flushed.'

'Would you like some tea?' I said offering to pour a cup. 'You don't look quite the thing.'

'Bit of shock,' said Harvey. 'Never occurred to me you didn't like men.' He scratched his head. 'I suppose that explains the driving.' Then he put up his hands. 'Each to his own. No matter to me.'

I stared at him. 'Good gracious, no,' I said as the penny dropped. 'No, she does not mean I am a sapphist,' I said crossly, kicking Bernie under the table. 'I doubt she knows any more about that than Queen Victoria did. I simply haven't found a man whose company I have preferred to a decent book.'

'Well, if you're going to compare them to your love of books,' said Bernie. 'I'm not surprised there's never been a front runner.'

'Gawd, you pair!' said Harvey. 'I need my cuppa.' He poured the tea, topped his up with milk and three sugars, and slurped some with evident enjoyment. 'How we going to do all this then?'

'I fear we shall have to split up,' I said. 'Much of what you discover must be on your own recognisance.'

'Yeah, well, I'm up to nosing around a bit. I take it you want me to be discreet?'

'As you can be in that appalling suit,' said Bernie.

Harvey ignored this comment. 'I'll see you back here in a couple of hours, ladies? We can't leave it too long before we head back, or your precious reputations will be tarnished, and you'll turn into pumpkins.'

I nodded my assent. As we watched him walk out, I remarked, 'It's curious isn't it, that I never need to explain my more complex language to him?'

Bernie shrugged. 'Everyone reads the papers nowadays,' she said. 'I find it more curious he didn't want any of these delicious cakes.' She picked up a meringue bursting with cream. 'Still, all the more for us.'

'Eat your sandwiches first,' I said, placing a couple of crustless cucumber ones on my own. 'This is a jolly good tea.'

Bernie said something through her full mouth that signalled agreement. I have mentioned she can skip meals with no obvious ill affect, but she likes a cream tea almost as much as I do. We both tucked in and chewed and gobbled our way through it in a way that would have had us struck off the debs list.

'Oh, so much better than all those silly shrimps and caviar blinis!' She actually rubbed her stomach in public. I sympathised, but I was not American. The table lay in a state of devastation, but we had not finished everything. I feared even one more mouthful would make my waistband pop. I dug in my purse for change and placed the fee, plus a large tip, on the cloth. I looked over at the door and wondered if I was now too wide to pass between the tables.

'I suggest we waddle over to the door and walk into town to try to get the feel of the place. I have never been to Brighton and I think our first impressions may prove useful,' I said. 'Besides, I'm not going to be able to do any serious thinking until I've walked off some of this food.'

'Oof,' said Bernie as she levered her way out of her seat. 'I must be the size of a whale now.' She stood, turning from side to side, so I could admire her tiny waist.

'You break all the laws of physics,' I said. 'Let's go.'

Outside we linked arms. In the end I hadn't paid a waitress to watch the vehicle, but I could not see any suspicious characters within sight. 'You couldn't have parked your motor anywhere better than outside a shop full of snooping old biddies,' said Bernie.

'The windows are fogged.'

'Oh, their sharp glares can see through trivial inconveniences like that,' said Bernie. 'Harvey practically wilted on the spot when he came under their collective gaze.'

'Poor Harvey,' I said with a smile.

'We'll make a man of the poor slob yet,' said Bernie overemphasising her accent like a Chicago gangster.

We walked along the street away from the tea shop. The pavement was wide and freshly swept. Lots of little shops lined the way, from milliners to haberdashers with a few little chocolate shops in between. My mother would have said it was decidedly middle-class, but it was upper middle-class at worst. Perhaps on holiday visitors lowered their standards.

Bernie broke in on my thoughts. 'You're thinking that Charlotte would be about as impressed with this town as we are?'

I nodded.

'Mommy would say it was shabby-genteel,' said Bernie. 'I mean, there's nothing precisely wrong. It's all very neat and clean, but it's not of the best, is it? More the kind of place you'd bring your mistress than your wife.'

'You're outrageous,' I said. 'But accurate.'

'I'm steeled now, fortified with good English Indian tea. I think we should walk along the front, arm in arm, and pass by the beach where she was found – a few times.' She smiled at me. 'I do believe we are becoming detectives, like that man with a funny hat.'

'Deerstalker,' I said.

'No, that wasn't the name. It was more like Shamrock. Was he Irish?'

I sighed deeply. 'You are shockingly illiterate for an Oxford graduate.'

'Nothing will make me smoke a pipe,' said Bernie.

I ignored this. 'If the worst comes to the worst and anyone we know spots us we can say we fancied an afternoon break from the metropolis. I'm known to be a country girl and, being an American, no one feels able to predict what you might do. There can be no real harm done if we do run into anyone.'

'Are you trying to convince yourself or me? I might not be British, but I know Brighton is the place where reputations are lost.'

'All right, at the first sign of anyone we know, we leg it into the back lanes and make our way zig-zagging back to my motor.'

'It sounds like a lot of walking,' said Bernie.

Chapter Nine

The sun shone, but what might be termed by the hearty as a 'fresh' breeze blew off the sea. Bernie kept patting her hat to ensure it was on her head. I took the more forthright step of simply jamming mine down over my ears. Another win for cloche hats, even if everyone but me hates them nowadays.

Bernie has an expressive face and it clearly showed her discontent as we walked along the prom. Personally, I found the rails along the seafront, with their wide bars topped every now and then with large balls and painted a pale blue, quaint and delightful, as if we had stepped back into the nineteenth century. I could picture damsels, all bustles, corsets, enormous hats and frilled bosoms, tottering along with their parasols overhead. No doubt many of them would each have been towing a pug dog on a lead. I would have shared this image with Bernie, but the wind did not allow us to converse. It was then I saw my vision come to life.

We had rounded a gentle curve in the promenade, by the bandstand, when two ladies such as I had imagined came into view. I stopped for a moment thinking I had been transported in time, only for Bernie to stumble and give me an evil look. As the ladies neared I realised that their clothes might be from another age, but so too were they. Each of them was sixty if she was a day. I dug Bernie in the ribs and steered her towards these two impressive personages. Askance, she gave me another filthy look, but short of digging her heels in like a mule, she could hardly refuse to accompany me as my arm was threaded through hers.

'Excuse me, ma'am,' I said to the stouter of the two ladies. Closer to, I could see she had at least four chins thanks to her rigid collar and corseting, and that each had at least one mole with hairs growing out of it. I dragged my eyes to hers and found myself gazing into orbs of cornflower blue that glittered with intelligence.

I had turned my body to the side, so the wind didn't steal my words. She did the same, but her voice was hearty enough that it was hardly needed. 'Yes, girl,' she said. 'Speak up. I'm almost deaf, you know.'

'I hope you do not find this an impertinence, but are you the Dowager Duchess of Langdon? My mother specifically asked me to look out for her.'

'And accost her in a public place?' screeched her companion, a much thinner lady, who appeared to be nothing but flounces and sourness.

'Hush, Antoinette,' said the first lady. 'I'll take being mistaken for a duchess, even a dowager, any day.' She looked me directly in the eye. 'I am not she. Why, pray tell, are you seeking her?'

'We are new to the area. My friend and I have arrived for a few days of rest. The London season has been so tiring.' Bernie's eyes fairly bulged at this. 'But because of the incident, Mama said I should seek counsel about where it was best for young ladies to disport themselves.'

At this the lady broke into a delightful chuckle. 'Do you hear, Antoinette? This young girl requires our assistance in ensuring her . . .'

'That is quite enough, Diamond!' said the thin companion. 'If you do not cease to speak now you will say something regrettable. Excuse us, girls, but we must be on our way.'

'Oh, dear,' I said, 'could you not even direct us to a pleasant tea room? The wind is so shrill.'

'I can see how it would be for a skinny thing like her,' said Antoinette, eyeing Bernie, 'but you're made of stronger stuff. Dowager Duchess my foot. Who sent you?'

'Oh, good grief,' said Bernie. 'They're . . .' I stood heavily on her foot.

'Ladies who know exactly what is happening around here,' I said, giving both older women a level look. 'Would you care to join us for tea?'

'We can't,' hissed Bernie. 'We've just had tea.'

'Yes, we can,' I hissed back.

Diamond watched us with amusement. 'We would prefer sherry,' said Antoinette. 'Sherry and Madeira biscuits.'

'I'd prefer a good stout,' said Diamond, 'but I think your friend would faint if we took her into the lounge of a public house. At least the ones that admit the likes of us.'

'Then,' I said, 'we shall go to the Grand.'

'They won't let us in,' said Antoinette.

'And to think we used to be a permanent fixture on their private menu,' said Diamond. 'Don't grow old, girls, that's my advice. Either that, or marry a rich man while you still have your looks.'

'Oh, they will let us in. This is the American Ambassador's daughter, and I'm the niece of an Earl.'

'You might even be what you say, but I doubt it'll do the trick,' said Diamond. 'Still, might be fun to try. I can't remember the last time I was thrown out of the Grand.'

There was indeed a little trouble with the head waiter when he saw our guests, but after I had pointed out the slight stain on his white gloves, that the creases in his trousers were not what one would expect from such an establishment, and then offered that he ring up either my uncle the Earl or the American Embassy, he became quite docile and tame. Though admittedly he showed us to a section that was screened from the rest of the lobby by tall foliage in scattered pots.

'Oh, this won't do,' said Bernie. 'I won't be put among the plants.'

'I think that's all we're going to get,' said Diamond. 'I'm quite happy if you are.'

103

'There is only so much I can do to the maitre d' in public,' I said, making the two older ladies laugh. 'And we do have a lovely view on the other side.'

We could see the sea out of the long windows that looked on to the beach front.

'Pah, the sea,' said Antoinette. 'I've seen it every day for the last twenty-five years. Should it dry up tomorrow, I wouldn't object.'

We were off to the left of the grand chandelier-hung lobby with its black and white marble floor and majestic sweeping staircase. The seats were fulsomely upholstered. We had been given a set of seats close together, with a low table between us. In short, we were partly hidden and partly indulged.

Diamond settled her large frame into a seat, chuckling heartily. 'You're quite right, my dear,' she said, nodding at Bernie. 'The place has positively gone downhill. I believe the staircase could do with a good polish. Why, I remember you used be able to see your face in it. There was that private party that I slid naked down in into the arms of the Viscount of . . . well, never you mind, I'm sure he's a totally respectable old codger now.'

'Is Diamond your real name?' said Bernie, trying hard to look comfortable.

'Heavens, no. It was – you know I can't remember if it was old Bertie or Sammy who first coined it.' She gave a little flourish of her hands. 'I was the diamond of Brighton. Everyone wanted to have me.'

'Have you?' Bernie started to say, but I kicked her under the table.

'We're debutantes,' I said. 'A friend of ours was murdered here recently. We're looking for clues. The police think she died by accident, but we don't.'

'The girl who went skinny-dipping?' said Antoinette. 'No one in their right mind paddles in the sea at this time of year, let alone swims. They'd catch their deaths.'

'Yes, but she was snowed up to the eyebrows by all accounts,' said Diamond. 'Now, about that sherry?'

104

I ordered a mixture of delicacies. After imbibing an astonishing quantity of sherry, both ladies became quite relaxed. 'If she was coked,' said Diamond, 'there might be a gang involved. Who was the man?'

'Trask, heir to an arms company.'

'Good Heavens – son of Marcus Trask?' she said.

'Didn't we both . . .' said Antoinette. I noticed tendrils of hair escaping from under her hat, and although she remained sitting bolt upright, she swayed gently. A sharp tap from Diamond's parasol shut her up.

'How is the old bugger?' said Diamond.

'Dead,' I said.

Diamond gazed off into the distance for a moment. Then she sighed. 'So many of them are. Of course, we lost a lot of them in the war. Those that made it back were never the same, poor dears. And the ones too old to go, most of them are pushing up daisies now.' She sighed deeply and produced a lace handkerchief from the depths of her bosom. She briefly dabbed her eyes. 'I take it the Trask estate was being held in trust for his son?'

'I guess so,' said Bernie. 'Everyone talked about him as an heir, never an owner.'

'He'd have to wait till he was thirty-five to get the money,' said Diamond. 'Trusts are often set up like that by fathers who'd been a bit wild themselves. Not that Marcus was like the others. Always saw you right, and a little more. Kind man.'

'You were soft on him,' said Antoinette and hiccupped loudly.

'And he was soft on me,' said Diamond. 'Nothing either of us could do about that. But to think his son dead, and in all that scandal. The newspapers went on and on about the girl, simply said she was found within a few yards of her beau.'

'One of them must still have family alive to have leashed the press,' said Bernie.

Diamond nodded. 'So, you do have a head on you.'

'Do you think there is anything you could tell us that would help?' I said.

'She could tell which way his father preferred it,' said Antoinette, swaying violently. Diamond gave her a hard poke with her parasol and Antoinette slid off her seat and into a corner behind the chair. She didn't seem at all upset by this sudden change of circumstances, but instead folded her skinny body, tucking her skirts in tight around her, leaned into the corner and closed her eyes.

'Leave her be,' said Diamond, as Bernie rose to help her. 'She might be all prim and proper sober, but a few drinks in Annie and she has the lewdest mouth on her you ever heard. That's why places like this don't let us in. And I, for one, would like to enjoy this afternoon. It's bringing back lots of very happy memories.'

'Happy?' said Bernie, surprise obvious on her face, as she retook her seat.

Diamond patted her hand. 'Oh, there's always the bad times in a career like ours, but if you go into it with your eyes open like Annie and I did, it's not a bad life. We were skivvies in a big house. If we'd stayed there we'd have been bow-backed by thirty, worn out in mind and body. We knew all we had going for us was our looks. Anyway, if you know what you're walking into, and if you make a big thing of how choosy you are – that's the real secret. Then you'll have your golden days. Better bow-legged than bow-backed, that's what I say!'

For once Bernie appeared speechless. Sadly, I did not have time to relish the moment.

'About Charlotte and Trask,' I persisted.

'Well, as I recall his father liked a good time when he was young. He inherited the business at nearly forty. Came to tell me himself, all tearful like, that our days were over. I'd been expecting him to hand me my cards for a long time, I was no spring chicken, but like I said, he had a fondness for me, and I for him. I got a few letters from him. Mostly written in phrases and jokes that only we would understand. He married and got himself an heir. I remember him writing, 'Di, I've found myself a filly and I have to do my duty. Silly mare, none of your brains, but hopefully the foal will take after me.' I felt rather sorry for the girl. Never met her. And eventually the letters stopped – might have been when he died, I don't know. But I do know he changed. He became a hard man. Hated the business. Hated his new life. I fear he took it out on all those around him. When I remember what he used to be like – so sweet and romantic. Still, nothing is happier than the might have been . . .' She took a swig of her drink. 'What was he like, the son?'

'Bit of a cad, by all accounts,' I said. 'Not above trying to get a girl to go further than she wanted. Seduce her, and then when she gave in, he'd cut her loose. But he'd always gone for the ones who had a reputation for being fast. This girl, our friend, wasn't like that.' I noticed Bernie looking at me in horror. 'What? It was Harvey who told me.'

'Oh, well, if Harvey said it,' said Bernie.

'He admits himself he's a bit of a bounder, but he says he's not a cad,' I said.

'Sounds like a keeper,' said Diamond. 'I always liked the ones who knew what they were. Mind you, I expect the Earl would object. She might get away with it, being American.'

'I have no interest in getting away with it with Harvey,' said Bernie crossly.

'Your loss,' said Diamond. She turned back to me. 'So, Trask's son was a seducer. Was he the kind who would force drugs on a girl to make her . . .' She gave a ridiculous wink.

'We haven't heard anything like that,' I said. 'In fact, it's all rumour.'

'Yeah, and an odd thing to get into any sort of funny business at the start of the season. Still runs the same, doesn't it?' said Diamond.

'It was the night of the presentation,' I said.

'Hmm, that's all wrong. Of course, a lot of the drugs that end up in London come in through here. Quite a local trade. But then, if that's what it was about, I doubt they'd want to draw the police's attention to the area.'

'What if it was meant to be a warning to someone?' said Bernie.

'Maybe,' said Diamond. 'But why the girl too? Better warning if she's left alive. Or even the other way around. Kill her as a warning to Trask. Any idea if she got into his motor willingly?'

'We don't know. The police believe he convinced her they were eloping.'

'Police don't think. According to the paper, the girl had family, an aunt and an elder brother at least. There was a picture of the aunt, she looked like the back side of a busted boiler. Someone likely to cause a dust-up if ever I saw 'em. Tell you what, girls, I'll ask around my old contacts and see if I can dig anything up. Maybe someone saw something they wouldn't want to tell the constabulary because they didn't want to admit they were out and about.'

'I'd be very grateful,' I said. 'You could drop a note to me at the American Embassy in London.' I handed her my card and a couple of rolled notes. 'Of course, you will have to buy a stamp and some paper. I wouldn't want you to be out of pocket.'

'Thank you, my dear,' said Diamond. 'I will contact you in due course.'

I paid the bill and left Diamond in charge of the remaining goodies and her comatose friend.

'However will she get Antoinette home?' said Bernie when we were outside.

'That's not my problem,' I said. I checked my pocket watch. 'We're out of time. We need to meet Harvey. Damn, we never got a chance to see the murder scene.'

'It's a beach,' said Bernie. 'We passed loads of them. They all looked the same.'

'I suppose it doesn't matter. We did the important bit,' I said.

Bernie stopped. 'Now look, Hope. I don't always see where you're going with things but taking two old tarts for high sherry, or whatever that was, and then giving them my parents' address! I think you owe me an explanation?'

'It had occurred to me that there might some underworld involvement,' I said calmly, taking her arm and walking on. 'And when I saw them trundling along the esplanade towards us it seemed too good an opportunity to miss.'

'You'll never hear from them again.'

'I thought you were worried we would,' I said with a slight smile. 'Maybe not, but I think old Diamond plays by the rules. They might not be our rules, but she's got a code of honour. If she finds anything out, she'll tell us. Besides I want to know who the Viscount at the bottom of the stairs was, don't you?'

Bernie flushed a fiery red. 'Honestly, Hope, sometimes I don't know you at all. I thought I was meant to be the wild one!'

Chapter Ten

Harvey had already arrived at the tea shop and was mid-bun when we arrived. Obviously he had got over his fear of the dowagers. To be fair, the shop's custom had shrunk to half its previous size. Or perhaps, I thought hopefully, he was buoyed up with success. He gave us a cheery, 'Wotcha,' through a mouthful of Battenberg and motioned to us to sit down. He swigged from a cup of tea, swallowed and gave us a very self-satisfied grin. 'Nice walk, ladies?'

Bernie shuddered. 'Too cold for your delicate constitution?' said Harvey.

Bernie leaned over the table and spoke in a lowered voice. 'We had tea with ladies of the night.'

'Hope Stapleford!' said Harvey in shocked tones. 'I am shocked!' But he angled his face so that Bernie wouldn't see that he also winked at me. 'Dragging your innocent young friend into your terrible escapades.'

How, I wondered silently, had we become on such a familiar footing? I didn't think I minded exactly, but I was certain my mother would disapprove.

'Thank you,' said Bernie, so happy to find herself in accord with Harvey that she gave him a dazzling smile.

'Hope,' repeated Harvey. 'Why didn't you wait for me! I'd have given a lot to meet some real-life streetwalkers.' Bernie's expression changed swiftly from one of friendliness to one of a young lady who very much wants to throw a cream jug at someone but is clinging to her upbringing. 'Were they lookers?' Harvey continued, totally unaware of the danger he was in.

'I'm guessing their heydays were the Edwardian era,' I said, 'so unlikely to be your type. Though it's not my place to judge. What is it you say? Each to their own?'

'Hey, hang on . . .' said Harvey.

I proceeded to tell him about our encounter. 'So, you see,' I finished, 'I believe I was right in guessing they will have an "in" with the Brighton underground, particularly the drugs scene. I thought it better to try and attain some assets than attempt to infiltrate it ourselves.'

'Too bloody right,' said Harvey. He took some fortifying gulps of tea. 'But, from what you've said, you're checking out all the angles. You don't have any reason – other than there's a rumour the ill-fated couple had been powdering their noses – to believe this is the result of some kind of gang warfare.'

'I did wonder when Trask would inherit. He wouldn't be the first to get into debt while waiting for his inheritance.'

'Yeah, but you don't kill the golden goose. You might put the frighteners on it. But if you do it in, you lose out. Common sense, that,' said Harvey. 'I can ask a few chaps who know about this sort of stuff.'

'You know loan sharks?' said Bernie. 'I should have known.'

'No,' said Harvey, 'I mean bookies.' He said it with his nose in the air as if this was an entirely different level of criminal. I tried to stifle my rising giggle in a meringue and nearly ended my days right there and then.

After we had moved to a clean table and reordered, Bernie asked Harvey if he had anything to report. She did so in a scathing tone, but I could see Harvey was itching to boast.

'I went for a half down at the Waterman's Inn—' he began.

'A half what?' said Bernie. We both ignored her.

'Anyways, I get talking about all the hoo-ha of the dead girl on the beach and all that. Told 'em I was down from the Big Smoke on a day outing with the family to take the air, but I reckoned they were down for a noisy. Said I'd sloped off as I couldn't stand being cooped up with so many women. Said they'd brought me for protection, but I reckoned there wasn't anything scarier than my Aunty Maisie on the gin – washerwoman with arms like a navvy. Then—'

'I get the picture, Harvey. You established a realistic cover, made yourself empathetic, and got the other patrons to talk to you.'

'I did not get empathetic,' said Harvey crossly. 'I only had a half. Spent the rest of the money buying drinks for the others.'

I thought about explaining, but decided to simply say, 'I stand corrected.'

'To cut a long story short,' said Harvey, 'no one in the bar knew anything about Trask or the girl. They'd all heard the stories – which incidentally go from her being a Parisian can-can dancer to him abducting her from Buck House itself and being chased by the Royal Cavalry.' He took another sip of tea. 'Thing is, none of them knew anything in real terms about Trask. They'd read about him in the papers, but I got the distinct impression that he – let alone his flashy motor – would have been remembered if they were regulars down here.'

'Oh, come on,' said Bernie. 'There must be thousands of people in this town.'

'Ah, but only so many who work in the gentleman's clubs – of either variety, classy or more like the ones your *ladies* would have been familiar with. There's only so many shops that can clothe ladies of quality. If Charlotte had intended to spend some time down here she'd have needed clothes. There wasn't 'ide nor 'air of them.'

'What about the motor?' I asked.

Harvey tapped his nose and pointed at me. 'Right you are. The motor was sighted driving through the town the night they're assumed to have gone into the water. All anyone saw was two figures in it, well wrapped up as if they had been on the road for some distance.' He scratched his head. 'That put me in mind of an odd thing. When the police found the motor, the girl's silver bag was in the back and the roof was down. Now, the motor was found before her body was, so why did she leave her expensive bag lying out in the open?'

'Her kidnappers gave her no choice,' said Bernie.

'Maybe,' said Harvey, 'but if so, why, when the motor was found mid-morning by a copper, was the bag still there?'

'You mean why hadn't someone stolen it during the night?' I said.

'From the photograph in the paper it was a pretty enough little thing that, night or day, I'm betting someone would have tried to lift it.'

'You're thinking someone was set to watch it, so no one lifted it before the police found the motor,' I said.

Harvey nodded.

'That is something to think on,' I admitted. 'Well done.'

'I've got more,' said Harvey. He broke open a scone and enthusiastically creamed it. 'I have to admit, this is more down to luck than skill. I reckoned I'd just about milked the bar dry, and was on my way out, when this odd little man comes up to me. He's all greasy raincoat, flat cap, and the kind of moustache that looks like a bit of mouldy toothbrush. I was about to side-step him when he says, "I know your game".' Harvey bit into his scone. 'Now, me instinct is telling me to leg it, but as me old grandma used to say, I have one besetting sin . . .'

'Just one?' said Bernie.

I kicked her under the table. 'Do go on,' I said politely.

'Curiosity,' said Harvey, his mouth full of jam and cream. 'I asked him what he thought I was up to . . .' He paused dramatically. I calmly took a sip of tea. Somewhat deflated, he continued, 'He said, "You're with the press, aren't you?" I was about to deny being such a low-life scumbag when I thought, why not, so I says, "What's it to you?"'

'This blow-by-blow account is very riveting,' said Bernie, 'but we need to get back before midnight.'

I sighed. 'I like details, Harvey, but I'm afraid we are on the clock. If you could, as they say, "cut to the chase"?'

Harvey nodded. 'Turns out he was after selling a tip. I strung him along and he tells me his sister-in-law owns a boarding house where that man and "his totty" – his words, not mine – stayed. We bantered about price for a bit, but he takes me and shows me the place. He doesn't want me to go in, but I knock on the door anyway. His sister-in-law spies him and takes after him with a broom. Not only funny but spared me having to pay out. I go all polite and asks about the details, says I'm an agent of the dead girl's mother, blah, blah, blah. She tells me she got a note from Charlotte a week before she's meant to have come down, asking her to reserve a room. She says she's looking for somewhere discreet and would prefer to come and go unseen. Could she leave a key under the pot outside? She, this Mrs Williams, doesn't like it, but there's a five-pound note in with the request, for her trouble, and doesn't a widow like her need to make a living? She reads the gossip columns but has no idea who Charlotte was. And as she says, the letter promised her another five-pound note, so she assumed the lady in question is either married, one of London's classier ladies of the night, or a young lady on her way to a clinic overseas.'

'That is an awful lot of money for a place like that,' said Bernie.

Harvey nodded. 'And no, Hope, before you ask. I checked. She didn't keep the letter. She burned it like she was asked. She said the room was in a right state when she went to check on it, but she sorted it all out. She never got her other fiver, and she didn't want anything getting into the papers, so she didn't go to the police. She said there was nothing of interest to them.'

'Did you get any more details about the state of the room, or the letter?' I asked.

'No, I'm afraid not. I had to go careful. She just about swallowed the bit about me being from the girl's mother. Lucky I had that picture in my wallet. Maud looks awful like 'er.'

'Maud?' asked Bernie. Harvey ignored her.

'But she was starting to think I might be from the press after all, and I'd seen the way she used her broom, so I thought I'd better bring the interview to an end. Leave her happy, I thought, and

114

then if I had to, I could always go back. Though I'm not convinced there's that much more to get from her.'

'It's still tremendous work, Harvey,' I said. 'We've learned that someone who'd been to Brighton booked the room.'

'Because they knew about the pot outside,' said Bernie.

'Would have been a good guess anyway,' murmured Harvey.

'That it was booked in Charlotte's name,' I said.

Harvey slapped his hand against his forehead. 'Which almost certainly means she didn't book the rooms. Even an ingénue, like you said she was, would be fly enough not to leave herself open to blackmail by a Brighton landlady, wouldn't she?'

'I liked her,' said Bernie, 'but even I thought she was very silly.'

'But most important of all, we've learned these rooms were booked before the season started, so whatever happened was most definitely not a spur of the moment decision . . .'

'But something that had been planned for some time,' said Harvey.

'I'm pretty sure Charlotte was the type who would have spilled to us if she had a great adventure going on that night,' said Bernie.

'I'm betting she would have been crying all the time, or high as a kite and acting mysterious,' I said.

'Not sobbing over a tear in her train, certainly,' said Bernie.

Harvey looked from one of us to the other. Then he said, 'Blimey, it is murder. Who'd have thought it?'

Chapter Eleven

Somehow, we managed to make it back to London without further adventure or serious disagreement. Although at times it was a close call. Bernie kept up an anxious and increasingly ludicrous predictions that Brighton gangsters would chase us, catch us, and do terrible things to us.

'What terrible fings?' Harvey finally enquired, only for Bernie to tap the side of her nose, whereupon Harvey offered her a handkerchief. Naturally she threw it back at him, only for the wind to whip it away.

'Oi! That's me best 'ankie!' protested Harvey. He might have got an apology and a box of monogrammed handkerchiefs had he left it there. From the corner of my eye I could see Bernie's red face as she turned back and sat down in the passenger seat. 'I don't know how you behave when you're at home, girl, but my dad would have put you over his knee for that if you'd been his daughter,' said Harvey.

Personally, I could understand Harvey's wrath. The glimpse I'd got had suggested it was a linen handkerchief. No doubt bought originally as Sunday best and honouring us as a special occasion. It also looked as if it cost a pretty penny. Bernie, never having had her parents scraping money together to repair yet another falling chimney, as mine often had at White Orchards, possessed no real understanding of what it was like to lack money. She shot back a pithy retort that more or less likened his ancestors to a pack of mongrel dogs. (Language and imagery I will not repeat verbatim here).

'Why, you devil-begotten minx!' said Harvey.

I checked behind me then stood on the brakes. The automobile screeched as the brake pads rubbed together so hard they gave off an acrid smell. Harvey and Bernie, not expecting such a sudden stop, hurtled forward in their seats and got the breath knocked out of them. 'If the two of you wish to continue this argument you can get out here. I won't have such behaviour from either of you when I'm driving,' I said. Both of them regarded me like mice caught mid-theft by the kitchen cat.

Bernie was the first to rally. 'Then throw him out!'

'I know when I'm not wanted,' said Harvey starting to get out.

'Shut up, Bernie. Sit down, Harvey. We've had a trying day. I suggest you try thinking over what we've learnt for the rest of the drive. And keeping your mouths shut!' Where upon I took off at some speed, so that both of them were caught both mentally and physically off-balance. I endured a blissful, if slightly sulky, silence from the pair of them all the way back.

When we pulled up to my garage it was already dark. Bernie and I climbed out of the front seats with some awkwardness. By all rights Harvey, in the back with the boxes, should have been stiff as a board, but he vaulted over the side as if he had only been sitting down for a few moments. 'Want me to open the garage?' he asked. Then he realised I too had got out and frowned in puzzlement.

'My man will look after the motor,' I said, feeling a little self conscious.

'Right,' said Harvey. 'Your man.' I tried to think cold thoughts, so I wouldn't blush, but it was dark enough now the headlights were off that he couldn't see. A square of pale yellow had lit up in the flat above the garage. Obviously, he was waiting for my signal to take the vehicle inside. Harvey glanced up and gave a swift nod. He took a pocket watch from his waistcoat. 'Blimey! You girls be all right?'

'Of course,' said Bernie bristling. 'This is one of the better parts of the city.' I felt like kicking her. It was hardly Harvey's fault where he had been born.

'Catch you later,' he said without explaining how or when. Then he sped off into the night. His long legs ate up the distance until he vanished into the shadows. The last we saw of him was the soles of his shoes flashing in the few gaslights that lined the mews.

'He's fast,' I said.

'The mysterious Maud?' said Bernie.

'No idea,' I said. I found it odd to think of Harvey with a girl-friend, if that was what Maud was. But why else would he carry her picture? 'We need to think of how we're going to get back into the Embassy without arousing trouble. No one will believe the gymkhana went on this late.'

'Riding by moonlight,' said Bernie and twirled with her arms outstretched. 'It's a lovely moon.' She saw me frown and patted my arm. 'Don't worry, Hope. Aunt Bernie has thought of every-thing.' She pulled a case out of the back that I had paid no previous attention to. 'I told Mommy that after the gymkhana we would be going on to the Leighton-Smythes' ball. They're terribly nou-veau riche, but as I told Mommy, we're American. She didn't have an answer to that one.' During this extraordinary speech Bernie had opened the case and pulled out what even I had to admit was a divine evening dress. With a beige underlining, it looked as if stars and moonlight had been dappled across the top. Of course, it was only sequins and beading, but it had been done with excellent skill.

'Mine,' said Bernie, extracting a pair of pearl-coloured shoes. Then she pulled out a swathe of emerald green fabric and handed it to me. 'Yours! Hang on a moment, I know I put shoes in for you too. Ah, here we are.' She thrust a pair of strappy silver san-dals at me.

'I'm a debutante, Bernie,' I said. 'I'm not meant to wear bright colours.'

Bernie shrugged her shoulders. 'So? In the right light, my dress looks like I'm nude, except for a little stitching. I'd hardly say yours was dashing in comparison.' She attempted to take me encouragingly by the shoulders, but we were both carrying too much material for this to work successfully. 'C'mon,' she said. 'This whole season is proving to be such a bore. Let's shake things up a bit.'

'Charlotte has been murdered,' I said coldly. Standing there on the lane, my arms full of party dress, while Charlotte Saulier lay in a morgue somewhere, the whole concept of the season seemed tawdry.

'Oh, I know. It's awful, but there's nothing we can do tonight. And now you're on the case I'm sure we'll catch the killer. Besides, the Leighton-Smythes know some dreadful people, we might pick up some clues tonight.'

'But green?' I said, gazing at the dress in my hands.

'The dead are dead, and the living have to live,' said Bernie. 'It sounds harsh, but it's true. Besides, maybe another girl will be abducted tonight. Wouldn't you feel terrible if we weren't there to stop it?'

'You're terrible,' I said, torn between a smile and truly meaning it.

'Great,' said Bernie, obviously taking this for agreement. 'Can you unhook?'

'Dear God,' I said, 'we shall ask my mechanic if he can lend us a room. We are not getting changed in an outside garage where anyone might walk in.'

'Pity,' said Bernie pouting. 'I doubt they would have. It's hardly Piccadilly Circus, but it would have been a thrill.'

Johnson is well paid, so he gave us access to a small, neat bedroom. He's an ex-army man with a bad limp but a genius with vehicles. By the time we exited the room he had found us a taxi-cab. 'I'll have your belongings sent over to the Embassy, miss,' he said, his bland face devoid of curiosity. 'Unless you want me to send them up to your family.'

'Oh, dear me, no,' I said. Then I corrected myself. 'As some of the property is Miss Bernie's I think it best to send to the Embassy. Thank you, Johnson.'

Once we were seated in the taxi-cab, Bernie hissed to me, 'How well do you know your man? I don't like the thought of him pawing through my drawers.'

'Your drawers?'

'You can't wear underwear in a dress like this!'

I gave the red-eared driver directions for the ball. Then I leant back in the seat and closed my eyes. The drive had taken more out of me than I had thought. I also needed to remind myself why I had let Bernie in on this mystery. I could tell she was in her most mischievous mood.

'Do you think I should try and get myself kidnapped?' she whispered.

I groaned inwardly. It was going to be a long night. 'No,' I said. 'I do not. No one would try to kidnap you. You're too . . .' I groped for the right word, 'feisty to kidnap.'

'I can be demure,' said Bernie. That was too much for me. I was still laughing when we pulled up at the entrance to the ball.

I guessed the Leighton-Smythes had spared no expense, but to my somewhat jaded eyes, it was yet another large London house, lit up like a beacon with servants milling everywhere, carrying glasses of champagne and caviar on blinis. If it wasn't so expensive I had always wondered if people would eat fish eggs, because that is all caviar is. Disgusting, really. But then, quail's eggs too are enormously popular. It's as if the Beau Monde love eating the unborn babies of the animal world.

There were already a great many people at the ball. The actual dancing was in another room, away from the champagne-bearing servants, which I thought an excellent idea. Instead, the salon seemed to have been allocated to parading and gossiping, in quite an old-fashioned manner.

'I'm off to get my dance card filled,' said Bernie. A quick kiss on the cheek and she was gone. I decided what I needed was champagne, and I was hopeful the enormous picnic we had devoured would have lined my stomach. There had been no chance for dinner. I wondered if the ball was of the kind that came with supper and who I could ask about this discreetly. From what I could gather, debutantes were meant to be thin, white-gloved, and averse to food. Yet another reason why I made a terrible deb.

So it was with unalloyed delight that I saw there had been a table laid out with delicacies. Devils on horseback, oysters, smoked salmon on tiny pieces of brown bread, more wretched caviar, and some little pastry cases filled with highly processed ingredients. I mean by the latter that whatever the meat, fish, or vegetables had started out as, now they were within the cases there was no indication of what they had once been. They were exactly the kind of mystery that I do like to solve. I piled a small plate as high as I dared and promised myself that I would return as many times as my stomach required. At least my dress had a certain amount of give to it, so I didn't need to worry about eating. Bernie would be lucky if she could swallow a pea.

'Nice to see a gal with an appetite,' said a smooth male voice. He'd caught me mid-devil on horseback – I had the choice between trying to hold it, sloppy and half-eaten, and not spill it down my dress, or be unladylike. I looked him over briefly and decided he wasn't worth wasting food over. I shoved it in my mouth, making speech impossible.

I guessed he was mid-forties. He had a little frosting in his hair, but otherwise most females would, I believe, find him attractive. Reasonably tall, he wore his tux well and not a blond hair was out of place. He had a square jawline and an adequate nose. But it was his eyes I most noticed. If such a thing as blue fire exists – then that was their colour. There wasn't a chance he wouldn't know how good-looking he was and would thus likely to the most terrible bore. (Good-looking people never need to make themselves interesting to be invited to a party. They are decorative.)

'I would offer to shake hands, but yours are somewhat engaged. I am Danville, but you can call me David. Our population has grown so small I think that the separation of elders and youngsters cannot be what it was once was. Although, forgive me, but I don't think you are the youngest of the debs present.'

121

By now I had swallowed the hors d'oeuvre, but it had left my mouth sticky and I longed for a drink. Danville, I recalled, was a minor noble. Viscount, possibly? He was distantly related to the King and was rumoured to be a friend of the Duke of Windsor, who had abdicated in '36. His social standing was thus up for debate. 'I am Hope Stapleford,' I said. 'You probably know my uncle.'

Danville nodded. 'Excellent chap. Holds the best shooting parties. Blue blood through and through. So, you're young Hope. Is Eric Milton your godfather?'

This caught me by surprise. Uncle Joe does tend to know everyone, but he is very choosy about any party he frequents. He is even pickier about who he invites to his shooting parties. But for anyone to know about Uncle Eric, who is more close-mouthed than a proverbial oyster about his personal life, was truly remarkable.

'Are you acquainted with my godfather?' I asked.

Danville smiled at me in a way that looked perfectly normal, yet felt extremely uncomfortable. 'Ah, no. We don't mix in the same circles, but we have heard about each other. Dear Eric, he does so try to be a forward-thinker, but he doesn't see the danger we are all in.'

I blinked slightly at that. 'Danger?' I asked. I assumed he was speaking of our growing animosity with Germany, but I had an instinct not to tell this man anything I did not have to.

Danville took my plate from me and placed it on the table. At the same time, he dextrously replaced it with a goblet taken from a passing waiter. He linked his arm through mine, so that it would seem extremely rude if I was to pull away. He guided me, to my horror, away from the food. I had mistrusted this man and now I positively disliked him. He also, like most handsome and rich men, seemed to think his status allowed him to control women at parties. However, disobliging him of this view would not be conducive to furthering investigations, so I counted internally to thirty. Ten was nowhere near long enough.

Once we were standing a little apart from other groups, he stopped. We were still in full sight of the room, so no indiscretion could be thought. 'I mean, my dear, that so many of us died in the Great War. There's plenty of his type around,' he indicated a passing waiter, who I recognised with a jolt as Harvey. So, it hadn't been Maud he was rushing to, but an evening's paid employment. 'But we need men of strength and character to run this country. Men with the right blood. There's only one leader in the modern world who appreciates how a country needs to be run. And, by Jove, hasn't he done it well? Dragged his people up out of the ashes. He knows who the real enemies are.' He leant in close. 'If I say the money-lenders, you'll know who I mean, won't you?'

I was regretting eating my one-half egg. I felt extremely sick. 'I take it you are talking about Herr Hitler,' I said.

'Clever girl. I knew there had to be more to Eric's goddaughter than your average, silly little deb. I'd like you to meet my son, Henry. He's about your age. Clever chap. Knows the right people.'

Of course, the primary reason for the season has always been match-making, but I was quite taken aback to be caught by a match-making father. I could only be grateful he wasn't offering himself for consideration. I failed to think of a reason to excuse myself and let myself be led over to a young version of Danville. I was also, distressingly, getting further and further away from the food. 'Henry, come and meet Hope Stapleford. Her people have that small estate in the Fens, but her uncle's the Earl. Still not married, is he? Is it entailed, or will it come to you?'

I couldn't quite believe what I was hearing. 'The title is entailed, but not the property. Uncle Joseph can dispose of it as he wishes. But, as you doubtless know, he is still a young man and has plenty of time to marry. I have no expectation of being his heir.'

'Just your parents' place in the Fens, then?'

I doubted I could keep my reply civil, so I merely nodded.

'G-gosh,' said Henry, stammering horribly. 'D-d-doesn't it flood awfully?' I didn't reply at once as my attention was caught by his enormous Adam's apple. Was there something about this year's crop of eligible young men, I wondered. But I shook the thought off and held out my hand. Papa would have made a remark about the inbreeding of stock and Mother would have scolded him.

'We have been quite innovative about draining our fields. My father likes to think of himself as an armchair engineer.'

'J-j-jolly good. Need to keep our agriculture up,' said Henry. 'Isn't that right, Father?'

Danville nodded. 'I'll leave you two young people to get acquainted. Why don't you take Hope for a quick whirl around the dance floor, Henry?'

'Oh, I say, Father. I'm not much of a s-s-shoe s-s-shuffler, you know!'

'I'm sure Hope will understand. She has the breeding.'

As soon as Danville moved off. Henry's face fell. 'I s-s-suppose we'd better do as Father says. Hopefully, I won't h-h-hurt your f-f-feet too much during one dance!' Then he made the most hideous sound. Harvey, I suddenly thought, would have described it in terms of a donkey having something unspeakable done to it. Only Harvey would have been specific. A small smile curled at the corners of my mouth. I assumed it was Henry's version of an encouraging laugh.

'That's a g-g-girl,' said Henry, misreading that smile and whisking me away to the ballroom. To say Henry was a bad dancer is like saying my mother is a woman of some fortitude; a vast understatement. When I finally got him to lead me back to the salon on the pretence of meeting up with a girlfriend, my feet were already turning black and blue. For a skinny youth, he had a tiresomely heavy tread.

I was dismayed to see all the food vanished and the tables cleared away. The tiny silver lining in my fast accumulating cloud of a ball was the appearance of Bernie, who took one look at Henry and rushed over. 'Oh, darling, I couldn't think where you had gone,' she said. She held out her hand to a startled Henry. 'Bernie, the American,' she said. 'Positively everyone knows me.'

Henry's Adam's apple seemed to go into a dance pattern of its own as he took in Bernie's dress. Although it covered her perfectly decently, it looked absolutely outrageous. It was also perfectly clear she wasn't wearing a stitch underneath.

'H-h-hello,' said Henry. His eyes had now joined his Adam's apple in going up and down as he took in every inch of Bernie. 'You g-g-gals should come to our meeting on Saturday. There's going to be a parade and everything. I'll get Father to send a vehicle, shall I?'

'Oh do,' said Bernie, showing her teeth and giving a shameless wiggle of her backside. 'I do love a parade. But now we must love you and leave you, Henry. Hope and I have an engagement. A girls' thing. If you know what I mean?'

Henry clearly had no idea what she meant but let me go with a confused grace. Once we were out of earshot, I snapped, 'Why did you say we'd go to his wretched parade?'

'I love a parade,' said Bernie innocently.

'We don't do American-style parades,' I said. 'It will be some kind of march about something political.'

'Oh no, that would be awful! Never mind, I didn't tell him where I lived.'

'As you said, my dear, you're Bernie. And even if everyone didn't know you before, after that dress you're going to be the talk of the town.'

'The price of beauty,' said Bernie, pouting and waving at a man behind me.

I groaned. 'Can this night get any worse?'

'I've found us two lovely young men to escort us . . .'

'Where now?' I groaned, but then she said the magical words, 'in to supper,' and all thoughts of Danville and his Henry vanished from my mind.

Chapter Twelve

Supper was excellent – well-cooked, and the servants circulated enough to allow me to eat more than the average deb without anyone being any the wiser. We were sat at an extraordinarily long table with, quite shockingly, no seating plan. But from the moment the group walked into the room it was clear many had indulged in a quantity of champagne and that managing the silverware alone was going to be challenging enough without the puzzle of trying to adhere to a seating plan.

Bernie's choices of escorts were, naturally, most interested in her. When I confirmed my love of books and that I was an Oxford scholar, I was left quite alone. Bernie's eyes flashed with warning when I mentioned Oxford, but I didn't betray her academic background by so much as a flutter of an eyelid. Besides, I doubt anyone would have believed me. She was certainly gushing enough to match the most vacant of debs. There were also a great many epergnes on the table so that between them, the candlesticks, and the flowers, I was able to keep out of line of sight of anyone who might have wished to talk to me. I suppose I should have been seeking clues, but the level of conversation around me did not bode well for anything as complex as an investigatory question.

Afterwards though, I was overcome by tiredness to the extent I could hardly keep my eyes open. 'Come on, ladies. Let's put on our dancing shoes,' proclaimed one of our escorts – Algernon or Cameron or something, I forget which.

'I have no intention of changing my shoes,' I said. 'Nor of dancing.' I swayed slightly.

'Is she pickled?' asked one of the two beaus.

Bernie came over to me and took my arm. 'Darlings, wait there. I do believe my dearest friend is very tired. I'll see her sent home.' She got the butler to summon me a cab.

'Good idea,' I said. 'I wonder how long they'll wait for you.' I yawned. 'Must have been the driving. I am completely tuckered out.' Bernie patted my arm and helped me into my coat. I really was almost asleep on my feet and was very grateful for her help. The cab arrived, and I happily entered, but at the last minute, instead of climbing in beside me, she closed the door and waved. It says much for my state of mind that it was only at this point that I noticed Bernie wasn't wearing her coat and had obviously never had any intention of accompanying me.

Having lost Bernie to the party weighed heavily enough on my mind that I seriously thought about waking her mother and sending someone to get her. The beaus she had obtained seemed a harmless enough sort, I didn't doubt she could control them. If it had been someone like Danville I would have tried to intercede. I knew full well how Bernie would take such an affront, and to be perfectly honest, I was glad I hadn't needed to. I wanted to stay in London and press on with the Charlotte Case, as I had taken to calling it in my head. If Bernie was interrupted in her fun, it might annoy her enough that she would make my stay at the Embassy untenable. She isn't a spiteful soul at heart, but she can be – how can I put it – reactive. I would doubtless receive a fulsome apology within a week, two at the most, but by then the case leads, such as they were, would have gone cold. I could decamp to Uncle Eric's, except I wasn't entirely sure where he stayed. I imagined an apartment in the Albany or even a peripatetic existence spent between gentlemen's' clubs. If the latter, he would be no help to me at all. In fact, the thought of that made me quite angry with my absent godfather. How dare he exclude women from his life in such a way? This made me realise two things. One, Uncle Eric would always go where the people with power gathered, and secondly, I was far more drunk than I had realised. It was this that mainly caused me not to speak to Amaranth when I arrived back at the Embassy. Instead I drank a pint of water and pinned my hopes on Harvey.

I came down to breakfast the next day feeling much the worse for wear. One look in the mirror showed me bags under my red-shot eyes and skin the colour of curdled milk. Bernie, against all laws of nature, looked as fresh as flowers in May. She was up at the buffet serving herself from various hot dishes. No one else was there.

'How disgusting,' I said taking a place at the table and pouring myself a coffee.

Bernie, who was helping herself to devilled kidneys, paused with a piece of offal dangling obscenely off the serving tongs. 'Me or the kidneys?' she asked.

'You,' I said. 'By all rights you should feel like I look.'

Bernie came and sat down. The kidneys swam in some inedible ichor. 'And the kidneys,' I added. 'Yuck.'

'You do look a bit peaky, old girl,' she said.

'I feel dreadful and I didn't drink half as much as you.'

'Maybe you're coming down with something,' said Bernie brightly.

'Oh, thanks.' I scraped a small amount of butter onto some toast from the rack on the table. It was cold and had a nasty rubbery texture. 'What did I miss?'

'Danville, despite his great age, is rather a lot of fun. Of course, he was pushing that awful son terribly hard on any decent girl. What was his name again?'

'Henry,' I supplied. Mentally, I cursed not interfering. I should have known she would end up with him. Bernie had always shown more interest in older men. She complained the younger ones were silly and empty-headed. For the most part she was quite correct.

128

'Yes, Henry. Anyway, Danville got up a big group of us after the party and said he knew a nightclub he could get us into where we could have some proper fun.'

Now alarm bells really began to ring in my head. 'You didn't go?'

'I most certainly did. And you'll never guess who else came along?'

'That gormless chap you met outside the jewellers, Timmy? Lord of ancient tweed?'

'Actually, I think he was there, but no, that's not who I meant. Harvey! Picked up a white tie from somewhere and suddenly he's not a waiter, but the younger son of someone important.'

'Who?'

'I don't think he ever said. More hinted at it.'

'Clever boy,' I said.

'Anyway, we all pile into a couple of chara-thingys and off into a part of London I've never seen before. I tell you, if Danville hadn't been with us I'd have been a tad worried. He leads us down into this cellar and suddenly it's all red velvet, live jazz, and free champagne. It was lovely.' She dipped a piece of kidney into a soft poached egg. I had to look away. 'Not the kind of place I'd take Mommy. I think she would have found the waitresses a bit underdressed. Not that any of the men minded. Harvey even danced with one! But Timmy and . . . what was it?'

'Henry.'

'They just sat there with their tongues hanging out.'

'Was it the five of you?'

'Oh heavens, no. That would have been a bit off. Loads of us. At least twenty. Other debs, some men who were clearly men-about-town on the make – is that what you say? But quite a few respectable beaus we'd met at other season parties. It was perfectly fine.' She pulled a face. 'The worst bit was everyone seemed to assume I was with *H-h-Henry*.'

'It's hardly his fault he stammers,' I said.

'But he couldn't take his eyes off the waitresses, so he was a

129

total failure as an escort. Then, when most of the men went through the back . . .'

'To do what?'

'Play cards for money, I think. Anyway, Danville was going to leave. He said he was too old for the party. He said he'd only come to get us in.' My opinion of Danville dropped even lower. 'I said I was bored stupid, so he stayed and danced with me. We had some champagne and some delightful little pink things in sauce with crackers.'

'I don't think that was wise, Bernie.'

'Oh, it was fine. They tasted lovely and I haven't felt a mite ill,' said Bernie, waving a hand and swatting my misgivings away like a fly. 'Why, when someone came over to sell us some snow, he chased them away.'

'They were selling cocaine there?'

'Oh, don't be so snotty, Hope. All the best people use it. It gives the evening an extra buzz.'

'Good Lord, you didn't?'

'Only because Danville didn't let me. I'd rather like to have tried it. A lot of the others did. We almost argued about it, but he made it up to me by giving me all the details of the parade. Apparently, he'll be in it. We're meeting Henry in about an hour. He'll have been holding a spot for us. Oh, and Harvey is coming too. Not quite sure how he wangled that.'

'We're meeting them?'

'Oh heavens, yes. What would Mommy say if I went on my own?' Bernie gave me a sweet smile and cut into another poached egg, which oozed yellow all over her bacon. I excused myself from the table and ran to the cloakroom, where I parted company with my meagre meal of toast.

Some people are no less than a force of nature and Bernie is one of them. This is why I found myself on a wet London street around 11.30am with Henry and Bernie. I felt like death warmed over. Of Harvey, there was no sign. Caro Littleton, a deb renowned for her foul mouth and pointed opinions, did her best to ignore Henry, except for asking him every few minutes when Timmy would get here. With her chopped locks and mink coat she was as out of place as an otter at dinner party. Although Bernie, in her emerald green coat with purple gloves and hat, also stood out like a peacock among pigeons. I did my best to integrate myself with the scenery.

The people around Henry mingled with others on the pavement, but I managed to make out there were about fifteen in Henry's group. Apart from myself, Bernie, and Caro, the only other person present I knew was Beth Setton, a deb who carried a book bag with her to parties and sat in the corner reading titles like the *History of Plato*. She showed no interest in anyone or anything around and why she was a deb was a conundrum to me until I'd met her mother: a middle-aged beauty with suspiciously red hair, who revelled in every event and flirted outrageously with boys young enough to be her sons. Certainly, there was no sign of her parents today. I had felt rather sorry for her. However, she had never responded to any overture of friendship from me except to be civilly distant and I had left her alone.

But today Beth wore a grey mackintosh like the one worn by women from the factories, and small circular black glasses I had never seen her wear before. If I hadn't met her at one of the season's parties I would have thought her a factory girl – this, I was later to realise, was exactly the idea. The men in our party were largely unknown to me. Some wore suits that had obviously been hand-stitched, and others had shrugged themselves into cheaper versions. But having seen Beth's disguise, I didn't read that much into it. All the men were young – certainly none over thirty, and far too many of them had thin, Mosley-like moustaches.

Our group perched at the front of a wide pavement outside a hardware shop. Behind us stood a crowd maybe ten deep. On both sides of us the 'sidewalks', as Bernie called them, bulged with crowds. Mostly men but a few women. They were almost uniform in their attire of cheap trench coats and off-the-shelf standard hats. Clothing ranged from grey to black, but never got brighter. Expectation hovered, despite the bad weather, in the closed, serious expressions those around us wore. Despite their dour demeanours I felt a suppressed excitement in the air. It was not an excitement I shared. Instead I became increasingly uneasy.

The rain had begun as a light drizzle, but after Bernie and I had been there no more than ten minutes it was coming down in what my nanny would have described as 'stair-rods'. Once again, my cloche hat came into its own. Bernie's, on the other hand, was making her look like a drowned spaniel. She wasn't happy. I sneezed. The temperature appeared to have dropped alarmingly.

Then we heard a drumming sound. I say sound, because it wasn't drums, but it was rhythmical. A smile split Bernie's face. 'It's people,' she said. When I continued to look puzzled she added, 'Feet marching.'

Henry piped up, 'Daddy's c-c-chums are on their way.' He drew himself up a little taller and lifted the small nodule of bone that served him as a chin. I almost tipped off the pavement when a body pushed past behind me.

'Morning, workers of the world,' said a plummy voice. Caro squealed and threw herself at Timmy. He hooked one arm around her and edged his way in to speak in undertones to Henry. This made me push back against Bernie, who remained irritated about her hat, and while she didn't exactly force me into the road, neither did she give me quite the room I required. Weirdly, though, this balancing act seemed to warm me up to the point of overheating.

I teetered on the edge of the kerb. A murmur ran through the crowd. People leaned forward, craning their necks out like baby birds seeking food. The sound intensified. I felt a vibration through the soles of my feet. Then, around the corner, came the head of a march. In a triangular formation marched three over-weight middle-aged men, dressed in black shirts and trousers with overly large belt buckles. Two of them had silly moustaches and all of them wore their hair short and greased back, even though in one case there wasn't much hair to grease. Behind them came rows of four marchers, again mostly men, but some lines were entirely female. As the columns passed us they saluted the crowd, launching their right arms out directly in front of them. More than one member of the crowd saluted them back. Every third row an unhappy-looking police constable marched beside them. The police had their cloaks and their hats, and the male marchers no more protection from the rain than their shirts and trousers (only the women appeared to be allowed coats). But of the two sets of individuals, the police looked the more edgy. Indeed, as one young policeman passed closed to me, I saw that his knuckles were white as he gripped his truncheon.

'Are they waving at us?' asked Bernie. 'Are we meant to wave back?'

'No,' I said curtly. I found myself physically shivering at her idiocy. I could not see a way through the crowds. We had no choice but to stay put.

'I think it looks jolly fun,' said Bernie and tried out a salute. Henry brayed approvingly.

'That's a g-g-gal,' he said. 'Did you see Papa at the front? Looking damned dapper for an old c-c-codger, don't you think?'

I realised then that one of the foremost trio had been Danville. I had paid no attention to the individual faces once I realised what we were in for. My whole attention remained on the mood of the crowd and possible exits. 'Do you know who these people are?' I hissed at Bernie. I couldn't believe her naivety. I sneezed another three times.

'British Union,' she said. 'I thought it sounded awfully jolly. All Brits together and that. Should have known the great British reserve would keep everything muted. But I like the waving.'

'They're fascists,' I said. The mere thought brought on another round of shivering. 'The remnants of Oswald Mosley's lot. Your precious Danville is a fascist – like Hitler.'

Bernie paled. 'Oh, cripes. I thought there was something famil-iar about the wave. It's the Nazi salute, isn't it. I can't be seen here.'

'Let's hope no photographer caught the Ambassador's daughter *Sieg Heil*-ing.'

Bernie said a word I didn't even think she knew. 'Hope,' she whispered, 'how could you let me come to a thing like this?'

'I had no idea it was going to be like this,' I retorted. At least my temper flaring was keeping me warm. 'It's not the kind of thing I put in my diary: must go and wish the Nazis good luck today! Besides, I didn't think even you could be so naive as not to know what the British Union is!'

'What do you mean, even me? I know about *American* politics. Global stuff. Not what your silly island gets up to.'

Our exchange was becoming heated and I felt eyes in the crowd turn towards us. 'Hush,' I said. 'Let's wait it out and back out as soon as we can.'

At that moment I spied Harvey through the marchers on the other side of the road. I recognised his face at once. He wore an expression of disgust and horror. My heart beat a little faster in my chest. Obviously, he did not support the marchers. 'Ooh, Harvey,' called Bernie, who had spotted him too. She jumped up and down and waved. 'I'm sure he can . . .' but that was all I heard her say.

My position on the edge of the kerb, always precarious, succumbed to the influence of Bernie's jiggling. I fell forward into the marchers. Fortunately, not into a policeman, or I suspect I would have been strong-armed off to a cell at once. Instead I collided with a solid little man, who swore viciously at me and pushed me off him. I reeled backwards, sneezed again, and lost my balance. I landed against someone else, who swore and shoved me hard into another marcher. I thought, very faintly, I heard Harvey's voice, but I couldn't be sure. I was far too busy reeling from person to person, like a child's spinning top. I imagine it might have been amusing to watch, but to me, in the midst of it all, it was bruising and confusing. A mixture of calloused hands and whirling, swearing faces. Normally, I was good at extracting myself from physical interactions, but I couldn't seem to find my focus, let alone control my feet. The one good thing in my favour was the pace of the march was such that while I was bouncing from marcher to marcher I remained more or less level with Bernie.

Sadly, Bernie has never been one to act in crisis. While I was becoming far more intimate that I would ever have liked with the nation's remaining fascists, Bernie, I saw in brief glimpses, was jiggling in frustration on the spot, flapping her arms like a goose fearing Christmas, and shouting. I couldn't hear what she was saying. The noise around us, not simply of the footsteps but of the crowds murmuring en masse, drowned almost everything out in an unpleasant dull roar. I did still hear, and will never forget hearing, the braying laughs of Henry and Timmy, who apparently found amusement in my predicament. Though, in retrospect, I realised both were probably too dim to realise I was in grave danger of being trampled underfoot.

I bounced off my fifth or sixth person. I was losing count. I caught a glimpse of Harvey pushing into the march from the other side. 'No,' I cried out, but my words were lost. I saw his face briefly between the dark-clad bodies and it seemed to be mouthing 'Hang on'. However, I knew I should be able to take care of myself. I tried to give myself a mental shake and almost went down under the next pair of marching boots. I pulled myself up – goodness knows how. The laws of physics would have said it was impossible for me to recover, but against the odds I managed. Then I saw that Bernie had done something useful. She pushed a cane towards me. 'Catch this,' I saw her lips move. I realised she intended to reel me in. Not a good idea.

If I acted quickly enough Harvey would be able to retreat to his side of the street before he . . . I pushed the thought to the back of my mind. A girl being bounced from marcher to marcher is seen as an inconvenience, even an amusement, and most certainly not a threat. Their mistake.

I yanked the cane from Bernie's startled hands. Now I had a weapon, I felt much more in control. The next person I collided with, as soon as he tried to push me, I bent forward, slid my cane under his arm. Then using my weight as leverage, I pushed the cane through and across his back. This bent his forward. Using the momentum of this action, I swung him round. His lumbering form propelling me out of the way of the marchers and onto the pavement next to Bernie. This, of course, disturbed both the pattern of the marchers and those on the pavement. I hated the decision I made next, but in a fight, I had to back Harvey over Bernie. I had to assume he could make it out on his own.

I yanked the cane free from my reluctant human riot shield, grabbed Bernie by the hand, and flourishing the cane before me, made a rush though the crowds. Behind me I heard the start of a scuffle. A glance over my shoulder showed me Harvey deep in the middle of it all. He looked like he was going down, but I'd made my choice. All I could do for him now was pray.

The sight of a young woman forcibly waving a cane in front of her proved to be innovative enough that I managed to clear a path. As soon as I could, I dived down an alleyway and started putting as much distance between the march and ourselves as possible.

We came to a wide street and I spied a taxi-cab. I have little memory of how I got us inside, but I did, and then I collapsed. It seemed that rather than simply being hung-over, I was actually unwell. Consciousness did the decent thing and shut everything out.

Chapter Thirteen

When I opened my eyes the dawn sun shone through the window. 'Why are the curtains open?' I demanded. My throat rasped and my voiced sounded rough.

'Well now,' said Bernie coming into view and sitting on the edge of my bed. 'Do you want the English Rose explanation or the down-to-earth American one?'

I signalled the second. 'All right. Well, you see, you vomited an absolute sea of bile. Despite changing the bedclothes and scrubbing the floor, the servants couldn't get—'

I held up my hand for her to stop. She smiled down at me. I noticed my friend looked different. Her face was devoid of make-up and her hair decidedly tumbled. 'Have you been here all night?' I croaked.

'Most of it,' said Bernie. 'Mommy made me leave the room when the doctor was here. Do you not remember anything?'

'The taxi-cab,' I said. Bernie passed me a glass of water. I struggled to sit up. My head span and for an awful moment I thought I was going to be sick again. But some determined swallowing and small sips, and I began to feel as though I might possibly live.

'I'm so sorry I took you to that awful parade,' said Bernie, an expression of genuine remorse on her face. 'I never imagined you would get hurt.' Tears hovered on the edges of her eyelids. I tried to remember when I had seen Bernie so upset and failed.

'Not your fault,' I said, continuing to sip the water. My throat soaked up the water like a cracked, dry riverbed.

'But it must be,' said Bernie. 'All those men battering you.'

I closed my eyes. Tattered memories of the march whirled in my head. It was akin to trying to reassemble a jigsaw puzzle when someone was tossing pieces in the box. 'Blackshirts,' I said. 'I got knocked off the pavement. Bounced.'

'I'm so sorry.'

I put my hand on my stomach under the covers. Even the pressure from my fingers made me wince in pain. I peeked under the blanket. I didn't see any bruises. I couldn't remember anyone actually striking me. If Bernie was right about my night of acute stomach distress, and I had no reason to believe she wasn't, I could find no connection to the march. 'No,' I said. 'But I must have been already ill. Sneezed.'

'A cold wouldn't make you this ill. You almost died,' said Bernie, verging on the edge of hysteria.

Fortunately, at this moment, a swift knock at the door heralded Amaranth's entrance. 'Oh, my darling girl, so good to see you awake.' She came up to the bed and gave me a kiss on the cheek. She looked at her daughter. 'Out,' she said. 'You're overwrought and exhausted. You're too disruptive for an invalid. Go away and sleep. I'll keep Hope company.'

'Oh no,' I said. 'I think I'll go back to sleep.'

'Excellent. Then I will stay with you until you sleep. Go, Bernadette! I will not argue with you.'

Somewhat cowed, Bernie slid out of the room. Amaranth pulled up a chair next to my bed. She patted my hand. 'I was a nurse in the Great War. Volunteered. Nothing worse than someone bouncing on the edge of your bed when you're feeling sore, is there?' She took the glass from me and expertly altered my pillows. 'Bernie can be terribly melodramatic, but she does love you, Hope. You are her dearest friend – and not simply because you put up with her. She admires you enormously. She's always boasting of her clever friend.'

For no reason tears prickled my eyes. Amaranth patted my hand again. 'I know. When you're feeling lousy emotions always

138

come to the top. I'll let you sleep, but I need you to help me make a decision. Should I call your parents?'

I shook my head vehemently. Pain echoed between my temples as if someone had beaten a giant gong inside my skull.

'I know your papa isn't in the best of health, and now you're out of danger, I'm worried about alarming him. But your mama is quite another matter. Between you and me, she scares the bejesus out of me. Don't get me wrong, she's a lovely lady, a close friend for many years, but not someone you want to get on the wrong side of.'

'Uncle Joe?' I croaked. My throat had gone dry again.

'Oh, an excellent idea!' said Amaranth, catching on at once. 'I'll send Joe a telegram, to explain things and ask him to pop down to see your parents. Much better than a telephone call from me. I find that machine quite dreadful. It makes me say the oddest things. I accidentally ordered fifty-three lobsters last week rather than sixty trout. The Ambassador was not amused. But at the time all my brain could remember was it was from the sea and more than fifty.'

'Does my family need to know?' I said with some effort.

Amaranth frowned. Normally, I realised, she went to enormous lengths not to do so. 'Darling, I know you're much more sensible than Bernie could ever be, but I think we should talk about this later.'

I did my best to emulate my mother's most mulish face. Amaranth gave a small laugh. 'Goodness, my dear. How frightful. Don't do that, it might stick. You look just like Euphemia when she's on the warpath!' She gave a little sigh. 'All right, I'll tell you, and it's probably better to do so rather than let you imagine things. The doctor thinks it was likely you were poisoned.'

It took me at least a minute to understand what she had said. 'Me?' Amaranth nodded. I wondered what on earth she though I could have dreamed up that would have been worse than someone trying to kill me. Amaranth continued to talk as if, once started, she had to let it all tumble out.

'I've got the security team going through the kitchen with a fine tooth-comb, but honestly I think it must have happened away from the Embassy. I cannot see how they could have got to you without affecting the rest of us. You'd been out at that gymkhana all day, and Bernie said you'd eaten stuff from Fortnum's – good choice – but did you eat anything else the others had brought?'

I was surprised Bernie had managed to lie so well under pressure, so I shook my head.

'I could pester Fortnum's,' she continued, 'but it all depends on how much fuss we want to create. It's not the kind of thing anyone wants in the papers. But I have to weigh that against whether you could possibly still be at risk.'

I looked at her with wide eyes and shrugged. It didn't seem to have occurred to her to establish if I was the only one or if there were others. If I was the only one, then this was serious. But to explain it all I'd have to come clean about the wretched gymkhana. It seemed likely to have been something I'd ingested at the party last night. Now that she knew I had attended, I decided, partly because my throat was sore and partly because I didn't want to mention the trip to Brighton, I would simply listen and see if she hit on the right course of action.

'I suppose it could have been nothing more than bad oysters,' she said. I nodded. That was certainly true. Although I expect a decent doctor could have told the difference. 'They can be especially vile to one, but I am still worried.' She reached into a pocket. 'That reminds me. Somehow your Uncle Eric heard you were ill. He came by earlier this morning. I've got a letter for you. He wants to take you to lunch, when you're well enough, at his club.' She tucked the envelope behind the water jug. 'Charming man. The Ambassador was delighted to see him. Apparently, they go way back. Don't ask me how! They went off to smoke those revolting cigars.'

'I'm safe,' I said, sliding down my pillows. 'If Uncle Eric knows I've been ill he can always tell Mama and Papa if he thinks he should.'

'I suppose, as a close family friend, it's his choice,' said Amaranth slowly. 'I've never quite understood his relationship to your mother. I know he's your godfather, but since I first knew them he's always been hanging around in the background. Popping up when one least expected him and often whisking Euphemia away to goodness knows where. Mind you, your father never seemed to have any concerns, so I guess I should mind my own beeswax. Especially talking to you!' She patted my arm again. 'He's still a very handsome man. Maybe I should check he and the Ambassador have everything they need . . .'

She seemed almost to be speaking to herself now. I gave a little cough and she started slightly.

'Very well,' said Amaranth. 'We'll let things be, for now. You get some good sleep. I'll stay with you until you nod off.'

It could only be a few minutes before I slid down into sleep. I vaguely heard the door shut softly. I turned over on my pillow and snuggled down. I had barely closed my eyes, before they flew open. Harvey. What had happened to Harvey?

I tossed and turned for what seemed like hours. I seriously considered getting out of bed, but one half-hearted attempt at sitting upright had me flopping back down on the sheets like a freshly landed fish. I could only hope that Bernie finished her nap, or whatever she was actually doing, before long. It crossed my mind to ring the bell, but it would most likely summon Amaranth and I could think of no way of explaining my concern about Harvey without her jumping to the conclusion that I had formed an improper alliance. And as for telling her about researching Charlotte's death, that was simply unthinkable. If only Uncle Eric would come by and see me. But it wasn't as if I was a little girl any more. I should stop calling him Uncle too, I thought sleepily. After all, he'd never actually been one. I nodded off again.

Eventually, Amaranth returned with my lunch on a tray: a clear consommé, with garlic croutons and a light salad of leaves and herbs. It didn't look enough to sustain a mouse. As this thought crossed my mind, I realised how hungry I had become. Amaranth must have read my face. She set the tray down before me.

'The doctor said you would have to eat lightly for two days at least. He will visit you after that and ascertain whether you are to be allowed up.'

'In bed for two days,' I said, horrified.

'I know it's a disappointment, darling. But there's still plenty of time left in the season. It's not uncommon for young ladies to take a couple of days out due to exhaustion. That's what we're saying has happened to you.'

'How's Bernie?' I asked.

'Up, and ripe for mischief as usual,' said her mother. 'I was going to let her come in and see you after lunch, but you've got black circles under your eyes. Did you sleep at all? Maybe I should get the doctor back.'

'Oh no, it's not that,' I said quickly, 'I'm not worse. It's simply that I had arranged to meet some friends tonight and I need Bernie to get a message to them. You know how it is, friendships we make this summer could last us a lifetime, but at the same time if someone gets a reputation for being flighty, it'll stick.'

Amaranth gave a light laugh. 'I can't imagine anyone ever thinking you flighty, dear Hope. But I will get Bernie to come in and see you — for a short while — if you finish your lunch.'

As I was fairly sure I could bolt the lot down in two minutes flat I agreed, trying to seem meek and dutiful. Amaranth seemed content and left me to eat. The soup transpired to be tomato and despite its lack of colour, tasted exquisite, while the salad, dressed only in lemon juice — an odd, acidic choice I thought — was equally lovely. The pairing of flavours by the chef obviously superseded any suggestion of illness. Although the quantities on the tray were pitifully small, by the time I had finished my stomach felt so bloated I might have eaten ten courses. I pushed the tray to the end of the bed and lay back to digest.

Bernie burst into my room. 'Oh, thank goodness, you're

awake,' she said. 'Mommy said it would be unfair of me to go to this afternoon's picnic without you. I am so bored.'

'You have a very ego-centric version of reality, don't you?' I said.

'I don't want you to be ill for your own sake, too,' said Bernie. She moved the tray to the bedside table and pulled up a chair.

'I know,' I said. 'You're not selfish, but you do forget things that don't affect you.' I paused. 'Like Harvey.'

'What about him?' said Bernie.

I searched my memory of the march. 'Didn't you see what happened to him?' Bernie looked at me blankly. 'He tried to get through the march to me and got into a fist fight with some men.'

'I should think that's nothing he isn't used to,' said Bernie.

'I saw him go down on the ground, Bernie. I had to decide between getting you out of there and trying to go and help him.'

'I don't see how you could have helped. We were both too busy running for our lives. It's women and children first,' said Bernie. 'One expects someone like Harvey to be able to take care of himself. Are you saying you think he might really be hurt?'

I nodded. Bernie sprang up. 'I'll be back in a moment,' she said and left. My concern levels rose. Now, not only was I worried about Harvey, but what Bernie being 'ripe for mischief' might also do. I was on the verge of ringing the bell, when Bernie returned, sheaves of paper clutched under her arms. She sat down on the edge of my bed with an 'oof' that sent a disproportional shock through the mattress. 'Took some doing, but I got the information,' she said, spreading out newspapers over the bed.

She picked through the papers, pulling out various double spreads from each. 'I had to bribe one of the security men to go out and get these.'

'Bribe?'

'A kiss. If anyone hears about it, he is so fired.'

'He certainly sounds like a security risk,' I said.

'Pooh, he was merely getting yesterday's and today's newspapers for me.' She glanced at me. 'Oh, you mean the kiss? I shouldn't think kissing me was a national security risk. Daddy is his boss. Could be a major health risk. For him.' She grinned evilly. Then she folded up the sheets she'd picked out to show me various passages. 'Right, here's the first report of the march. It says about five hundred Blackshirt marchers passed through the streets of London and two thousand spectators gathered to watch. It also says there was some trouble around Bights Hardware store, but otherwise the appalling spectacle passed without incident.' She picked up another sheet. 'This one came out slightly later. It cites "seven hundred and fifty followers of Oswald Mosley marched through the streets of free London in scandalous display of Fascism" and that "a scant thousand witnessed the disgrace". But it does go on to say, "three respectable citizens were drawn into a brawl with the raging protesters."'

'Oh Lord, does it mean us?' I said.

Bernie shook her head and picked up another paper. 'This is yesterday's late edition.' Bernie read, '"During this afternoon's parade by the notorious Blackshirts, a fascist organisation led by former MP Oswald Mosley – and one which this reporter is happy to say is well in its decline – several Londoners were injured in a brawl that broke out opposite Bights Hardware." Then he goes off to deplore it, etc., etc., talks about the ban on uniformed marches caused by Mosley, mentions the evils of Germany and Herr Hitler "whose influence could be seen in the number of ridiculous moustaches sported by male members of the march". Then right at the end he says, "all injured parties were taken to St Mary's hospital, but, this newspaper understands, have been subsequently discharged with no serious injury."'

'Thank goodness,' I said flopping back against my pillows in relief.

'Don't get too comfy yet,' said Bernie. 'This morning's newspaper talks about the march – blah, blah, blah – but mentions two men from the East End were kept in overnight as they displayed signs of concussion.'

'Does it name them?'

'Harvey Clayton, also known to the police as Lenny Partridge, and Bill Higgins, also known to the police as William Hodges, both of the Canning Town area.' There were two black and white smeary photos next to the piece that could have been any young men. I couldn't even tell which of them was meant to be Harvey.

She put down the sheet. 'Partridge! I have to ask him about that. And known to the police! You do find the most fascinating people, Hope.'

'What does it say in the latest edition,' I said, pointing to the last sheet.

'Pretty much the same,' said Bernie. 'Although they have printed a correction, "while it is correct both men are known to the police, this newspaper wishes to point out that neither of them is a known fascist or has ever been known to be involved with the fascist movement."'

'Faintly damning praise,' I said.

'Did you honestly make a choice between me and Harvey?' said Bernie suddenly. 'I mean, I was with Henry and Timmy and the others.'

'None of who, you'll recall, made any effort to help me. So it seemed a good bet they wouldn't spring to your aid if things got nasty – as they did.'

'It's was Timmy's cane I used.'

'Did he give it to you?'

'No,' said Bernie. 'In fact, he swore when I took it off him. I don't think I'm going to be getting those earrings any time soon.'

'Well, I am very glad you did,' I said. 'I am still concerned about Harvey. The newspaper reports were hardly consistent, were they?'

'No, and I didn't read out the half of it,' said Bernie. 'There's more speculation about war with Germany, how many Mosley supporters remain in the country, and who they are. There are even suggestions that the fascists are seeding themselves into British industry, so they can sabotage any war effort, should it come to that.'

'Does your father think it will?'

Bernie nodded. 'And Daddy's usually right. He's expecting to be recalled any moment.'

'You'll go too?'

'Not if I marry someone by the end of the season,' said Bernie with a determined pout. 'Do you think I would leave you to face a nasty old war on your own? Did you really choose me over Harvey? Only it seemed to me you were rather fond of the dope.'

I smiled. 'No point thinking about all that now,' I said. 'There's nothing we can do about it. But I do think as soon as I'm up we need to go and find him.'

'You want to go down to Canning Town?' said Bernie. 'Even I know we wouldn't be welcome there. It's the very definition of rough.'

'I know,' I said. 'I don't want to go either, but how else can we reach him? It's not like we have a postal address.'

'I could go around to the editor's office at the newspaper and try to sweet talk it out of them. I'm enjoying the opportunity to expand my kissing skills. All in a good cause, of course.'

'You're outrageous. Besides, they may not have it. I can't imagine Harvey giving his address out willingly, or saying he was known to the police.'

'I rather think the latter is a badge of merit in Canning Town,' said Bernie tartly. 'I could try and get it from the police, but unless there's a very gullible sergeant I don't think I'd get away without having to explain why I needed to find him. And I do draw the line at kissing policemen.'

'Blast it,' I said. 'We're going to have to hope he comes to us.' I tried to smile. 'It's not like everyone doesn't know your address.'

Chapter Fourteen

It took three full days for me to recover, but on the third I ventured down to the usual family buffet breakfast. Amaranth's perfume still hung in the air, but only Bernie was present. She sat at the head of the table with a plate filled with sausages, bacon, and scrambled eggs. 'Does your father ever come down to breakfast?' I asked. 'I'm beginning to wonder if I imagined him.'

'He joined us the last two days,' said Bernie. 'But usually he has coffee and toast at his desk.'

I collected a plate and filled it with scrambled eggs, smoked haddock, and one crispy rasher of bacon. I intended to be careful of my stomach, although I couldn't resist the chance to make heavy inroads on the gorgeous white bread baked at the Embassy. I selected three thick slices from the buffet and helped myself to a pat of butter in a little saucer. (There is no doubt Americans have some strange eating habits. There were also pancakes and waffles, alongside jams and syrups on offer. None of which I would object to later on in the day, but not at breakfast. Goodness!) I sat down to the right of her. 'Either that or I'm beginning to think he doesn't like me,' I said. 'I haven't seen him since I got here.'

'Daddy doesn't generally see anyone without an appointment,' said Bernie. 'Even me.' Her mouth was full of sausage, so I couldn't tell if she was joking or not. I let it lie. Yet I couldn't help remembering he had put aside his schedule to see my godfather. Surely a guest in one's house merited a bit more consideration than the passing impulse visit of one's guest's godfather?

Bernie swallowed. 'There's lots of talks going on,' she said. 'Don't ask me about what. Long faces, serious conversations, and Mommy's being extra bright and charming which always means she thinks things are about to take a nosedive.'

'Oh,' I said.

Bernie shrugged. 'Anyway, what are we going to do about Harvey? I checked with my friend in security and no one has asked to see either of us – except your Uncle Eric. I don't remember ever meeting him. Is he your mother's or your father's brother?'

'Neither. He's my godfather. The uncle is a courtesy title. I should stop using it now I am an adult, but it's a well-worn habit. Besides, he can be a bit formidable when he wants to be.'

'Is he old with a busy beard? Looks like Santa and sends you sweets at Christmas?' asked Bernie.

'No.' I spread some fine creamy butter on the bread and answered without thinking. 'He's probably in his early fifties. Quite distinguished-looking when he wants to be. I remember last time he put on a tux for one of Mother's parties, he looked distinctly dashing. Quite took me by surprise.'

Bernie's eyes glinted. 'Interesting,' she said. 'You must introduce me. I admit, I'm rather disappointed I made so little impression on the London set. You think someone would have missed me.'

'Considering he's involved with the fascists I don't imagine either Danville or his son would turn up here.'

'Why not?' said Bernie. 'I overheard Daddy saying that America isn't interested in taking sides. Besides, there was a time when all the best people were fascists and Danville says a lot of them still are.'

'I wouldn't trust anything that man says,' I said. 'Let's think about how we could get to Canning Town. I take it there's transport of some kind?'

'Tube, I think,' said Bernie. 'I could do a little visit.' She saw my expression. 'To the local tube station, not to Canning Town. I'm the one who thinks we shouldn't go there at all.'

'Harvey must be shockingly poor,' I said. 'Yet, he's always so well turned out.'

'Maybe that's what he spends his money on,' said Bernie. 'Trying to be a dapper gent. If I lived in the East End, I'd want to find a way out, or at least a way to hob-nob with the toffs.'

'Us,' I said.

'Don't look so horrified, Hope,' said Bernie. 'You must realise, to Harvey, we are top-of-the-trees rich, affluent to an extent he can never aspire to.'

'My family is not that wealthy.'

'Says the girl who has an Earl for an uncle and who is sole heiress to a sprawling estate.'

'A soggy estate in the Fens,' I said. I sighed. 'But yes, I get your point. We must seem like spoiled brats to him. I've been doling money out to him like I'm giving him treats for being good.'

'Like a pet,' said Bernie. 'It's been rather cute to watch. The way you've tamed him to take money from your hand.' She made a gracious blessing gesture. 'Hope Stapleford, saint to all cocky con men. Benedictions this way.'

I pushed my plate away. 'Oh, shut up,' I said. My appetite had vanished. At that moment, the breakfast parlour door opened. Briefly, I thought it might be the elusive Ambassador, but it proved only to be a butler, who presented me with a calling card on a silver tray. 'A gentleman to see you, miss,' he said. His voice had the refined, cultured edge that belies a natural London accent.

I looked at the card. It read 'Paul Saulier'. 'Good Heavens,' I said. 'I do believe it's a relative of Charlotte's. Saulier isn't that common a name, is it?'

Bernie got up and came over. She examined the card. 'I think I remember her mentioning she had an older brother, or was it a cousin? She had some male relative she quoted as the arbitrator of all things if the conversation got tricky,' she said. 'Let's go and see him.'

'Ah, I'm afraid not, Miss Bernie. The gentleman was quite

insistent that he needed to see Miss Stapleford alone.' He looked down at me. 'If you would like to me to send him about his business, it would be a pleasure, miss.'

'Thank you, but no,' I said. 'Please ask him to wait and say I will be with him shortly.'

'Heavens,' said Bernie after the door closed. 'I've never heard Burns say he would like to send someone about their business before. Are you sure you want to see him alone?'

'If I scream, how many security men would come running?' I said.

'Good point,' said Bernie. 'Just promise me you'll tell me everything!'

Paul Saulier waited for me in a small, garishly decorated anteroom. It probably had a name, but if the discreet gentleman who led me there mentioned it, it bypassed me. I was too caught up in wondering why Charlotte's brother had come to us now and what, if any relationship, this might have to my being poisoned. Then again . . . had I been poisoned deliberately, or merely been the unfortunate recipient of some bad oysters?

My escort melted away into the shadows without a word. I entered the room to see Saulier standing by the window. In outline, he did not resemble his sister, being much taller and broader-set. In fact, the idea that this man could in any way be related to the waif-like Charlotte seemed ridiculous. But no sooner had the door closed behind me than he walked swiftly towards me. As soon as he was away from the back lighting of the window I saw he had the same golden shade of hair as Charlotte, and while his features remained wholly masculine, around his eyes I saw an echo of Charlotte's face. Seen together, it would have been obvious they were siblings. It struck me then that I could never see them as a pair and a sharp pang of loss surged through me.

I suppressed all visible signs of my reaction. I knew it to be ridiculous and even self-centred. I had hardly known the girl, and this was her brother. His loss was immeasurable compared to mine. I knew my response was rooted in the suddenness of poor

150

Charlotte's death. I was young and had lost very few people. I was not yet used to the way the dead are suddenly ripped from our world and how everything around us continues on regardless. It is not only a reminder of our own mortality, but also our insignificance. For most, myself included, it is the latter that chills us to the core. To not matter, to not achieve something with the gift of life one possesses, would be to me the worst crime. Charlotte's life had been over scarcely before it had begun. Not that even in my kindest thoughts could I have envisaged her changing the world, but she had been kind, if vacant, and she had presumably loved her brother, if she had spoken of him as frequently as Bernie implied. The world was less without her. 'I am so sorry for your loss, Mr Saulier,' I said.

I held out my hand to greet him, but his advance towards me did not stop and I was forced to drop my arm awkwardly. He came up to me, nearer than seemed necessary. 'Are you Hope Stapleford?' he asked in a taut voice. This close, I could see the lines around his eyes and the sides of his mouth. I estimated he would be eight to ten years older than his sister.

I gave his bad manners the benefit of the doubt and ascribed it to grief. I said, 'I am. I am so sorry about Charlotte.' I knew I was repeating myself, but he had not responded to my first condolence and I wondered if he was a little deaf.

'Well, if you indeed are,' he said, his tone now developing into anger, 'kindly leave my sister to rest in peace. I assume it was you who asked about her at the boarding house in Brighton.' I did not have a chance to answer before he pressed, 'I, my parents, and my wife, have suffered enough without watching you drag Charlotte's reputation through the mud.'

Somewhat rocked off balance I could only stammer, 'But I have said nothing to anyone.'

'Really,' he said, his sneer pronounced, 'and that tart who associates with you, Bernie Woodford, hanging around press offices is merely a coincidence?'

For a moment I could not follow what he was saying. To my

knowledge, Bernie had been nowhere near Fleet Street. Then I realised she had asked someone to gather a large number of newspapers for her. This exchange had obviously been seen outside the Embassy and someone had misinterpreted this.

'The Ambassador's daughter does not frequent Fleet Street,' I said sharply. 'And I advise you to watch your tongue when you speak about the American Ambassador's daughter when you stand in the American Embassy.'

He pointed a finger at me. 'And I advise you, young lady, to mind your own business.'

'And you yours,' I snapped. 'I assume you have been having us watched. That is entirely unacceptable. I have a mind to inform the police.'

At this I saw a fleeting expression cross his face. It was gone in an instant, so I could not be sure, but I thought it was fear.

He lowered his hand and took a half-step nearer me. Now, we were almost touching. I felt an urge to retreat, but I treated him as one would an ill-tempered dog and stood my ground. If you show fear to such a cur, it will bite you. I had to tilt my face up to look at his. This made him, I guessed, about 5'10". My neck protested but I continued to look him in the eye.

He lowered his voice and angled his form to loom over me. 'You have no idea what you have got yourself into,' he said. He swallowed. 'My sister was a bad lot. If you value your skin, you won't pursue your charade of an investigation any further. I warn you, entering the society she mixed with, you're liable to end up the same way she did.' Then he walked directly at me, forcing me to turn to the side, but still giving me a fairly hard knock on the shoulder. He stormed out. I stood looking at the closed door for a few moments as I rubbed my sore shoulder.

Later, back in the lounge with Bernie, I found myself rubbing at it again, as I retold the story. 'Do you think Charlotte was a bad lot?' said Bernie, her head tilted to one side. 'I can't see it myself.'

'I think she might have had a persuadable personality,' I said. 'But to get herself mixed up in so much trouble so early in the season, she would to have had to be a fast worker. I mean, before the presentation I'd never heard of her. If she'd been up to her ears in cocaine and loose men – does one call men loose or just cads?'

'Just cads,' said Bernie.

'All right, if she had been finding cads with whom to consort, would her parents have allowed to come to London under the auspices of an aged aunt? And where had she been finding the cads? Some rural backwater where she lived? I'll admit most places play host to a cad or two, but not the kind of rampant caddishness Saulier seemed to be implying. I need to find a word other than cad.'

'Maybe her parents threw her into the season to get her off their hands. A quick marriage to cover up previous indiscretions,' said Bernie. Then she shook her head. 'I'm only playing devil's advocate here. As one of the more modern young ladies of today, I can categorically state that I don't think Charlotte had an ounce of stuffing in her. If she was a wild woman then she utterly deceived me, and that's no mean feat!'

I gave a slight smile. 'That's the weird thing. I don't think even her brother believed what he was saying. There was real grief and loss in his voice, under the anger. And even that wasn't real. If I didn't know better, I'd say his overriding emotion was fear.'

'You can still love a wicked sibling,' said Bernie. 'I've imagined myself at least two, so I know. A sibling is a sibling. I mean, one of Daddy's brothers ran off with an heiress and spent all her money. I'm not meant to know about him. The pair of them now run a small inn in Kentucky. I've never met them, but I know Daddy visits at least once a year and still sends Christmas cards. Sometimes even money. Mommy would have a fit if she knew the extent of it.'

'How do you know?'

'Oh, Mommy and Daddy almost never argue, so when they do I know it's worth listening in on. Afterwards Daddy tends to come explain to me that everything is all right. Then I turn on

153

the waterworks and get the whole tale.' She raised her eyes and fluttered her lids. 'I'm such a black-hearted schemer.' She paused and became more serious. 'It's awfully tough on them both, this diplomatic business. If I know what's happening I'm more likely to be able to help. Don't you think?'

'I don't know,' I said slowly. I felt taken aback that Bernie's parents were not on as good terms as it seemed. Silly really, but I'd thought they were a happy couple. 'My parents have flaming passionate rows, but they manage to make up fine.'

'Oh, your parents!' said Bernie. 'Everyone knows they were a love match. Mommy calls them soul mates. Says it's the most romantic thing ever. Why, your father was the shortest man courting your mother at the time. Mommy said she had her share of beaus, but despite the Fens and lack of height, she still chose your father.'

'Really, Bernie!' I said faintly. 'You can't talk about my parents like that.'

Bernie clapped her hands. 'You didn't know! How jolly. Are you shocked your mother was a sought-after beauty? Apparently, she was always getting into trouble too.' She stopped. 'That's a thought. Do you think we should go to the police about Harvey? Or I could get us a security escort. Even the mere sniff of someone following me would get us a small army of men in black suits to escort us.'

'That's what I'm afraid of,' I said. 'And if that happened there wouldn't be any way we could take this investigation further.'

'Oh, do you intend to press on despite brother Paul?'

'Certainly,' I said. 'His intention might have been to scare me off, but he's achieved exactly the opposite. I am more determined than ever to find out what happened to poor Charlotte.'

'Jolly good show!' said Bernie, almost sounding British. 'But what about Harvey? If he's already been beaten up for us once, can we involve him again if Saulier is on the warpath? That is, if he's even well enough.'

'If we can find him,' I said, 'we will tell him everything. And see if he's still willing to help us.'

'So, you don't think it was him that sold us out to Paul?'

I paused. 'That hadn't occurred to me, but I don't think so. Besides, for the next part of our investigation, I need Harvey. If only we knew how to find him.'

'Ah, I think I might be able to help with that,' said Bernie, looking unbearably smug.

Chapter Fifteen

Bernie arrived in my room pre-breakfast. My previous experience of her lifestyle had suggested she normally saw this time of day only from the other end. But she bounced on the end of my bed with disgusting chirpiness. She wore a spring frock and no make-up. This demeanour made her look quite girl-like. If it wasn't for the wicked grin spread across her face I might not have recognised her.

'Guess what?' she said.

'You've forgotten my tea,' I said as I pulled up myself against the pillows. 'It should be outside the door.'

'Oh no,' said Bernie. 'That was taken away ages ago. You missed breakfast.'

Now that jerked me awake. 'No!'

'Table cleared and brushed. I had to wait for ages to get Burns alone.'

'Burns the butler?'

'Yes, Hope, the butler. You've seen him thousands of times. Older, greying man with a face like a constipated walrus.'

I sat bolt upright. 'Oh, God, tell me you didn't kiss him too?'

'What? No! Urgh! How could you think that of me? No, I did something far cleverer.'

I felt as awake as if I had plunged into an icy lake. 'What?' I managed to say despite the sudden dryness of my throat.

'Well, I cornered him in his den – the butler's pantry, you Brits call it. Then I asked him about how to get to Canning Town. For a moment I was on one of your sticky wickets. He was so alarmed he threatened to tell the Ambassador about my request. But I made up some rubbish about a man at the disturbance rescuing you from the brawling Nazis.'

'As I recall, I rescued you.'

'Piffle,' said Bernie. 'Spreading rumours about your cane-waving ability will do nothing for your marriage chances. Anyway, I said you wanted to thank him, or at least send him a little something. I thought it was rather smart of me to come up with something on the spot.' She pouted.

'It would have been even better if you'd planned it out properly before you went in.'

'Who does that?' said Bernie. 'Honestly, Hope, I love you dearly, but you are an oddity. But you'll never guess what.' She paused.

'I want my tea, or to go back to sleep,' I said.

'He asked the name of this man. It's possible he didn't believe me. When I told him, it turned out he knew Harvey.'

I yawned widely. 'Great. Well done. That was a stroke of luck, not brilliance. From your behaviour I take it Harvey is fine. Good. I'm pleased. I can go back to sleep now. Close the door quietly.'

'What's more, Burns is his uncle by marriage.'

'He's *what*? Does that mean *Harvey*'s married?'

'I've no idea. They say London is a big city. Your entire country is a tiny island! You could probably drop the whole of England in one of our big lakes. But anyway, you should have seen the look on his face when I said we wanted to thank Harvey!' said Bernie. 'He said must be the first time a toff wanted to find Harvey and not put him in bracelets! Apparently, that means handcuffs.'

'I know,' I said, trying to dent the smugness.

'Anyway, Burns has the afternoon off and he's going to contact Harvey and ask him to pop across. So, we can have a nice leisurely luncheon while we wait.'

I brightened at the magic word. 'You think he will jump at our summons?' I said.

'Burns says if he thinks that if money is involved, Harvey would crawl his way out of his own coffin.'

'How nasty,' I said.

'That's what I said, so Burns coloured up and explained. Apparently, our Harvey is the sole supporter of his father, a disabled veteran of the Great War, and some siblings. Burns said his — Harvey's, that is — mother died of the Spanish 'flu. He's been taking care of the family ever since he was old enough!'

'Good grief.'

'I know. Anyway, it turns out, though Harvey might be a con man, he's super strict about his siblings attending school and getting them decent apprenticeships.'

'I wonder how he justifies his own actions?' I said. 'Does he see himself sacrificing his reputation and lowering his behaviour as the price for their ticket out of Canning Town?"

Bernie shrugged. 'I have no idea. Harvey's never struck me as the self-sacrificing sort. He seems to enjoy what he does. Anyhow, we might be having a little visitation before luncheon. I noticed your wardrobe was a tad on the sober side.'

I groaned. 'No more clothes,' I begged. 'Mother already had loads sewn for me.'

'I've got Madame Avoir to come and show us some gowns. She's all the rage. Don't give that look, Hope. Whatever happens, one has to dress!'

The 'petite promenade' of gowns and tea frocks supplied by Madame Avoir was anything but petite. Avoir herself was, in my judgement, about as French as jellied eels. Then came the inevitable measuring, 'just in case', and arguing pointlessly with Bernie about not buying me frocks. By the time lunch came I was exhausted. However, Chef's pea and mint soup, followed by a cold pigeon salad, and finishing with a plate of exquisite petits fours he was experimenting with for some forthcoming political event, quite set me up again. I declined the ubiquitous cup of coffee that Americans drink at the slightest provocation and settled for a nice Earl Grey with a slice of lemon, and absolutely no milk.

(You'd think after all that fuss in Boston the Americans would have learned how to drink tea!)

Post-prandially, Bernie and I sat back in the lounge with our feet up, both of us feeling content with the world, when the door opened and in walked Harvey. 'Gawd, look at the pair of you!' he said. 'Lying around like you're Lady Muck while honest men like me are working our bleedin' socks off.'

Bernie scoffed at the honest men reference, but I was too aghast to speak. It took all my self control not to rush at Harvey and embrace him. He sported a bloated black eye, walked holding his left side taut like a man with cracked or broken ribs, and his right arm was in a sling. 'Good God,' I cried. 'If we had known you were this bad we would never have asked you to leave your bed.'

'Worse than it looks,' said Harvey, sitting down and helping himself to the coffee pot. I noticed he used the arm in the sling to pour and my eyebrows rose. He grinned and slipped off the bandage. 'All right, that one's not real. Going for the sympathy vote can be useful in my line. Mostly bruises and aches. Though my side hurts something rotten.'

'What did the doctor say?' asked Bernie.

'Doctor? Doctor? Do you think I'm made of money? Thanks to Burns, you know where I live. So, you'll know it's not the most prosperous of areas.'

'You might have broken a rib,' I said.

'You think?' said Harvey, scooping up three petits fours in one hand and popping them in his mouth. 'Had one before, have you?' The latter was said through a full mouth and took me a moment to distinguish.

'And she is a Lady,' said Bernie. We both looked at her. 'You said,' she said to Harvey, 'we were lying around like Lady Muck, which isn't true. Hope's been terribly ill. But she is a Lady.'

'Actually, I'm an Honourable,' I said. 'My mother became a Lady when her brother became Earl.' I turned to Harvey. 'I broke three ribs when I fell off my horse once,' I said. 'I am not a good horsewoman.'

159

"'Ow have you been ill?' demanded Harvey, ignoring what I said. 'Did those bastards hurt you?' He said this most fiercely, and with his black eye looked quite murderous. Despite my feeling that a woman should be able to look after herself, I was both charmed and impressed. I tried very hard to show neither emotion.

Bernie sidled out of the door. From some comical miming I guessed she was getting a doctor and so did my part in distracting Harvey with a shorted and sanitised version of my illness. But eventually I had to mention the possibility of poisoning. Bernie was taking her time.

'Someone really tried to off you?'

'The doctor suggested it. It might not even have been aimed at me. People do try and poison the Ambassador. I remember Amaranth saying once how she had to be so careful with kitchen staff, which is why they got a fortune out of her. But no one else got ill. And it can't have been the stuff I got from Fortnum's for our picnic, as you two are fine.' Harvey raised an eyebrow. 'I meant on the inside,' I said. 'I do realise a whole load of fascists laid into you at the parade. I felt dreadful leaving you, but I had to get Bernie out of there. She's no idea how to take care of herself.'

'What, did you think you could come to my rescue?' said Harvey in astonished tones. 'I may not be one of your toffee-nosed friends, but I know how to look after myself. I don't need rescuing by a girl.'

'Two women,' I corrected him. 'Well, one. As I said, Bernie is useless when it comes to physical encounters.'

'Not all o' them, I'd bet,' said Harvey under his breath. I chose to ignore this. Then he said, 'But you were at that party later on, weren't you? The one with that blighter Danville. Could it have happened there?'

'Possibly. I was very tired and left before they went to some nightclub. You went along to that, didn't you? But when we were at the march I was sneezing like billy-o.'

Harvey nodded, looking relieved. 'Sounds like a nasty case of stomach influenza and everyone over-reacting a bit.'

160

'I'm glad you agree,' I said. Then I told him about Paul Saulier's visit. I finished with, 'It was a most unusual encounter. The man seemed torn between anger, grief, and fear.'

'That's a strange one, but grief can take people funny ways,' said Harvey. 'I ain't ever come across him before, so I can't tell you anything about the geezer.'

'Is it the setting that's making you come over all common?' I asked with interest.

Harvey sniffed. 'You want me to talk better?' he asked.

'Well, obviously you can,' I said. 'Or you'd never be able to jump between being a waiter and a guest the way you often do.'

'Fair enough,' said Harvey. 'To be frank with you, my way of speaking is a right mix-up. Me Dad married way above his station. Not that it did either of them much good. Love matches. You won't catch me in one of those. A nice girl with a steady income, that's what I want. Sense of adventure might be nice too - within reason, of course.'

I was about to pursue this interesting line of enquiry when Bernie came back with the Embassy nurse. I should have realised calling in a doctor would draw too much attention. A small, curly haired blonde thing, Harvey made a show of objecting to her taking him away to remove his clothing and examine him, perhaps too much of a show. In fact, when he had gone I felt positively cross with him. I finished the remaining petits fours.

Harvey returned alone, walking much more easily. 'Two cracked ribs,' he said. 'Nothing broken. She strapped me up good and proper. Feel like I can walk without tearing a hole in me lung now.' He sat down without being invited and said, 'So what do you want me to do now, girls? And what's it paying?'

'We mostly wanted to know you were all right,' said Bernie. 'I'm not quite sure where we go from here. I take it Hope told you about Saulier coming here?'

'Yeah, right odd it sounded,' said Harvey. 'Almost like the blighter was deliberately blackening his sister's memory – though

161

that's what he accused you of. I don't like the idea he was watching you either. It might mean I have police watching me – and I don't know how to tell you this . . .'

'It's all right, Lenny,' said Bernie, almost snorting her coffee down her nose she was laughing so hard. 'We know Mr Partridge sometimes helps the police with their inquiries.'

'It was in the newspaper,' I said.

'Bleedin' 'ell! Burns might have mentioned that to me. He knew I'd been laid up,' said Harvey. 'That's a right bugger. I'll have to keep my head down for a while.'

'Which is exactly what I have in mind for you,' I said. 'How do you fancy doing a little bit of reconnaissance work with me?'

'And me!' said Bernie.

'Darling, I love you,' I said, 'but you are about as discreet as a Macy's parade.'

'Don't know what that is,' said Harvey, 'but I agree, you're not the discreet type. Best if I do it alone. Have you got a picture of the geezer you want followed?'

'It's Paul Saulier,' I said. 'And no. I'll need to come with you.'

'And why is that?' said Harvey in a stern voice.

'May I remind you I am the employer here?'

Harvey muttered something under this breath, but this time I didn't catch it. Then he said, 'Do you know where he lives?'

I shook my head. 'No address on his card either. I think we will have to start off by taking a stroll around some of the better parts of the nightlife the city has to offer. Together we can pass as a couple walking out together.'

Harvey went slightly red. 'Bit of a long shot,' he said.

'I don't know that we have much else,' I said. 'Or were you referring to anyone thinking I might walk out with you?'

'I'll have you know people have remarked how well I scrub up,' said Harvey. 'I've danced with at least half of this season's debutantes.'

'Lucky them,' I said. 'Bernie and I are going to the Worthingtons' dance tonight. I'll meet you outside. It's at . . .'

'I know the place,' said Harvey. 'Would have been working it if I didn't look like this. Had to cry off.'

'Bernie can cover for me.'

'And be at the dance on my own,' said Bernie pouting.

'You'll have enormous fun without my restraining presence. Besides, I normally slope off to the library. You're always complaining about it. Tell anyone who asks I'm in the other room.'

'What other room?' said Bernie.

'Obviously, the other room to the one you're in,' said Harvey. 'Haven't you got a brain in that pampered head of yours?'

The two of them might really have laid into one another, when we heard Amaranth's voice in the hallway. Harvey left by the window with a dexterity that spoke of many such exits in his past.

Chapter Sixteen

The decorations at the Worthingtons' dance proved to be the high-light of the whole affair. Even from the street I could see the rose-coloured swags and climbing briar roses. 'Oh my,' said Bernie, 'they're using the same style of decoration as the Wells did.'

I eyed the flowers. 'I wouldn't be surprised if those were exactly the same roses. They're looking pretty wind-blown.'

'Oh, and I can see a stain on the swag on the far-left window,' said Bernie. 'This is going to be so much better than I hoped. Now one is beginning to know the others, one can really talk.'

'She means gossip,' I said into the shadow on our left.

'Gawd, what you lot concern yourself about! It don't bear thinking about to a sane man,' said Harvey from the depths. He didn't seem particularly surprised I had spotted him. I felt rather disappointed.

'Pah,' said Bernie. 'I've seen you swaggering around in your borrowed feathers. You enjoy gate-crashing these affairs. You want this life.'

'Never,' said Harvey. 'And how long do you think you two can hang about here without attracting attention? It's time you ditched Hope, and she and I went off.'

'Not yet,' said Bernie. 'That's Eileen Kensington over there and she's spotted us.'

'What's an Eileen?'

'It is difficult to tell, the way she's dressed,' I said. 'But she

164

might be an aid to our purpose. Let's go in with her, Bernie, and then a few minutes later I can slip out.'

'Sure,' said Bernie. 'Eileen's got a mouth on her as wide as the Atlantic. She'll tell everyone you're here. My only problem will be how to ditch her. If I don't she'll hang around my neck like a millstone all night.'

'Want me to wait round the back?' said Harvey.

'Under the trees by the park across the road,' I said.

Harvey snorted. 'I hope there aren't any coppers roaming around. They'll have me down the clink in no time if they find me lurking in the bushes.'

'I said trees,' I hissed into the shadows. I then laughed loudly, causing heads to turn. Then I linked my arm through Bernie's and we entered, sweeping a grateful Eileen up in our wake. Bernie said, far too loudly, 'Oh, you are a hoot, Hope!' By the time we entered the ballroom all eyes were on us.

I thought it reasonable that I stayed half an hour before sneaking out. It didn't look as if it was going to rain, so Harvey would be fine, though doubtless grumpy when I came out. Fortunately, although the hour was early, a buffet of nibbles to accompany the free-flowing champagne had been set up. I stationed myself alongside this. This served the dual purpose of ensuring as many people saw me as they passed along looking, but rarely picking, at the buffet, and also allowed me to get some sustenance. I anticipated being out with Harvey until late into the night and missing supper. Obviously, it was necessary to build my strength up for such an adventure. I did consider wrapping something up in a napkin, but firstly I wasn't completely confident about my sleight of hand skills. Secondly, and more importantly, it appeared that the only easily portable hors d'oeuvres all had a fishy component. Having such an aroma around one is not conducive to being stealthy when necessity requires, and it also tends to attract cats.

Most of the other debs wore silk gloves which did not allow them to so much as touch a sandwich. Now, while I am not adept with a needle and thread, I had contrived a way to slit the sides of the fingertips of my gloves so they could be discreetly rolled back. Unless someone held my hand close to their eyes – unlikely – I felt confident they would not see my adapted needlework. Midway through attempting to surreptitiously free my fingers, I caught sight of Paul Saulier, pausing on the threshold of the room. I was so surprised I tore the fingertip clean off and had to hide it behind a salad dish.

Saulier's eyes swept over me, lingering only for a second to register my presence, then he appeared to find whoever it was he searched for and strode into the midst of the crowd. I made my way to the exit by way of the ladies' dressing chamber. I collected my coat, which I had stashed behind a stool, and left.

Harvey, as arranged, waited under the trees opposite the house. 'About bloody time,' he said, 'I'm freezing me . . . ah . . . fingers off here. I tell you, a London summer evening ain't what it used to be.'

'It's no use,' I said. 'Saulier's in there.'

'Oh, right, can I get off home then?' His voice became quite cheery.

'I'd be grateful if you could help me find a taxi,' I said.

'No reason for you not to enjoy the party, is there?'

I held up my glove. 'Ruined,' I said. 'Can't stay at a party with ruined gloves.'

'If you say so,' said Harvey. 'I would've thought – no, never mind.' He peered closer, realising what I'd done, and gave a chuckle. 'Quite a clever idea. Pity you can't sew.'

I was about to protest that my glove only tore when I saw Saulier come out of the house. I grabbed Harvey's arm and dragged him backwards towards the railings. He opened his mouth to yelp in surprise, but despite being shorter I managed to get my hand over it in time.

Pressed up against the park railings, the shadows swallowed us entirely. I took my hand off his mouth. 'Er, Hope,' said Harvey in my ear, 'I've enjoyed working with you too, but I didn't think . . .'

'Shut up!' I hissed. 'That's Saulier, over there. What luck! He's leaving, and on foot. We can follow.'

'Yeah,' said Harvey very quietly and with no apparent sincerity, 'what luck.'

Saulier set off at a smart pace. I slipped my arm through Harvey's and pulled my collar up close against my face. 'Let's walk,' I said.

Harvey proved surprisingly adept at following our mark. He held back, taking the occasional detour, but never let our quarry get out of sight, and stopped at various pretty landmarks as if we were actually a courting couple. When he pulled me up to admire a particularly lovely pastoral view from a bridge, I had the uncomfortable thought that walking out with Harvey would not be the worst way a girl might spend an evening.

'Do you know the direction in which we are headed?' I said sharply, seeking to keep the evening on a professional footing.

'Away from the posh end.' Harvey bent and spoke into my ear in the way a lover might whisper sweet nothings. 'Into the sort of area that caters for drivers while you lot are off enjoying yourself. Not too rough, but don't go speaking if you can help it. Your accent could cut glass and it'll stand out down here like a ballerina in a butcher's.'

The metaphor struck me as a creative one and I wondered where he had heard it. But I took Harvey's counsel and kept quiet from then on. As he appeared to be a competent tail I did not interfere in his decision-making. From the way he set his shoulders, I got the distinct impression Harvey thought he was running our little adventure and I saw no harm in allowing this. At least it stopped him moaning. Also, the poor chap needed something to cheer him up after the beating he'd taken. Hopefully, this evening's escapade would restore both his confidence and his interest in the mystery at hand. I determined to take as back a seat as possible tonight.

Saulier stopped outside a public house entitled, rather unimaginatively, the Dog and Duck. By the light of the tavern's windows we saw him pull out his watch. Harvey whisked us into shadow as, for the first time, Saulier checked up and down the street to see if anyone was watching him. His eyes passed over us and did not pause. I held my breath. Beside me I could feel Harvey doing the same.

Seemingly convinced he was alone, Saulier entered the inn.

'Is this place known for anything I particular?' I whispered to Harvey.

'Like?'

'Drugs, loose women . . .'

'Enough. An Honourable shouldn't know anything about those sort of things,' said Harvey with distaste.

I opened my mouth to object, but then remembered by resolution to let him take the lead. I kept quiet. I knew he'd never swallow a quiet 'Yes, Harvey', from me. A sullen silence perhaps. It worked.

Harvey sniffed. 'Besides,' he said, 'it's an ordinary pub. The kind your average taxi-cab or limo driver might frequent. 'Ere, why would you think I would know about pubs that loose women frequent anyway?'

'Then we should go in,' I said, tactfully avoiding a response to Harvey's question.

'He's gone into the public bar,' said Harvey. 'No women, loose or otherwise, allowed in there.'

'Damn,' I said.

'Looks like that's it for tonight,' said Harvey. 'I'll walk you back into town.'

'Oh no,' I said. 'We've much more to do tonight.'

'I might have bleedin' well known,' said Harvey. 'Ain't nothing that stops you, is there, girl?'

Chapter Seventeen

'How well do you know the place?' I asked.

'Been in a few times,' said Harvey. 'Why?'

'Is there an alley behind?'

'Yeah, I think so,' said Harvey. 'Why?'

'Windows that look out?'

'I expect so,' said Harvey. 'What's all this about?'

'Show me,' I said. I linked my arm tightly through his so, short of letting me fall flat on my face, he had to follow as I set off at a brisk pace, heading across the road a little beyond the inn. 'I assume the alley runs down here?'

'Don't know if I should go down a back alley with you,' said Harvey, trying to joke. 'Me, a respectable man and all that.'

I tugged harder. 'Come on.' He seemed genuinely reluctant. The alley smelled terrible. I almost slipped on something slimy underfoot, but Harvey caught me. 'They throw all kinds of stuff out the back,' he said, making me glad that the place was only dimly lit. 'I would throw out those shoes when I got back to the Embassy, if I were you.'

'An excellent idea,' I said. 'Perhaps even before I go inside. I don't think I want to see them in the light. I presume this is why you did not want us to come this way.' I hoped the latter would be a sop to my dragging him over.

The alley sloped downward slightly. On one side ran a high brick wall, but on the side nearest the Dog and Duck, the buildings had backyards, of a kind. A wooden fence ran along these in varying states of repair but, typically, the part immediately behind the public house seemed well-kept. 'We need to get in there,' I said. 'How do you think we should do it?' I already knew what I would do, but I wanted Harvey to feel in charge again.

'Are you kidding me?' said Harvey.

'No one will see us,' I reassured him. 'The lights are blazing in there. And they've got coloured glass halfway up the windows.'

'That might be,' said Harvey. 'But who's to say they don't have a dog out the back.'

'Are we scared of a doggy?' I said and then bit my tongue. 'Sorry, that was very rude of me. I realise some people do have a phobia of dogs, but I am sure you have dealt adequately with canine obstructions before.'

'Hmph,' said Harvey. 'Canine obstructions that can wake the whole neighbourhood with their barking while they can rip out the seat out of your trousers. Not an experience I'm keen to repeat.' He sighed. 'You're going in there anyway, aren't you? If I don't get you over there, you're liable to walk through the front door.'

'That's about the size of it,' I admitted. 'I would much rather have your help doing this subtly.'

Harvey heaved an enormous sigh and, despite his injuries, hauled himself agilely over the fence. I waited to see if any barking ensued. When it didn't, I followed. Uncle Eric has ensured I am adept at scaling fences. Despite the gloom I could feel the evil glance Harvey gave me. I contained the bubble of laughter that rose within me. No doubt he had hoped I would scramble pathetically at the side of the wall.

We were now in a rough sort of yard where barrels and rickety-looking chairs were stacked against the walls. Littered around were a number of potato peelings, so I guessed the nearest door must lead straight into the kitchens. I jerked my head to indicate to Harvey we should move away from the door.

From an open window above us we heard sounds of male voices and the clink of glasses. It sounded much like I had imagined a public house would – in other words very noisy. Certainly, there was no meeting or function taking place that might have meant people would talk in turn rather than all babbling at once. We would learn nothing by simply listening. Unfortunately, the windows were well above both our heads. I crept back towards the rusty chairs. Harvey caught my arm.

'Whatcha doing?' he whispered.

'I need a chair to see in.'

'You'll go straight through one of those,' said Harvey bluntly. 'Wouldn't take the weight of a rabbit.'

'The cook obviously sits on that one,' I said, indicating a lone one sitting by the door. 'And cooks aren't known for being thin,' I said.

'Yeah, but he doesn't stand on it. Besides, it's more likely a kitchen boy that uses it when he's peeling spuds. Probably a skinny lad.'

I concentrated once more on being professional and counted mentally to ten. By the time I reached nine the itching in my hand to slap him had mostly subsided. 'What do you suggest?'

'I can't believe I'm saying this, but you'd better sit on my shoulders,' said Harvey. He saw my expression by the light from the windows and added, 'If I thought there was any way you'd leave here without getting a gander in there, I wouldn't even suggest it.'

'If you're sure,' I said, and placing my foot into the impromptu stirrup that his interlinked fingers provided, I hoisted myself up onto his shoulders.

Or at least, that was my idea.

The problem, in part, was that Harvey was totally unprepared for how nimbly I could climb up onto him. 'Like a squirrel after a nut,' was his uncomplimentary comment.

The other problem was, not to be too indelicate, that I had quite forgotten I was wearing a ball gown. Jodhpurs, trousers, or even shorts, would be my preferred raiment for such activities. I can only offer as an excuse that the idea of climbing Harvey, like a child would a tree, seemed so forthrightly bizarre to me that I lost my usual sense of decorum.

I landed with a leg either side of Harvey's head, which was fine – exactly as I intended – but in the process of doing so I also covered his head with my skirts. Fortunately, my modesty was preserved as I had mounted the nape of his neck. But all Harvey knew was that it had suddenly gone dark. Add to this the rough and sloping nature of the garden, and it really was a testament to Harvey's sense of balance that we didn't end up crashing to the ground.

I now had a clear view into the bar. My dress was pale and my shoulders bare. Harvey was blinded and swaying from side to side. He was complaining, but his voice was muffled by the volume of material over his head. I paid him no heed. Any minute this charade could come to an end. I focused on my mission and attempted to see what Saulier was doing. Luck was on my side, as I spied him immediately, and even better, I got a clear look at the man he was talking with.

Then a drunken old soul, staggering between the tables, glanced up at the window. He raised a hand to shield his bleary eyes from the light inside and, with horror, witnessed what he thought was a spectral form floating outside. He dropped his pint, uttered a yell of terror and stumbled backwards into a table full of the Dog and Duck's roughest-looking patrons. Beer, glass, and fists flew through the air.

I pulled my skirts off Harvey's face and nimbly jumped down. 'Come on,' I said earnestly. 'We need to get out of here.' For once Harvey was only too keen to agree, so hitching my gown up in a most unladylike manner, we dashed up the lane. As I hoped, it came out at the top of the street, bringing us almost full circle to the point when we had originally seen the pub.

'Bleedin' hell,' said Harvey. 'That was . . .'

I pulled him into the shadows of a nearby wall. 'Remind me never to wear a white gown when we do this kind of thing again,' I said.

'Again . . . ?'

'Shhh, do you see that man leaving the Inn. That's the one Saulier went to meet. Do you know him?'

'I don't know everyone in bleedin' London,' said Harvey, but he stood up and, using a tree as cover, peered down the street. 'Blimey,' he said quietly. 'I reckon I do know him.'

'Who is he?'

'Hush up and let me think. I've seen him before somewhere,' said Harvey scratching his head.

I tried to bite my tongue and failed. 'He's getting away.'

Harvey tensed beside me. 'He was working the ball the night the girl disappeared.'

It was all the confirmation I needed. 'Right,' I said, 'after him.' Having kicked off my shoes, they were ruined anyway, I abandoned them and, inwardly cursing my gown, I hot-footed it after Saulier's companion, keeping as close to the shadows as I could. Behind me, I heard Harvey's gasp of horror, then to his credit, the sound of him following. I sped up. The last thing I wanted was him for him to catch my arm and to try and stop me. In his current state I would probably damage him quite badly.

Lined with trees, the street suited my purpose. Houses on both sides, set back from the road, showed no lights. Even one of the street lamps had gone out. I took this as a favourable sign. In my stockinged feet, I sprinted towards my target. If I could get him down on the ground, between us, Harvey and I, should be able to subdue him. Although I had only observed games of rugby, I assumed a flying tackle really could not be all that difficult. Certainly, the players I had seen did not appear to be overly endowed with brains. If I had been close to him from a standing position I doubted I would have needed Harvey's help, but Uncle Eric had never shown me how to capture a moving target. I would have to tell him how remiss he had been.

The road began to slope down slightly. Conditions were as good as they were going to get. I put on an extra spurt of speed, extended my arms, and launched myself forward.

However, instead of colliding with my target's upper thighs,

173

an amply padded area, I discovered how very hard the backs of a man's knees can be when hit with your bare shoulder. His knees naturally buckled as I hit them. For a moment, the universe tumbled, along with the two of us, and all I was aware of were stars spinning in night sky and the rank smell of cheap beer. The pavement quickly rose up to meet me and I retained enough sense to put out my right arm, tuck in my head, and manage a rather clumsy roll across the shoulders. The paving stones felt very different from a tatami. It hurt. I would have to wear a shawl for some days to hide the bruising. I had probably bruised my upper back too, but it was far better than landing on my head.

I scrambled to my feet. I saw Harvey pelting towards me, my shoes clutched in one hand and an expression of extreme concern on his face. He skidded to a stop some feet from me and we surveyed the man lying on the ground between us.

'Oh my Gawd,' said Harvey. 'You've killed him.'

I tutted at that, but as the prone man lay there, a motionless puddle of bad tailoring, I squatted down beside him and felt his neck. 'There is a strong and regular pulse,' I told Harvey. 'He is merely unconscious.' I rolled him onto this back. A bump the size of an egg had already risen in the middle of his forehead.

'What the 'ell did you think you were doing?' said Harvey.

I looked up at him. 'Oh, you brought my shoes. How sweet.' I held out my hand. Automatically Harvey handed them over. I put my hand on his shoulder to steady myself as I put them back on. 'Yuck, as you said they're quite ruined, but it will look less suspicious if I'm wearing shoes.'

Harvey opened and closed his mouth a few times. I took the opportunity to do my best to rid my dress of dried mud and leaves. I even managed to pin my hair up again. 'It won't do for anything close to decent,' I said to Harvey, 'but for coming out of a public house with you, I think I'll pass.'

Harvey gave me a look that could have melted stone. 'What will?' he said. I raised an eyebrow. 'What will look less suspicious?' persisted Harvey.

'Oh, when we put this gentleman in the back of the taxi-cab you're about to hire. It must be near closing time, so there will be a few in the vicinity. Or, at least, one can hope so. I'd rather you didn't have to go back into town to find one. Who knows how long he's going stay unconscious?'

'You can't leave him lying in the middle of the pavement,' said Harvey.

'You're quite right,' I said. 'Help me roll him over towards that wall. I can tell anyone who passes that he had a few too many and took a tumble. Maybe I can find a few stones to scatter around the path that he could have stumbled over.' I knelt down again and put my hands under his shoulders. 'I think it would be more appropriate if you were the one to move his hips.'

Harvey knelt down to help me. 'I must be dreaming,' he said. 'It's a bleedin' nightmare, that's what it is. I'll wake up any moment.'

I stood up and dusted myself down once more. 'I do not want you to think badly of me,' I said. 'I do not usually undertake action without a plan. It was simply that a collusion of circumstances inspired me to take a chance.'

'Collusion of circumstances . . .' repeated Harvey. 'You're mad. I should get the coppers on you. You need to be locked up.'

'I hardly think you will do that,' I said sweetly. 'Your part in this is far from innocent. Besides, Mr Partridge, you are well known to the police.'

Harvey winced. 'Don't call me that.' He ran his hand through his hair, his hat had disappeared earlier in the night. 'I wouldn't do that to you, but crikey, girl, you've got to admit you're acting as if you fell out of your tree.'

'Get me a taxi-cab and we can move this man to somewhere more comfortable.'

'All right,' said Harvey. 'I guess if we drop him off at the hospital we can scarper before they ask too many questions. They must get loads of drunks who've fallen over.' He stood staring at me for a minute. Ran his hand through his hair twice more. Then realised this was the hand that had been holding my shoes and swore roundly. 'Right, don't move. Our story is he had one too many and knocked himself out. I'll go and find a cab. Right.' Then he patted me awkwardly on the shoulder. 'It'll be all right, Hope,' he said. At least he still felt he was in charge. I intended to keep to that as long as possible – not that it would be so very long.

He walked off up the street, turning his head from side to side, listening for the sound of anything approaching. I sat down on the wall. I wished I had asked Harvey to leave his coat as mine was too thin to be of much use. I considered getting the jacket off my prone companion, but I decided I'd rather freeze than be seen in something so terrible. The man only stirred once. I hit him with my shoe just to be sure. The impact made an odd sound halfway between a squelch and a thud.

What seemed a lifetime later, a taxi drew up and Harvey jumped out. 'It's all right, Maud,' he said. 'I'm here. Help me get Charlie in the back.' His diction might have been a little forced, but it pleased me he had prepared a cover story. I wondered how he would hold up when he heard we weren't going to the hospital. Not that it mattered. What I really wanted to know was, who was this Maud whose name he kept borrowing?

Chapter Eighteen

Between us we got 'Charlie' into the cab. I gave the driver the direction of my little garage, trying to modify my vowels slightly. Harvey, who had sandwiched the man between us, gave me a startled glance. "Ang on a minute, darlin'" he said. 'I thought we'd agreed we were taking Charlie to the 'ospital?'

'Don't you think it's a bit pointless, seeing as h . . . as 'ow 'is wife is a nurse,' I said. 'I'm sure 'e'd be better off at home. He lives above one of the little garages in the mews,' I said to the driver.

'I'm pretty sure I 'eard him say his wife was working at the 'ospital tonight,' said Harvey, frowning and very clearly wishing looks could, if not kill, then give me a good spanking.

'Really?' I said. 'Well, then 'is sister must be minding the baby, and she's a nurse too, don't forget.'

'I don't care who does bleedin' wot,' said the driver. 'Meter's running. Where am I going?'

Harvey opened his mouth, looked and me, and crumpled back into his seat. 'Where she said.'

'Quite right, mate,' said the driver. 'Never argue with a woman. 'Specially when she's right. Them hospitals are nasty places. He'll be better off at home. Why, I could tell you some stories . . .' He then proceeded to do so for the rest of the drive. It transpired that he, his brother, his friends, and probably even his dog, knew of someone who'd gone into hospital with a tiny cut, nothing worth bothering about, and come out minus a limb, or dead, or both. I said 'goodness' a lot and that kept him happy.

Harvey sat in silence, staring determinedly straight ahead like a French nobleman in a tumbrel on the way to the guillotine. That is, if French noblemen had ever worn pinstripe suits.

As we drew up outside the garage, the light clicked on in Johnson's small apartment. By the time the taxi drew up, he was standing by the open door, light spilling out across the mews. 'Oh, Johnson,' I said, jumping out almost before the motor had stopped, 'Charlie's 'ad a bit of fall. Can you help us get 'im inside?' Much to his credit Johnson did no more than nod agreement. Despite his limp, he lifted 'Charlie' easily in a fireman's hold and took him inside. I followed, leaving Harvey to pay the driver.

Inside, Johnson made as if to go upstairs. 'I don't think so,' I said. 'Is there a part of the shed we could put him. A part that isn't particularly recognisable?'

Johnson, balancing the man on his shoulders, swung round to look at me. 'Pardon me, miss, but you won't be requiring of me to dispose of a body later this evening, will you? Only I had hoped to have an early night. It's my godson's Christening tomorrow.'

I heard Harvey, who had entered behind us, make choking sounds at this statement. 'No, I certainly shall not,' I said. 'I am hoping that, if we can bring this gentleman round, we can let him on his way again in under an hour or so. I just need a little information from him.'

'Oh, that shouldn't be too much trouble,' said Johnson as calmly as if I had asked him to polish my motor. 'I can bag him up and drive him a few miles before letting him off. I take it he's not the sort that's liable to go to the police about a little kidnapping?'

'I rather think not.' I said. 'In fact, I think he may have been involved in some kidnapping himself. That girl in the newspapers, who went missing from the Ball?'

'What, that pretty little blonde thing they found dead on the beach? I thought she'd run off with some fellow.' He pointed to the man on his shoulders. 'Him?'

I shook my head. 'Harvey, do close the door,' I said over my shoulder. 'No, and she didn't run off. It was staged to look like that. She was murdered.'

Harvey closed the door. 'Or so we think,' he added. He sidled up to me and tried (and failed) to say discreetly, 'Are you sure we can trust this fellow?

'If Miss Stapleford said it was murder, then it was murder,' said Johnson. 'I'd take her word over the newspapers' any day. Now, if you'll follow me, I know just the right corner for him. I've got some ice water too, that will work a treat. I take it you want to stay out of the interrogation, miss?'

'Why, Johnson,' I said. 'I've always known you to be a loyal soul but you are displaying rather surprising depths.'

'Me too,' echoed Harvey faintly.

'I was in the spotters, miss, in the Great War. Sometimes we got places before the last of the Hun had moved out. I could normally get them to help us answer a few questions before – err – you know.'

'How impressive,' I said. I heard Harvey gurgle behind me. 'Sadly, we will have to leave this parasite alive.'

'Of course, miss,' said Johnson. 'We don't have authority to do otherwise. What do you want me to ask?

'I am extremely grateful for your help, Johnson. I rather thought I would have to do this bit and I wasn't looking forward to it.'

''Ere!' said Harvey.

'Did you want to take the lead?' I asked him.

'No, I bleedin' well don't,' he said. 'But I resent the implication I am useless.'

'What exactly can you do to help?' I asked.

Harvey blinked at me blankly. Then he said, 'Stop you and get the police.'

'Oh, I don't think that will be necessary,' said Johnson. 'Seeing as how I'm here. I'd take it kind of personal if someone were to try to get Miss Stapleford into trouble.'

'Thank you, Johnson. I won't forget this. There will be something extra in your next pay packet.'

179

'It's no trouble, miss. But I'm grateful.'

'How about Harvey and I stay on the other side of the door and we can whisper instructions?' I said.

'Fair enough, miss. But it would be good to have an opener.'

'How about, tell us in your own words how you came to kill Charlotte Saulier?'

'Sounds like one of those awful essays you used to get in school,' said Harvey. 'What did you do in the summer holidays. Everyone wrote about fruit picking.' He looked at Hope. 'What? I went to school. Well, sometimes I went to school.'

I turned to Johnson. 'We'll head around the back. I'll tap on the door when we're in position.' Then I turned to Harvey and took him by the arm. 'This way,' I said. 'We need to go out into the Mews, along a bit, and then double back to get behind the door.'

'Don't look like you'll be needing me now you've your professional on the job,' said Harvey.

'Buck up, Harvey,' I said. 'You've seen Johnson's limp. He'll need help bagging the man up before he drops him off. But if you do a bunk I won't be able to stop him driving out to find you. He's very protective of me. It's rather sweet.'

'Ain't it just,' said Harvey. 'And there was me thinking Bernie was the wild one. You're a dark horse, you are, Hope Stapleford, and not one I'd dare bet on.'

I tugged at his sleeve and he came along quite easily, like a dog on a leash, except he continued to moan about my inadequacies and general madness. I wondered if he had gone into shock.

We took up our station behind the door to hear Johnson say, 'Seeing as how we're liable to get well acquainted, I should introduce myself. I'm your worst nightmare. So, what's your name?' I thought he was laying it on a bit thick, but I heard the other man whimper. I pressed my face against the wooden door, but Johnson had kept it in good enough repair for there not to be any holes or splits between the planks. Typical military man, I cursed inwardly.

'Your name!' thundered my chauffeur, loud enough that Harvey, beside me, jumped in the air.

'Godfrey,' said our prisoner. 'Godfrey Kew.'

'If he's given up his name that easy,' said Harvey in tones of disgust, 'he'll tell you anything.'

'If that is his name,' I said softly.

'Look, mister,' said Godfrey. 'I ain't got to no money to speak of. Tell me what you want and if I've got it, I'll give it to you. I don't want no trouble.' He nodded his chin towards his chest as his arms were tied behind him. 'I got a weak chest. The doctor says it's me heart. It's going like a ruddy steam train against me ribs.'

'Crafty,' I said.

'I want to know why you murdered Charlotte Saulier,' said Johnson.

'Oh, bleedin' hell,' said Godfrey. 'I knew it. I knew it would come back and get us. We'll swing for this.' We heard the sound of him struggling for breath. 'It weren't meant, you gotta believe me. All we was asked to do was take the girl for a drive into the country. We weren't going to do her no harm. We had a nice place set up for her. He said we'd need to watch her for a week or two and then he'd let her go.'

'Who said?' said Johnson.

'The geezer wot set it up. If that bloody drunken toff hadn't have got in the way it would have been an easy job. A nice stint at the seaside. The air would have set me right up. But, oh no, nothing goes right for poor old Godfrey.'

'He's very chatty, isn't he?' I whispered to Harvey.

'He's having trouble breathing,' said Harvey. 'We should go in there.'

'Nonsense,' I said. 'He's playing for sympathy. Johnson's not even threatened him properly yet. We have no idea if any of this is true. He's giving it up all too easily.'

'He's a lightweight,' said Harvey. 'Probably the driver. Not that they would have needed much muscle to kidnap Charlotte.'

'So, you were going to hold her for ransom?' said Johnson. His voice had grown deeper and more growly.

'I weren't getting it,' protested Godfrey. 'He was getting it. We was getting paid, like, but it weren't much. He said he was the one taking the risks.'

'Who?' demanded Johnson.

'The man in the red tie. That's what we called him, sir. He didn't give us no name. Honest.'

I tapped on the door. 'Ask him what happened to Charlotte,' I whispered.

'Is there someone there? Help! Help!' called Godfrey. 'They've got me . . .' There was the sound of an open hand hitting flesh. Godfrey gave a small cry and began to whimper. 'Don't hurt me. Please don't hurt me. Me heart. Me heart's not right. I can't take this.'

Harvey put his hand on my shoulder and tried to pull me away from the door. 'We have to stop this,' he said.

'Not yet,' I said, pushing hard against him with all my weight. 'Let's hear what he says about Charlotte.'

'Hope!'

'Shhh, he's talking again.'

'. . . grabbed her right easy when she came out of the powder room. Tom, the other bloke, had wanted to grab her as she went in, but I said how we had a long drive ahead of us and it wouldn't be fair to make the poor girl so uncomfortable. Davie, he was standing lookout, didn't care one way or the other. But I did.'

'Right nice of you,' growled Johnson.

'I was going to be nice to her. I respect women. Always have. Ask anyone.' We heard movement, then Godfrey bleating, 'All right. All right. So, I had a handkerchief and a bottle in my pocket. I was meant to pour the stuff on the hankie before I grabbed her and put it over her face. But when Tom called out to her, quiet like, as we'd planned, saying he needed to speak to her urgent, something about a message from her aunt – we was pretending, see, like in a play. That's what the man in the red tie said we should do. Think of it like a play . . .'

'Get to the point,' said Johnson.

'So, Tom calls her over. I get out my hankie and step up behind her. Then I put one arm round her waist and one arm up round her face, so I can get the hankie over her mouth.'

'What went wrong?'

Godfrey swallowed audibly twice. 'You ain't from the man in the red tie, are you? Cos if you are, I'm sorry. We'd practised it again and again, just like he told us to do. I had the move down real smooth.'

'What went wrong?'

'I did it exactly as we'd practised, me and Tom – him pretending to be the girl and all. Exactly.'

'Oh, the blithering idiot,' said Harvey under his breath. 'This beggars belief.' I couldn't work out the problem. But Johnson did. Obviously, he and Harvey had both given more thought to kidnapping than I.

'You forgot to use the bleedin' bottle, didn't you?' said Johnson.

We could hear Godfrey crying openly now. 'That I did, sir. And, as I say, I am sorry. It might have been all right, even then. The girl tried to scream, but there weren't no one else about, and I had her mouth covered with me hand, still holding the hankie. We'd took her out the back as all the drivers were off down the pub. We should've been able to get her into the motor easy enough. Tom picked up her feet. She squirmed like a buttered eel, but between us we held her. We'd have got her to the motor and all, no more problems like, if it hadn't been for that toff deciding to piss in the yard rather than in the gents.'

'The other man you took for a ride,' said Johnson, who had indeed read his newspaper.

'That's the one. Trask. Not a small bloke by any means, but drunker than my granny on a bank holiday. So, Tom drops the girl's feet and goes for him. Grabs a tyre iron off one o' the motors that were lying about and I'm well worried. I think he's going to do the fella in, and I'm not in this for the killing.'

'Of course not,' said Johnson with deliciously dry irony.

'I weren't. I told you, sir. I didn't mean no harm to no one. So, there's me, still holding the girl and her still trying to scream, her head twisting back and forth, almost enough to pull me arms out of their sockets. For a tiny thing, she weren't half a squirmer. I begged her, I did. I begged her to quiet her noise and stay still. I promised nothing would happen if she did. I wanted to get over to Tom before he killed that fella, so I got a bit rougher with her than I meant to.'

There was a long pause.

'Go on,' said Johnson.

'You gotta understand, I still hadn't worked out why the hankie wasn't working. The man in the red tie said it was guaranteed. Said he'd given me enough to take down an elephant. 'Course, in the midst of it all, I'd forgotten that I hadn't put the stuff on the hankie.'

'So, what did you do?'

'I crammed it harder over her face,' said Godfrey. 'Dear God, forgive me. I thought she hadn't got a good enough whiff. But she was twisting and turning like she was possessed, and I didn't realise that in all the struggling, me hand and the hankie was covering both her mouth and her nose. Her thrashing about seemed to weaken after a bit, and I thought she was finally calming down, then it stopped altogether, and she went all limp-like.'

'She suffocated,' said Johnson. 'And the other man?'

'Davie, the lookout, heard all the fuss and came up in time. Between him and Tom they laid the gent out without needing to use the tyre iron. Then we put the bodies in the motor and drove off.'

I tapped on the door. 'Ask him how they got the drugs in Charlotte's body?' I said.

'The girl had drugs in her system.'

'That were Davie, injected them both with the drugs.'

'You injected drugs into a corpse?'

'It was that powder the toffs like. He'd said how it would keep him quiet on the trip if he woke up. Davie split it between them. I thought maybe she was out cold like the other gent. Davie ain't

184

much of a bright spark, so he just did what he'd been told. I thought maybe it would bring her round. Jolt her back to life, like. I didn't want her to be dead.' Godfrey broke down and wept again. We heard Johnson pace back and forward.

Eventually Godfrey stopped. 'What happens now?' he asked.

'What do you think happens now?' said Johnson.

'Oh God! Oh God! You're going to do me in, aren't you? Please, sir. Please, sir. Don't do it. I'm not worth it.'

'I'm going to put a bag over your head. You won't even see it coming,' said Johnson. 'More than you did for that poor little cow.'

Godfrey screamed. 'No! No! I don't want to die.'

'We need to get in there,' said Harvey. 'He's taking it too far.'

'He won't hurt him,' I said. 'He's giving him a bit of a fright, that's all. Can't say I blame him after what he's done.'

On the other side of the door, we could hear Godfrey alternatively screaming and pleading. 'I'll not be a party to this,' said Harvey and pushed me. 'If you won't stop it, I will.'

He burst open the door. Johnson stood over Godfrey, a hemp sack in his hand. Godfrey had gone remarkably quiet and was slumped forward. An eerie silence descended over the scene, which Johnson soon broke, 'Seems like he was telling the truth about his heart, miss.'

Harvey stared in disbelief. I didn't need to feel for a pulse. The glassy look in his eyes told me all I need to know. Godfrey Kew had gone to meet his maker.

Chapter Nineteen

'Happens,' said Johnson stoically. 'Do you want to get the police involved, miss?'

I took a deep breath. Kew was dead. Obviously, I hadn't wanted that to happen. I didn't hold Johnson responsible as he had been acting on my instructions. Did I feel culpable? I wasn't entirely sure. There was a clear argument that if Mr Kew hadn't got himself mixed up in some decidedly dodgy dealings, then he wouldn't be in his now deceased condition. We make choices and we accept the consequences.

'No, Johnson,' I said. 'I think things might get a bit too embarrassing for all concerned – especially as I am currently a guest at the American Embassy. I dare say, considering his background, he was known to the police, and it would probably all be tidied away without too much fuss. But I don't think we should take that chance. Did he struggle much against his bindings? Are there marks?'

'I don't believe this,' cried Harvey. 'The man's dead.'

'No one wanted him dead,' I said calmly, as I helped Johnson check his wrists. 'And unless you know some remarkable way of reversing his situation, we have to think of those left alive. I presume you don't want to go to jail?'

'Me?' said Harvey. 'I never wanted any part of this.'

'Indeed,' I said, straightening. 'And I would be happy to supply the police with a statement to that effect, but once ambassadors, plus their children and their guests, are known to be involved, it might be decided it was prudent to pin this unfortunate situation on someone – and you would make a suitable "patsy", I believe is the appropriate term.'

'That's the thanks I get for trying to help you,' said Harvey bitterly. 'I should have known. You toffs are all the same.'

'No real marks, miss,' said Johnson. 'But you can never be quite sure what will show up after the blood settles and rigor sets in.'

I nodded in a way I hoped suggested I understood. I turned my attention to Harvey. 'Don't be silly,' I said. 'Of course I won't let you get sold out to the police. I'm simply explaining why it is better if we deal with this ourselves.' I didn't say out loud that the whole situation was making me feel a little sick, but then it could equally have been the lack of dinner that had stimulated extra bile in my stomach. 'We can't undo what's done,' I said. 'And it's not as if this man wasn't involved in the kidnap and death of two people. He's hardly an innocent.'

'Don't you see?' said Harvey. 'We've done exactly what he did. Accidentally killed someone. We're no different.'

'He may not have killed Trask himself, but he aided in doing so, and set up the apparent suicide scene,' I said. 'We are very different. He helped commit murder.'

'I imagine if we could see his police file, sir,' said Johnson, 'we'd find a whole lot of other misdemeanours. Miss Hope has it right, it's best we manage this ourselves.'

'What do you suggest?' I said.

'Now we've got the ropes off him, I suggest I get him into the motor and find a place to dump him. Which pub did you say he came out of?'

'The Dog and Duck. He was heading east when I caught up with him.'

Johnson nodded. 'I reckon I can find a nice little spot where he might have wandered off to attend to a call of nature and been overcome by a heart attack. He was eager enough to tell us about his heart, so the people that knew him would have known it might happen. If I do a bit of trampling around as well I can always leave a suggestion there might have been others there, so he might have run into some rough sorts and that brought it on.'

'In that case, you'd better take his wallet, and destroy it,' I said. Johnson bent and took out the wallet. He gave a low whistle. 'There's a betting slip in this and fifty quid. He must have a good day on the horses.'

'You keep it,' I said to Johnson. 'If he'd been boasting in the pub that he'd won, it'll lend more to the story that he was mugged.'

'Right-o,' said Johnson, sounding slightly less stoic and a little more upbeat. 'I reckon, with respect, miss, you two had better scarper and leave me to it.'

'Thank you, Johnson,' I said. 'I do hope you will still be able to make your godson's Christening.'

Johnson folded the notes and tucked them in his jacket. 'I'll be up like the crack of dawn, as usual, miss. This shouldn't take me too long. A little straightforward disposal job.'

'I really am frightfully grateful, Johnson.'

'Always happy to be of service, Miss Hope,' he said.

'Right, come on, Harvey,' I said. 'You need to walk me home. I'm going to tell Bernie I went to the cinema with you. She's going to be so jealous.'

Harvey trailed out after me, like a dog unwillingly being tugged along by its master. I tucked my arm through his. He flinched slightly at my touch. 'I am honestly very sorry about dragging you into this,' I said. 'I never intended the evening to end like this.'

Harvey looked down at me. His face white, and his lips thin, 'Hope, we killed a man.'

'No, we didn't. He had a heart attack brought on by his guilty conscience. He said himself, he knew he was living on borrowed time from the moment he killed Charlotte. For all we know, having bungled the kidnapping, and creating a media circus in the process, this man in the red tie might well have done for him anyway.'

'How can you be so calm?'

'I don't see how my going into hysterics would help either of us,' I said. 'It is all very regrettable, but at least we know now that the plan was to kidnap Charlotte. But why? We need to find out more about her brother. Was he the man in the red tie, and if so why did he want to kidnap his own sister?'

'Oh, no,' said Harvey, springing away from me. 'We let this drop now. No more investigating. No more nothing. I'm out. You're out.'

'I'm afraid it's not as simple as that. Godfrey Kew was not working alone. When his body turns up, his gang are going to be spooked. If they work out our connection . . .' I let the sentence dangle.

'Why the hell should they?' snapped Harvey.

'Brighton,' I said. 'There's a good chance we were noticed.'

Harvey paced around in a tight little circle, like a caged animal. He muttered under his breath, but I chose not to hear. 'Let's leave Bernie out of this,' I said.

'That's the one thing we agree on,' said Harvey. We had reached the road the Embassy was on. 'I'll watch you go in,' he said.

'How shall I contact you?'

'I'd rather you didn't,' said Harvey. In the light from the street lamp his face looked waxen. He closed his eyes and shook his head. 'You'll only come after me though, won't you?' I said nothing. 'I'll be in the park opposite at three p.m. for ten minutes, by that bench. That's all I'm prepared to offer.'

'Every day,' I said. 'Every day for the next week, at least.' Then I turned on my heels and walked away.

I had to do some fast talking from the moment I walked through the door. Bernie remained out. Despite all that had happened, not that much time had passed. Amaranth quizzed me closely as to her whereabouts. Fortunately, Amaranth has never been to a 'film house'. (Neither had I, but I had more of an imagination.) In short, Harvey became the son of a trusted friend of my godfather's and the movie was an uplifting morality tale of a young woman who saved her virtue for her wedding night. I threw in some jazzy music and amazing dancing routines. I almost got into trouble with the jazz, but I assured Amaranth we had sat in the best seats and I had been supplied with the best chocolates. Not that she had any real right to question me, but I didn't want to have to vouch for Bernie in any way.

'But no bar, you say?' said Amaranth. 'A kind of club? Does that mean anyone can go in?'

'The best seats are separated from the cheaper ones,' I said.

'Oh, like boxes in the theatre?' said Amaranth and I didn't correct her. Instead I chose that time to stifle a yawn. 'Oh, of course, darling, you must be tired. I have a few things to do for the Ambassador. I'll wait up for Bernie. The Ambassador has expressed some concern over the crowd she's running with. Not that there's any harm in Beth Setton, but the others . . .'

I opened my mouth to speak, but Amaranth lent forward and put a hand on my arm. 'Darling, I know how headstrong my daughter is. I'm more than aware that you've tried to get her away from those types – or so the Ambassador tells me.'

I decided to merely acknowledge this appraisal with a sad little nod. I then rose and said good night. But I went up to bed feeling extremely uncomfortable that the Ambassador, who I still had not met, kept such a close eye on his daughter. If I stood back from my personal qualms, it seemed not all that unreasonable, but the question was, was he also keeping an eye on me? I didn't like that idea one bit.

The moment I entered my bedroom the letter from Uncle Eric caught my eye. Recent events had driven it completely from my mind. It occurred to me that he would be the most amiable of my relatives if I admitted what had happened. But it seemed unlikely that even he would approve. Certainly, he had never included any instruction on how to dispose of a dead body in the frequent walks and talks we'd had when I was younger. How to wrestle a man to the ground, yes. How to escape from a capturer's grip, yes. But it had all been decidedly angled around keeping myself safe and not killing other people. A nasty pang of guilt stung me. I needed hot chocolate to calm my nerves. However, the letter must come first.

I closed the door behind me and could not resist looking around my room, even under my bed. The letter had been moved from behind the vase on my bedside cabinet to in front of it. I picked it up and looked at the flap. I had some vague idea from boarding school that letters could be steamed open. The girls used to joke about how the teachers read all our letters. However, I didn't stay long enough at the school to find out how it was done. I turned the letter over and over in my hands. I held it up to the light. It was thick enough that any writing within was shielded. I tested the edge of the flap with my nail. It seemed secure. I held it over the lamp. I couldn't see any tell-tale wrinkles from steaming. Then in a moment of pure paranoia, I wedged a chair under the door handle.

I told myself I was being ridiculous. I had no secrets worth knowing. And then I remembered I had contributed to the death of a man. I sat down heavily on the bed. What was more, I had paid and instructed my manservant to dispose of the body. Poor Harvey, no wonder he was in a funk. The letter dangled from my limp fingers as I went over the night's events. Really, I couldn't see any other way they could have gone. From the moment I tackled Kew, I should have known it wasn't going to end well. His dicky heart had set the seal on that. But if he hadn't accepted payment to kidnap Charlotte, we would never have crossed paths at all. He had sealed his own fate. The real question was, who had determined Charlotte's fate? I couldn't imagine that silly, sweet Charlotte had ever done anything to annoy anyone that badly. Did her brother want her fortune? Could this simply be a case of brotherly greed? I needed to know more. But I also knew I didn't want Bernie to know any more. I couldn't risk her being followed and thus all of us being followed. Therefore, I would need to invent something for her to do. Could she manage to find out about Charlotte's brother and if he would inherit her money? If she did it the right way it would seem no more than a little bit of tittle-tattle and gossip-mongering.

The letter dropped from my fingers. I picked it up and took it over to my dressing table. I had a nice letter opener that my god-father had given me. This evening was the first time I picked it up and realised what a nice weapon it would make. It even balanced on my finger, it was so well-weighted. I told myself I was imagining things. Uncle Eric wouldn't have knowingly provided me with a weapon. I slit open the flap and took out the single sheet of paper.

The crest on the top was from my uncle's London Club, where he had obviously written it. The paper smelled faintly of cigars and old whisky.

Dearest Girl,

What have you got yourself into now? Amaranth has promised to let me know if you get any worse. She seems to think you have been poisoned. I can only say, for someone who has had an attempt made on their life, you seem remarkably well to me. Perhaps the Embassy chef isn't quite so good as she makes out.

Anyway, I think it's about time I took you out to dinner properly. I remember coming down to see you at Oxford, but a proper dinner at my club is quite a different thing. There's a ladies' night during the last week of the season and as long as we can keep him, our French chef is quite superb. Wear something startling and pretty, but with taste and decorum, and I shall tease all the old buggers at the club that you're my new wife. We might even give one of them an apoplexy if we carry it off well enough.

In the meantime, if anything does come up that you need help with, don't bother your parents. Not to alarm you, but I think Bertram is feeling a bit frail at the moment. Your mother is feeding him up on beef tea and raw eggs. If he can survive that he can survive anything, but he could do without any additional stresses.

Any problems, leave a message at my club and I'll get a message back to the Embassy, or to that man of yours, Johnson, if you prefer. He's a good sort. I pointed him at your advertisement myself. We knew each other in the Great War.

Keep out of Amaranth's nonsense and don't let it bother you. Chances are she'll be out of the country by the autumn. You and Bernie could think of setting up in a little flat for yourselves. Bernie's got half the brains of her mother, and none of her guile, but she strikes me as loyal, and that, dear girl, is often the most important thing.

Fondest wishes
Your Godfather, E.

It was such an extraordinary letter I had to read it several times. My heart skipped a beat when my eyes ran over the word *apoplexy*, but the page was dated long before I had even met Kew. Uncle Eric might be many things, but I did not believe he was a clairvoyant. I had no idea what Amaranth's nonsense might be, but I had every desire to stay out of it. It seemed I had written Bernie's mother off far too quickly as a feather-brain. Apparently, I had misread her badly. That unsettled me. I thought Uncle Eric's opinion of Bernie a little harsh, but it intrigued me that he wanted us to set up a flat on our own. The idea hadn't occurred to me. I had assumed Bernie would either be married by the end of the season, or worse, that she might have been taken back to the States. This meant, of course, I would be heading back to the Fens as I had no interest in marrying anyone. The idea of us setting up home together had not occurred to me. I could feel my mood lifting at the thought of it. We'd shared a room up at Oxford and I knew we could rub along rather well. It might be the answer to both our prayers. I was pretty sure that, given the option, Bernie would prefer to be young, free, and single in London. The problem was how to persuade our prospective parents. We might both be of age soon, but in this sort of thing that counted for nothing.

I would have to ask Uncle Eric about that at dinner. If this was one of his plans, he doubtless had a scheme in mind. He'd never been a man to casually mention something, let alone write it. I knew him well enough to know that he thought carefully about everything he said and did. He had always encouraged me to behave the same way.

It didn't surprise me he knew about Johnson. I'd hardly kept it secret. I'd advertised openly in the paper. But I did get a warm feeling inside knowing I could call on Uncle Eric if I needed to. I wouldn't, of course. He wouldn't have meant he could help me with the disposal of bodies. What could he do, I wondered. I hadn't seen him on the season circuit, but everyone seemed to know him. He never mentioned his abode, and although he had often visited us at White Orchards I wasn't aware of my parents ever visiting him at his home. However, he certainly never seemed short of money. He must have some influence. Perhaps he meant if I got myself into any real trouble, he could always call in a favour or two? Regardless of whether he could or not, I liked the idea of him looking out for me. Of course, I could never tell him about the Kew situation. I sighed. Out in the world, away from home and academia, I needed to carry my own burdens. At least I had Johnson and the unwilling Harvey on side.

Chapter Twenty

Bernie had come in so late, she hadn't even surfaced by luncheon the next day. I decided she would have to wait to hear about my adventures, those that I was prepared to share of course, and told Amaranth, quite truthfully, that I fancied a walk in the park. I said I might also pop into a Lyons' to watch the world go by for a little bit.

'Oh, I quite understand,' said Amaranth. 'I'm a lover of people-watching too. Such fun spotting when someone is wearing last season's fashion, or with their best friend's husband.' She leaned in closer to me. 'If you ever see a woman pick a piece of lint off a man's coat sleeve, then you know they are . . . well, you know.'

I almost choked on my ice cream. My hand froze mid-air, while I accessed what she was telling me. 'You mean they are lovers?' I said.

'Hope,' said Amaranth, raising her hand to her mouth in faux shock. 'We don't say these things out loud, you funny thing.' She gave me a tap with the flat side of her knife. It stung a bit. 'But yes, darling, that's exactly what I mean. You English girls aren't exactly finished in the true sense, are you? That must be why the Ambassador wanted Bernie to go to university. I couldn't see the point of it myself. What does a girl like her need with a degree? Modern languages, maybe, if she had any interest in politics, but I don't think she does.'

I sipped the hot bitter coffee. 'She likes learning about people,' I said.

She laughed. 'Oh, you mean gossip. I suppose it can be useful.' Amaranth's laugh sounded false to me. Whatever had happened last night, I got the distinct impression I wasn't currently in her good books. I wondered what Bernie had said, or more importantly what she had done, without me.

'Thank you for luncheon,' I said, rising. 'If I go out now I shall catch the best of the afternoon. Growing up so secluded in the country, I miss nature.'

'How positively charming!' said Amaranth. 'For goodness' sake don't tell any of the other debs that. They'll eat you for breakfast.'

They can try, I muttered under my breath. Out loud, I merely attempted to give a light laugh and a smile. I'm afraid I didn't do it very well. London was beginning to take its toll on me.

I stopped only to pick up my hat. It would be hot outside and my nose is prone to freckles. I don't think I am overly vain, but I hate freckles. I always think they make me look like a schoolgirl.

I crossed the street and ambled into the park. I saw ducks on the pond and children playing under the watchful eyes of their nannies. I stood and admired banks of flowers of bright and varied colours. I hoped that by now anyone who might be following me from the Embassy, for my own safety of course, might be wholeheartedly bored and more than happy to report that the funny little English girl was doing exactly what she said and taking in nature. I could imagine Amaranth saying, 'Oh, how sad.' I felt a strong desire to slap her. I knew this to be totally unfair. Most of the people I had met during the season were pretending to be someone they were not. The thought had barely crossed my mind when I finally ran into Harvey.

'What if it wasn't her brother at all?' I said. Harvey looked at me blankly. 'He said he was Paul Saulier. Anyone can have a card made up.'

'Wouldn't the Embassy check him?'

'I don't think so,' I said. 'I expect they'd have checked him for weapons and all that, but otherwise he was a British gentleman, who spoke well and claimed to know me.'

'Could still have strangled you,' said Harvey. I didn't like the gleam in his eye as he said this.

'I always have security following me,' I said, and was about to add, 'when I'm with Bernie.' But I had to make a quick grab for his coat sleeve as he readied himself to jump into a bush. 'Not now, silly,' I said. 'But it does mean we shall have to think up things for Bernie to do that doesn't include anything – well, err –'

'I get your meaning,' said Harvey. He continued to dart furtive glances all around us. 'That looks terribly suspicious,' I said.

'I feel terribly suspicious. My entire skin itches,' said Harvey.

'Probably the cheap stuff you got your suit made from,' I said. Harvey adopted the look of a puppy that has been kicked.

'I'll have you know I paid good money for this.' He fingered the lapels of his jacket lovingly. 'Maud says I look very smart in it. Quite the gent.'

It was on the tip of my tongue to suggest that the mysterious Maud obviously didn't know a gent from her own ear hole, but I bit it back. There was no point in getting him riled. Whatever I might want, I was going to need his help. (As it transpired, it would be some time before I learned the truth about Maud.) 'Right, I'm getting Bernie to work the gossip angle and see what she can hear about this brother,' I said. 'If she can get a description from someone, we might even be able to rule him in or out. I hope he's not married. If he isn't, and he's recently inherited all of Charlotte's money, he will be a hot topic among the debs.'

Harvey pulled a disgusted face. 'I imagine Bernie loves gossip. Are you sure she's not going to let out as much hot air as she takes in?'

'She can only tell anyone what she knows,' I said. 'It's the main reason I'm not letting her in on anything else.'

'Just lucky old me,' said Harvey. 'Are your people definitely going to be talking about Saulier? Can you be sure?'

'If he's a bachelor he's a big prize. That's what the season is for,'

I said. 'Blending the right bloodlines and scooping up as much cash as you can at the same time.'

'Is that what you're here to do?'

I ignored this impertinent question. 'What I think we need to do is go back to the Dog and Duck and see if we can recognise anyone else.'

'So not only return to the scene of the crime, but repeat it too?' said Harvey, his voice dripping with sarcasm. 'I take it you never went to criminal school.'

I shook my head. 'I don't want to try and question anyone again. I agree that's too dangerous.'

'Hallelujah!'

'But we need to try and establish who these men work for. Perhaps you could get to know some of them over drinks and say you're in need of some work?'

'Over drinks? Will we be having canapés too?'

'You know what I mean. I take it you're working tonight's ball. I'll see you there.' I walked off quickly before he had time to argue. I felt I had sorted Harvey nicely. Bernie was going to be more of a challenge.

However, when I returned to the Embassy I found Bernie had finally surfaced. Having slept for the better part of the day, she looked rested and radiant. I found her in the yellow drawing room. She leapt up to embrace me. 'I had such a wonderful night,' she said. 'I feel bad you were out doing the serious stuff. Did you discover anything?'

'Nothing special,' I said. 'Harvey spotted where one of the men we think was involved in the kidnapping likes to drink. He's going to follow as many of them as possible and get addresses.'

Bernie gave a small sigh. 'Well, I'm sure he'll enjoy it. He looks like a man who knows his way around the inside of a pint glass. I doubt he'll do more than run up a bar bill. I suppose it was asking too much for us to solve this mystery ourselves. The season does keep one so very busy.' She gave a sly little smile.

'You've met someone,' I said.

Bernie giggled. 'Mommy roasted me for ages last night trying to find out what I was up to, but I held out. I told her I was spreading myself around.' She laughed so loudly it was almost a shriek. 'I thought she was going to faint. Then I explained I was taking my time getting to know all the options. For once in my life I wasn't going to jump in.'

'But you have?'

'I have, but I'm not even going to tell you, darling Hope. It's a teeny bit complicated.'

'Oh, my goodness. He's not married, is he?'

'It's a bit complicated,' said Bernie, 'but he totally adores me. Come upstairs. I need to show you something.'

On the way to the bedroom Bernie talked far too loudly about how she needed my help to choose her dress for tonight. Once we were inside her bedroom, Bernie closed the door and threw the security bolt. 'You've no idea how much I had to argue to get that put on the door,' she said. 'But I said, suppose a madman got into the Embassy? Or how about when guests get lost? I had one accidentally wander into my room once. That did it, but I had to promise I would never use it at any other time.' Then she went around the room checking in the lamps and under the dressing table. 'Modern recording devices are getting so small. Matchbox-sized. Would you believe it?' she said.

'You can't be serious. You think the Embassy bugs your room?'

Bernie threw herself dramatically down on the bed. 'It's an Embassy, darling. Who knows who might try to record us.

I sat down on a spindly chair. The pretty gold-cushioned seat gave no comfort at all. 'Do you ever think your parents might watch you?'

'I think Daddy is far too busy.' She shrugged.

To my surprise she bounced back up and took a flat tool from between the pages of the book beside her bed. (Trust Bernie to assume no one would ever look inside a book. I should have taken her to task.) I was even more startled when she began to prise off the top of the nearest bed-knob. But imagine my utter astonishment when, once the knob was completely removed, she reached in one slender arm and pulled out handfuls of multicoloured pearls all strung and tangled up. As she unwound the necklace the colours flashed between her fingers. She held the result up to her neck.

'Oh my,' I said. The drop diamond, as large as a plum stone, hung below three strings of smaller luminescent pearls, white, freshwater, and black respectively. The whole thing was extremely impressive and in very bad taste. I doubted a modern jeweller had made it. It looked to me like something that had been kept in the family vault because no one had had the nerve to wear it. Just the thing to flatter a young American girl, who supposedly came from a much more glittery and flashier culture. It could only mean one thing.

'He's married,' I said. 'Bernie, you need to end this.'

'Don't worry so much. I know how to handle myself. Or how to handle him.'

'You need to tell me who he is.'

The glow around Bernie faded. Instead of passing me the necklace, as I had thought, she put it back in the hiding place and screwed down the top. She placed the chisel back in the book. 'I don't need to do anything,' she said curtly. 'You've been a great friend to me in the past, but we are hardly the same, are we? We are going to have different expectations.'

'I did wonder if you could find out if Charlotte's brother inherited her share of the family wealth?' I said. 'I still very much need your help with the mystery. Harvey can't hold a candle to you.'

'I *meant*, you will want someone to come and live in the Fens with you. That's your end game, isn't it? For the season? I can't imagine you selling your parents' home. You have to admit, it's so out of the way, you're never going to get a man of substance up there. Much more likely to be one that will live off you. Whereas I need a rich man to take care of me – and if he's older and dies earlier, I'll have to marry again. Of course, I want to love my first husband or, at the very least, he needs to be handsome. I don't think I could bear . . . certain things . . . if I didn't like the way he looked.' She got up and went over to the mirror. 'I think I deserve this. Someone handsome and of influence. After all, I'm an heiress. A proper one with money, not a tumble-down property.'

'Do you think you could do that for me?' I said as if I hadn't heard her. Something was eating at her. This wasn't the Bernie I knew. But I also knew that pressing her for details when she was in this mood wouldn't end well. Instead I decided to keep trying to deflect her with the mystery. It seemed unlikely to me that the Ambassador would ever allow her to marry a divorced man – and whoever gave her the pearls doubtless knew that. It wasn't her hand in marriage the beau was after. Not that I would be able to convince Bernie of that now.

'If you're thinking of Paul Saulier for yourself, he's married. Besides, regardless of what the papers said, I don't think Charlotte had all that much money. She hadn't even been finished in Switzerland. I believe she said her brother worked in Government, but nothing important. Mommy knew of him.'

'She knows him?' I asked.

'She'd encountered him somewhere, at some function or other. She actually thought I might be interested in him! I said when he visited here, he'd come to see you. That's when she told me he was married and, if you were the one interested in him, I should warn you that he wasn't worth your time. Of course, I never did, because that wasn't why he came. Mommy said he even has children. He's not going anywhere in Government. Apparently, he's not thought to be bright enough.'

'I'd still like to know about how the money in the family was divided up. You're so good at rooting out gossip, Bernie. You can talk to anyone.'

'I suppose I could,' said Bernie. She ran her fingers through her hair, trying a new style. 'My new friend knows everyone. I could ask him.'

'I don't know if I would do that,' I said. 'We don't want anyone to know we've been looking into what happened to Charlotte.'

201

'I can pass it off as girlish curiosity,' said Bernie. 'Now, I need to get ready. Would you mind covering for me at the ball. I think I might be taking a little trip.'

I got up and took her hands. She let me hold them, but her expression had turned mulish. 'Bernie, please, please, be careful.'

She pulled her hands out of mine, but she did it gently. 'Sometimes you have to take a risk to win a prize. Mommy always thinks the worst of me, so I doubt I could do anything that shocked her. She's such a hypocrite. She's been sleeping with your uncle every chance she gets.' She sighed. 'Poor Daddy.'

'Eric?' I said astonished.

'Don't be daft. Your mother's brother. The Earl. Joe. Mommy has a thing for British aristocracy. She had a little chat with me last night about how things work and how I had to stop fantasising over him.'

My mind went completely blank. I couldn't think what to say. If Bernie had only just learned of the state of her parents' marriage, it would have been a dreadful shock. But Uncle Joe and Amaranth? That felt wrong on so many levels. In fact, so wrong, that although I had wondered about it myself I wasn't convinced Amaranth had been telling the truth. But why would she lie to her own daughter?

Bernie got up and opened her closet. I took this as a hint and left. As I walked to my own room, I thought how lucky I was to have the parents I did. They might fight like cat and dog at times, my mother could be over-protective, even overbearing, but I had never doubted that they loved me. Nor that they were anything other than devoted to one another. At university Bernie had been determined to be a rebel, but there had been a sweetness about her. Something that, seeing her in her home environment, appeared to have been extinguished. She had been at her best when we had been with Harvey. When she could escape everything that the Embassy represented to her. She was smart too and she must have felt my demoting her to a mere gossip hunter a slap in the face. She knew me well enough to know I wouldn't have given up my quest so easily. In fact, I thought as I entered my own room, it was probably why she had shown me the pearls. They were her success.

I sat down in front of the dressing-table mirror. The face in the glass looked older and more serious. My godfather had said I needed to get to know the right people. But the more I found out about people like Amaranth, Paul Saulier, and the nasty little group of friends Bernie had joined at the Blackshirt parade, the more I realised I didn't like people very much at all.

I remained determined to find Charlotte's killer, and save her reputation. However, it seemed I must also save Bernie from her self-destructive tendencies. I had a very bad feeling about this 'little trip'.

Chapter Twenty-one

The night's ball had a fruit theme. Every pillar, every frame, and every possible ledge bore bright oranges, bananas, cherries, green apples, and even the occasional wobbly pineapple.

'Looks as if they bought out the whole of Covent Garden, doesn't it?' said Harvey, appearing at my elbow, carrying a tray of champagne flutes. I took one and gave him the few pertinent facts I had learned from Bernie without any of the gossip.

'It was Saulier who visited, then,' said Harvey. 'Bernie's mother recognised him?'

'I think so. Bernie's in a bit of a mood. I'm worried about her.'

'She's like a cat, that one,' said Harvey. 'She'll always land on her feet.'

'She's going off with someone from here tonight. I think we should follow her.'

Harvey shook his head. 'No way. I'm not going anywhere until at least eleven p.m. If not later. Some of us have a living to earn.'

'I can pay you,' I said.

'I know you can,' said Harvey, 'but in a couple of weeks you're going to be away from London and I'll still be here looking for work. I can't afford to get a reputation as unreliable.'

'But you gatecrash these parties!'

'Ah,' said Harvey, 'but that's only after Harvey the waiter has completed his shift. I always make sure they see me do my work.'

'Fair enough,' I said. 'Let's hope the Dog and Duck has

lock-ins. Are you listening to me?' Harvey's attention appeared to be fixed somewhere behind my right shoulder and his eyes had narrowed.

'Your friend is getting in with a dodgy crowd,' he said. 'I'd warn her off if I was you.' I made to turn around, but he caught my wrist with his free hand. 'Don't be obvious. His name is Henry Danville, son of David Danville. Get someone to point him out to you later. He's a real . . . well, never mind. He's not someone Bernie should know.'

'I've run into him before,' I said.

'He's a cad.'

'Bernie boasted to me last night she had a boyfriend . . .'

'Not here. I've been standing by you too long. Meet me out the back.'

It might have been easy enough for Harvey to wander out to the rear yard, but not so for a lady in a ball gown. However, this time I had come prepared. I collected my carpet bag from where I had stashed it and retreated to the ladies' restroom – as Bernie usually calls them – to change. I then locked my bag and ensured the label indicating my ownership was clearly showing. I hid it behind some stairs. With luck, it would be returned to me unopened. People might think it odd, but it would be thought gauche to comment. And if no one returned it, the loss of one gown and one pair of silly shoes would not break my heart.

Looking thoroughly disreputable, I managed to slip out the front door by means of the old trick of rolling a shilling along the ground. The footman on the door obligingly ran after it. I only needed him to get a few feet away, so I could slide out unnoticed. My heart beat far too fast, and much too loud, but I managed to pass through the doorway and into the street. I immediately headed for the shadows. All I had to do now was get to the yard behind the house. Perhaps I should have told Harvey of my plans, I thought. If I was caught by a policeman and charged as a burglar, he might be able to vouch for me.

The idea of Harvey vouching to the police made me giggle. My mood lifted. This kind of leg-work, I had fast discovered, was not my kind of thing. Originally it was why I had roped Harvey in. How we had come to work together like this I couldn't fathom.

The ball had been at the townhouse of the host family. If we'd been at a mansion in the middle of nowhere I would have had no trouble. But in London, ladies and gentlemen who complained about being cooped up in the country made allowances for the London high life and lived in townhouses. Townhouses that were all squeezed together. Most of the horses might have gone, replaced by sleek shiny motor cars, but the old mews still ran behind them – often used as servants' quarters, and I counted on this.

I stayed under the trees until the last moment. I could see a flask being passed around among the drivers of the waiting vehicles. Admittedly they were taking small sips, but I didn't fancy being driven by any of them. I waited until there was a particularly saucy story being told, along the lines of what the butler saw – except it was what the driver saw – and stepped quietly out of the shadows.

I heard a familiar squeal of laughter. I glanced towards the house and saw Bernie exiting on the arm of a gentleman in a season-approved uniform comprising of a dark coat, white scarf, and top hat. He steered her towards one of the motors with such skill, neither of them passed under the street lamps. He was around the right height, but his build was hidden by his greatcoat.

I felt torn between exposing myself and grabbing Bernie or letting her go off with the man. I wanted justice for Charlotte, which I had to admit felt like it was slipping further and further away. On the other hand, I knew Bernie was more than capable of getting herself into deep trouble. Our earlier conversation had left me feeling raw, but that didn't mean I wished her any harm.

I heard the car door close and knew I had hesitated too long. I stepped forward into the road, but mud had splattered the number plate, so I couldn't make it out. I tried to convince myself the weather conditions had caused that, but I suspected it had been done deliberately. However, I could hardly chase after her on foot, so Bernie would have to fend for herself.

The task of eluding the other drivers didn't seem so huge. My fears for Bernie obscured some of the worry. I took a deep breath and crept down the mews lane behind the house as quietly as I could. My heart beat so loudly in my ears I was sure someone would spot me. I peeked carefully into yard after yard.

'Oi, you, 'op it!' said Harvey when I finally found the right yard. 'No work for the likes of you.'

'Harvey,' I said quietly, 'it's me.'

In the dim light of the yard I sensed, rather than saw, him turn red. 'Bleedin' hell, Hope! You can't go around like that, girl!'

'I take it you are referring to my disguise. I think it's rather good.' I had exchanged my ball gown for a pair of tight but flexible black trousers, a black polo neck jumper, a black cap, and soft black leather gloves. 'Besides, ladies often wear trousers.'

'Not ones that fit like that,' said Harvey. I heard him swallow audibly. He must have better night sight than me.

'I can hardly change now,' I said. 'Besides, Bernie has gone off in a motor with a strange man and, I expect, is about to get herself in deep trouble.'

Harvey swore again. This time much more foully. 'Do you think it's connected to Charlotte's kidnapping?'

I told him about the potentially married man and the necklace. 'Sounds like a set-up to me.'

'Blimey,' said Harvey. 'Do you think it's some kind of kidnapping ring?'

'I have no idea,' I said, rubbing my arms up and down my shoulders. Without a coat, the night air prickled my skin.

'Perhaps it's some kind of scheme to kidnap debs,' said Harvey. 'But having blown it once, you'd think they'd back off.'

'Greed often makes people stupid,' I said. 'But my gut tells me there is more to it. Why should her brother warn us off?'

'Because he's involved in all this and is, in all likelihood, kidnapping Bernie as we speak.'

'The only reason I can think he would take Bernie would be to ensure our silence. None of this makes sense. We need more information and besides, I'm freezing. Let's try the Dog and Duck for a lead.'

'Long shot,' said Harvey, 'but I ain't got any better ideas. Wait here a minute.' He darted off, only to appear a couple of minutes later with a small but heavy black coat. 'Belongs to the yard boy, so it might smell a bit.'

By now I suspected my skin had turned blue so, regardless of its unique odour, I quickly thrust it on. 'Right then, we'd better be off. I've got us transportation,' said Harvey. He reached into the darkness and pulled out a bicycle. 'You can sit on the handlebars, or the seat if you like, and I'll pedal standing up.'

I opted for the seat. The thought of sitting on handlebars seemed to be more of a romantic conceit than a practical reality. Harvey puffed and panted a bit, but within a few minutes he'd got up quite a rhythm. For the sake of discretion, he'd opted not to use lights. I found myself grabbing the underside of what was proving to be a most uncomfortable seat.

Despite a bumpy ride over the cobbles of the mews, we acquired a remarkable turn of speed. I resisted the urge to clasp Harvey as I swayed precariously behind him. I could hear his breath coming harder and faster; now was no time for conversation. I closed my eyes and prayed he'd thought about the route and that this ride would be as short as possible.

The wind whipped hard enough that it stole my cap. I released a hand in an attempt to catch it and almost unseated myself. Harvey corrected our balance with a swerve and a curse. How long we rode for I don't know. I only know that my posterior developed a relationship with the narrow seat in a manner that felt far too intimate for a first acquaintance. The road beneath us might be no longer cobbled, but every sharp turn of the wheel bruised me in places I could not even begin to mention in polite society. I had quite lost track of time, but we had to be near to our destination. I could not bear this much longer. I took a breath and opened my eyes. The bicycle had achieved such velocity that my eyes teared up. I blinked hard, trying to focus. I daren't let go of the seat again. Through a blurry haze I saw the hill that rose up before the Dog and Duck. We were almost there.

Harvey let the bicycle glide to a natural halt at the foot of the hill and I came to a realisation. 'This contraption has no brakes!' I said. 'We could have been killed!'

'Can't have everything,' said Harvey. 'Get off. There's no way I can push us both up that hill. Besides, we'd end up going faster than your driver once we crested over the top. I'm going to stash the bike in the bushes over there. We can get it later. C'mon, get off.'

This instruction was easier said than followed. I found I had become stiff in places I didn't know could become stiff. I managed to haul myself down and stumbled, ungainly, over to a garden wall, where I promptly collapsed. Harvey stuffed his scarf in his mouth, before moving the bicycle. I realised he was attempted to smother his laughter. 'I hope you choke,' I whispered as he passed me.

We made our way back towards the Dog and Duck. Harvey limped slightly, but the only word that could describe my gait was 'waddle'. By the time we had reached the summit I could almost walk normally, something which only ten minutes before had seemed an impossible dream.

'We're not doing a repeat of looking in the window, are we?' said Harvey as we started our descent.

'No,' I said. 'We can wait outside for someone you recognise from the night Charlotte was kidnapped.'

I could almost hear Harvey's scepticism. 'It's either that or I go to the Ambassador and tell him everything I know.'

'Hang on,' said Harvey, 'we don't know that Bernie hasn't just . . . you know. You were the one who said she was a wild one.'

'I know, and she's just found out her mother is cheating on her father. Maybe even has been for a long time. And worse yet, with someone she'd taken a shine to.'

'Bleedin' Americans. No morals.'

'Show a little sympathy. She's had her world turned upside down.'

'She's a tough one,' said Harvey. 'She'll work out that her parents are going through a bad patch. Doesn't mean she won't find true love one day.'

'You romantic!' I said. 'I agree she's unlikely to go and cry herself to sleep. She's more likely to rebel.'

'What's the difference?' said Harvey. 'You keep saying she's wild.'

'Yes, but not truly wild. I mean flirty, always up for going to a party. Nothing more wild than that.' I sighed. 'I have a bad feeling about this.'

'Oh really,' said Harvey with dripping sarcasm, 'I've had a bad feeling about this since . . .'

'The Lyons',' I said. 'When I blackmailed you.'

'Bloody toffs. C'mon, we can sit over here in the shadows and wait. Not that anything is likely to happen. Bernie might be many things, but you can't convince me she's enough of an idiot to throw away her virtue to spite her parents.'

'I hope not,' I said.

Harvey looked shocked. 'I thought she was your friend.'

'I don't mean she'd set out to do anything like that. Only that she might be reckless enough to get in over her head tonight.'

'Yeah, what say we wait here twenty minutes or so and then go back and try and track her down? Or we could go now before we freeze our ruddy arses off.'

I was on the verge of agreeing when the door of the Dog and Duck opened.

Chapter Twenty-two

A lone figure stumbled out of the Inn. Tall, thin, in a wiry rather than a scrawny way, and wearing a top hat and tails that, by the looks of it, had seen more than a few owners in their time, he attempted to navigate the steps. For every step he took he took a couple sideways, so his progress was quite alarming to watch.

'If you aren't the luckiest bleeder I've ever known,' said Harvey. 'I'll have to get you to mark my racing chit.'

'Do you know who that is?'

'I'm not saying there's a connection, but he lined up with the rest of us for the outside staff talk. It's a nice little chat the butler of the house always gives the hired staff, where he tells you how we will never have worked to such high standards and how he'll fry our livers if we don't deliver. It's like they get it out of a book. They all say exactly the same thing. The only differences—'

I tugged him by the sleeve. 'That hardly matters now. Let's follow him.'

'I ain't kidnapping anyone!'

'I hope he is walking home.' Even as I said this the man staggered over to the fence and extracted a bicycle. He then attempted to mount it. Harvey stared open-mouthed as the man tried to put one leg over and fell flat on his face. The bicycle flipped up and landed on top of him. 'Quick,' I said. 'Run and get ours. It's going to take him a while to get going.' He didn't move. I stood heavily on his foot and repeated my instruction. With a muffled grunt of protest Harvey ran off down the hill. I continued to watch our quarry. Really, he could go on the stage with an act like this, which made me wonder if it was all a bit too much. Almost as if he thought people might be watching him.

Even as this occurred to me, the man managed to mount his machine and, after a couple of wild zigzags, he began to pedal at a furious rate – straight towards me. I ducked back as far as I could go into the shadows. An owl hooted in the distance, the man on the bicycle puffed and from somewhere inside the Dog and Duck came the vaguest, muffled sound of revelry. Then, over Harvey's tuneless whistling, I heard the sound of another bicycle approaching. He and our quarry were set on a collision course.

I quelled an impulse to run into the middle of the street and prevent their meeting. Harvey had to deal with this alone. The man passed me without noticing. Despite being a good few feet from him I inhaled the sour smell of alcohol wafting off him. I gagged. I had to press my hand over my lips to stop myself being sick. As he approached the man, Harvey raised his hat and shouted, 'Good evenin'' and pedalled on past him. Our quarry wobbled alarmingly at this greeting, slowed down to recover his balance and then with a careful wave of his arm to signal him turning, he cycled off.

Harvey continued down the hill and I darted out of the shadows to meet him. He didn't have to say a word. I hopped on the bicycle as if I actually wanted to ride the darn thing. Immediately my bruises fitted exactly into what had previously caused them. I thought longingly of a hot bath filled with relaxing salts. But Harvey, newly energised, turned and cycled after the man.

Our quarry continued onward. I realised his roundabout route was taking us back towards town. Not once did he turn around, and his pedalling grew more and more steady. 'Could be a trap,' I whispered in Harvey's ear. He grunted softly. I had no idea what this meant. I held on tight to the seat as we sped down towards town and back onto the cobbled streets. I discovered it is hard to be fearful when one's posterior is in agony.

The man ahead turned onto a main street. We were now in the

city proper. To my relief Harvey switched to the correct side of the road. Our quarry cycled on and on. I heard the approach of a vehicle behind us but, as I turned my head, I saw no lights. A sleek enclosed car swished past us, spraying muck from the street all over my legs. The man in front wobbled violently when passed, but once again he recovered. I felt both relief and confusion that the motor had not used lights. There was no way he could have seen us.

We continued on. I could feel Harvey slowing. Considering he had been working all night, he had to pedal for two and he had recently been beaten up, I felt he was doing valiantly. Of course, I had no intention of telling him so.

We were now in an area of town that blended old and new together. The street we currently rode along had modern terraced houses on either side, but as we passed the side streets I spied larger, more mansion-like structures.

To probably both our relief the man finally turned right and stopped in front of a row of townhouses. Harvey slowed down but didn't turn yet. Passing the man a second time would risk alerting him. Behind us I heard a loud shout. Surprised, I turned too hard and too fast, upsetting the slow-moving bicycle. Even as the we tilted in an alarming manner I saw an open-topped motor careering down the street, lights blazing, filled with shadowy figures. One of them threw a champagne bottle onto the road, resulting in a smashing noise, accompanied by a loud 'Hurrah!' I briefly caught a glimpse of Caro Littleton's sour face before the sky and road suddenly, and dramatically, swapped places.

Midway through the fall I parted company with the bicycle and encountered stairs leading down. I half rolled, half bounced down these. I had the sense to put my hands up to cover my head. I landed, winded and shocked, at the bottom of the flight. I had no time to stand before the bicycle dropped down on top of me, its pedals still whirring, and Harvey, in turn, landed on top of that.

For a moment it felt like time stilled. One end of the handlebar was mere inches from my right eye. I blinked slowly to convince myself my eye was unharmed. Then I gradually eased my neck to one side to prevent my face from being impaled by the bike when Harvey moved. I kept a close watch on the end of the handlebar The rest of me remained trapped. The tendons in my neck felt like over-tightened violin strings.

Harvey groaned and rolled away. I gingerly stretched my limbs and, while bruised and sore, found them all to be in reasonable working order. Harvey lifted the machine off me and threw it hard against the nearest wall. I quite understood his feelings but uttered a 'Shhh' even as he held out his hand to help me to my feet. Thank goodness for the modesty preservation that trousers afford, is all I can say.

The bicycle lay on its side, looking distinctly misshapen. 'I think your machine has had it,' I said softly.

Harvey shrugged. 'Wasn't mine. What do you want to do now?'

'Do you think the man heard us?'

Harvey glanced around. 'Normally, I'd say that was a stupid question, but those idiots in the motor were making a hell of a lot of noise. So maybe not.'

'Maybe we should go and peek in the window. I saw which house he stopped outside before we crashed.'

Harvey gave me a look. 'It's a low window,' I said. 'The gate up to the house looks easy to slip through . . .'

'Oh goody,' said Harvey.

We climbed up the cellar steps. As Harvey said, there was no point in moving the bicycle. It would only make more noise and potentially attract the householders. As it was, I had to assume the servants all slept in the attic. Anyone on the basement level would surely have heard us.

Various different parts of me hurt. I believed everything would heal in time without medical intervention. Harvey, on the other hand, I could see limped even more badly than before. I definitely could not consider him my 'muscle' tonight. Although I suspected, in a hand-to-hand fight, I might fare better anyway. I assumed Harvey's experience would come solely from the odd bar brawl. And, as he was quite adept at talking his way out of things, perhaps not even that.

The trouble was, as always, I didn't look in the least bit menacing. Whereas Harvey, coming momentarily under the light of the street lamp, resembled a pugilist who had recently defeated a host of opponents, yet remained standing. Surely his appearance would be enough be for my purposes?

Once up on street level, I alarmed Harvey by taking his arm. 'You look like a boy,' he hissed.

'My hair is no longer restrained under a cap,' I pointed out.

'Well, dressed like that you look like an odd sort.' I let him go and walked a pace ahead towards the townhouse that had a bicycle propped up outside the gate. 'I think we should wait until he comes out,' I said. 'The main street is pretty quiet. We could sit on the steps of one of the other terraces.'

We both sat down with an involuntary sigh. The clear bright cloudless sky of the day had given rise to a bitterly cold night and I huddled down gratefully in the smelly coat Harvey had provided. I even tucked my hair inside my collar, so I looked less odd. Now would naturally be the time for us to share plans, perhaps even confidences. Neither of us spoke. I fixed my eyes on the house and slowed my breathing. I needed to calm myself and my thoughts for whatever happened next. Next to me Harvey blew into his bare hands and rubbed them together. He then proceeded to massage his upper arms, before bending forward to rub his shins. I did my best to shut him out.

In a short while the man came out of the house and climbed, with no obvious difficulty, onto his bicycle. 'Short meeting,' said Harvey.

'And a sobering one too. We must be cautious.'

'I was born cautious,' muttered Harvey.

We crossed the road, hugging the side away from the front window. When we reached the house, it became clear the gate was in full sight of the lit windows. 'Why aren't the shades drawn?' I whispered.

Harvey shrugged and put a finger to his lips. He crouched down and opened the gate. He darted through it, closed it quietly and slunk into the shadows. He clearly didn't expect me to follow, but after a quick check up and down the road that there were no constables in sight, I copied him. Or I tried to. The effect of the evening's events had stiffened my muscles and, crouching awkwardly, I toppled over. Mixed fortune ensured I landed in a rose bush. Harvey regarded me with horror. I made what I believed was a credible cat noise to cover my misadventure. Harvey slapped the palm of his hand silently against his head. Then both of us crawled towards the window. Harvey counted down on his fingers, three, two, one, and, in unison, we slowly raised our heads above the sill.

My hope had been that Harvey's bruised face would cause alarm rather than recognition if we were spotted. But neither of the two people within appeared to notice our presence. It was we who received the shock.

In front of us, locked in a passionate embrace, were Paul Saulier and Bernie.

Chapter Twenty-three

We ducked down below the sill. 'You are not going in there,' said Harvey sternly. I snorted, stood up, brushed myself down and strode over to the front door. Before Harvey could stop me, I had rung the bell.

A respectable butler took a respectable amount of time to reach the door. He regarded me down his long aquiline nose. Then he caught sight of Harvey and reached for an umbrella from the stand by the door. 'I shall summon the constabulary,' he said in admirably calm tones.

'Oh, don't be stupid,' I said in my most upper-crust voice and pushed past them. 'The Ambassador's daughter needs me.'

The butler automatically retreated from accosting someone who sounded like a lady. Harvey, however, did not fare so well. I left them struggling on the doorstep. The drawing-room window had been prominently placed and it took no great intelligence for me to find and swing open the appropriate door.

'Bernadette Woodford, what the hell do you think you are doing?' I demanded in a voice I hoped would strike her like thunder.

Paul Saulier released his prize, but Bernie only half turned, throwing her arms even more tightly round his neck. 'This is none of your business, Hope Stapleford,' she said melodramatically, and tossed back her hair like heroine in the movies. Saulier choked slightly on her long mane, diminishing the impact of the moment.

'He's married and a suspect in his sister's murder,' I said. Behind me I could hear grunting noises coming from the hall. I imagined Harvey must be getting the upper hand. Butlers never grunt if they can avoid doing so.

This time Saulier stepped clear of Bernie. 'I can assure you,' he said his voice low, 'that I had nothing to do with my sister's murder. I may have inadvertently been the cause, but I would never have willingly harmed her.'

'What are you talking about?' said Bernie, turning from admiring lover to shrew on the turn of a dime.

'I'm sorry,' he said. 'But I have a wife. Two small children. After Charlie, I had to do what they wanted.'

'Charlie?' said Bernie.

'Shut up,' I snapped. 'He means Charlotte. This is a set-up?'

Paul Saulier nodded miserably. 'You got too close. One of their men is missing. They're spooked.'

'Listen,' I said quickly, 'they never meant to kill Charlotte. The men sent to kidnap her bungled it. They aren't murderers. Is there a back door?'

'They killed Trask,' said Saulier. 'They're committed to action now. There's nothing I can do.'

'How long do we have?' I said.

'Minutes,' said Saulier. 'They're watching the house.'

'Someone was watching us?' said Bernie indignantly.

'You don't understand,' I said. 'This is a bizarre form of honey trap. They wanted to get the three of us in one place, so they could deal with us – permanently. They're threatening Paul's wife and family. That's why he began the affair with you. Because they told him to.'

'What?' said Bernie. 'Who the hell are they?' Her hands balled into admirable fists.

Poised for flight, but not knowing what to do, or what was coming, I couldn't follow her train of thinking. 'I was to show you this,' said Saulier. He took a folded newspaper from a bureau and passed it to me.

I unfolded it and read, 'Bizarre double suicide pact of ageing Brighton Belles'.

'Oh no,' I breathed. 'They killed them?'

Bernie grabbed the newspaper out of my hands. 'Gee,' she said. 'I never liked them, but this . . .' She looked at Saulier. 'You knew about this?'

'Only when it was over.'

'I suppose the necklace is paste as well?'

'Afraid so,' said Saulier. Bernie launched herself at his face, claws out. My attention turned to the door opening behind me. Harvey stood there, panting, with the butler in a headlock. 'For an old geezer,' he said, 'he can give it some welly.'

'Paul didn't kill her,' I said. 'Or order her kidnapping. It was done to threaten him.'

'Why? What's he got that they want?' asked Harvey, who seemed very familiar with the process of blackmail.

I turned to him. 'Where do you work?' I asked.

'The Foreign Office,' said Saulier, as he wrestled with Bernie.

'Bleedin' hell,' said Harvey, again sharper than I. 'It's the bloody Blackshirts, isn't it?'

'It must be,' I said. 'And they're on their way. Do you have a telephone?' I said to Saulier. He indicated the hallway behind us.

'How long do we have?' said Harvey.

'As long as it takes the man on the bicycle to summon his friends. Not long enough, I would imagine. They will have guns,' I said.

'And only we know he's a traitor,' said Harvey, nodding at Saulier.

'Sir!' said the butler from the headlock. 'I was only hired to provide drinks for the evening. I must protest!'

'You and me both,' said Harvey. He let the butler go and advanced towards Bernie and Saulier. I took the opportunity to dart out of the room and ring the number Uncle Eric had given me.

'Hope,' said my godfather, sounding remarkably alert for the time of night.

'I'm in trouble,' I said. 'I'm at Paul Saulier's house and I think there are Blackshirts after me.'

'Fascists, Hope,' said Eric. 'Do call them what they are.'

'What can I do?'

'Barricade the doors to prevent entry,' said my godfather calmly, 'and keep people away from the windows. I'll send help.'

'It's at . . .'

'I know,' said Uncle Eric and rang off.

'I need some help,' I called. 'Someone barricade the front door!' There was no immediate response to my cries, so I bolted down the hall towards the back of the house. There was a short staircase leading down to a deserted kitchen. With a strength born, I can only imagine, of fear, I pushed a dresser across the door that led to the back. I squeezed my way past a well-scrubbed table and checked to see if there were any another exits. I found a small scullery that led to what was the tradesman's entrance. The pine table wouldn't possibly fit there, so I jammed a chair under the door handle. Then I dragged the table over to the scullery entrance and, with some effort, flipped it onto its side. By this time, I was sweating and sore. Only sheer terror of what might be coming had allowed me to move such heavy pieces alone. I could feel adrenaline pumping through my system – that and a strong sense of being hard done by. Why had no one come to help? What on earth were they all doing?

Then I ran back upstairs. I found everyone occupied. Harvey was doing his best to choke the life out of Saulier. Bernie ran back and forth, helpless, looking for goodness knows what, while the butler valiantly beat Harvey over the back with a cane. Saulier had a faint blue tinge, but continued to utter guttural noises, so I had no real concerns.

'Help's on its way,' I cried loudly, to make myself heard over the scuffle. 'You need to get away from . . .' I had barely got the words out when I heard the screech of vehicles outside and I had an awful premonition. 'Get down!' I screamed.

The butler demonstrated admirably why he had lived for so long, dropping immediately to the floor. Harvey released Saulier, who staggered backwards and fell over a chair, landing in an untidy heap. Bernie as ever, began to protest. From the doorway, I saw her mouth open as I heard the first gunshot hit the window.

Then the world went into slow motion.

I saw one pane of glass explode, propelling hundreds of tiny, jagged shards through the air. I heard the sound of a second shot but, by then, Harvey had already flung himself across the room, hitting Bernie hard and taking her down before a second window pane blew in, spraying even more glass. Harvey gave a startled cry as glass showered down on him like rain, but he didn't move, protecting Bernie who lay underneath him. I threw my arms in front of my face but, even at the periphery of the room as I was, glassy needles tore at my coat sleeves. Thankfully, they appeared to bear the brunt of it.

I lowered my arms and saw Harvey lying quite still. A pool of red gathered around him and my heart almost stopped. My instinct was to run to him, but the shots continued. Dropping to the floor myself, I began to crawl towards him. 'Get out,' I screamed at the others. The butler scuttled past me with surprising haste. If we could get out of this room then maybe we stood more of a chance. Any moment I expected the gunmen themselves to erupt through the windows.

Bernie, having crawled out from under the still motionless Harvey, crept up to me. Her hands were bleeding from the glass on the carpet. 'I'll help you drag him,' she managed to say between the gunfire.

The shots stopped I heard the sound of car doors opening and closing. They would be here in a minute. Shots in a London street were almost unheard of and if this was to be a mass execution then they would want to be in and out as fast as possible. 'Help us,' Bernie said to Saulier, but he shook his head and pushed past us towards the door.

Bernie and I began to drag Harvey. 'Darn it! He's heavy,' protested Bernie. I could see that a bullet had penetrated Harvey's upper thigh and, while the blood flowed profusely, it didn't spurt.

'I don't think it's hit an artery,' I said.

'Hey, ladies,' Harvey's speech was slurred, and he was shaking.

'He's going into shock,' I said.

He started to say something else, but his eyes closed, and he went limp.

Bernie shook him frantically. 'Careful,' I warned.

'We have to get out,' she said. Seconds were passing like minutes. Surely the men would breach the windows at any moment? I turned my head to see how far we were from the doorway. I screamed in outrage. Saulier was barricading the space, having dragged several items of hallway furnishings to fill the gap 'Nothing personal,' he called out as he upended a sturdy console table that filled most of the frame.

'The bas—' said Bernie.

Suddenly there was a new sound, that of rapid gunfire. I expected Bernie to bolt for the back of the room, but she didn't. She and I hunkered down, both of us instinctively shielding the wounded Harvey with our bodies. 'You might be as annoying as all hell,' I said to Bernie, 'but it's a privilege to be your friend.' I have no idea if she heard me.

The next moment men poured through the broken windows. Bernie and I looked at one another and then turned to face them, keeping Harvey behind us.

Expecting to meet death, I looked up defiantly into the face of my executioners and saw young soldiers. One held out his hand. 'Sorry to take so long, miss, but traffic is awful on a Saturday night.' I took his hand and, finding my legs not quite as supportive as I would have liked, half stood. I pointed at Harvey. 'Medic!' yelled the young man.

Two soldiers began breaking down the makeshift barrier

that Saulier had erected. I heard him whimper and plead for his life on the other side. I realised, against the odds, we were now safe.

Then, rather embarrassingly, I fainted – right into the squaddie's arms.

Epilogue

My godfather carved through his steak as if it were butter. But having had the chance to finally see inside his club I had no doubt that the fillet cost more than Harvey made in a month – and a good month at that.

Uncle Eric dipped a small piece in pepper sauce but hesitated before raising the fork to his mouth. 'You made quite a few mistakes, Hope. You do know that?'

We were finally having dinner some days after the awful event. The dining room reeked of a different era, lined with oak panels. Tables with snowy linen tablecloths sported silver and crystal so well polished it glinted in the candlelight like jewels. Everywhere one looked, waiters moved with a slow elegance, carrying silver trays or pushing small trolleys with enormous meat dishes. The staff were almost indistinguishable from one another and all clearly disapproved of the presence of women. Still, it had excellent, if very British, food. Overall it was the sort of place I had imagined my godfather would feel very much at home: discreet, quiet, and highly selective.

I turned my attention from my Dover sole, presented in brown butter sauce and filleted at the table. 'I didn't tell you anything earlier on because I didn't appreciate you were – well, what you are.'

Eric raised an eyebrow. 'You mean a middle-aged gentleman, who deals with certain problems, in the employ of His Majesty's Government?'

'I don't believe anyone would ever call you middle-aged, Godfather.'

'Thank you.'

'They wouldn't dare,' I said.

Uncle Eric raised his left eyebrow but forked the steak into his mouth and chewed slowly. I watched his face carefully, not daring to look down at my own plate.

'Am I in trouble?' I asked.

He swallowed. 'I'm curious,' he said. 'What exactly did you think I was doing when I taught you all those skills as a child?'

'I thought we were playing games.'

'And when I insisted you learnt to defend yourself?'

'I thought you were being old-fashioned about me going up to Oxford alone in a world full of disreputable men.'

'Oh, my dear,' said Uncle Eric, 'I have always been a great proponent of the modern, independent female. I feel my gender underrates the fairer sex badly. But I was teaching you far more than that.'

'Oh,' I said.

'Your fish will be getting cold.'

Obediently, I went back to eating my sole. The waiter came over. Ignoring me completely he said, 'Is everything satisfactory, my Lord?'

'Certainly. I'll have the cheese and biscuits. My young companion will have the fruit trifle. Go easy on the sherry.'

'Certainly, my Lord.' He withdrew so silently I wasn't entirely sure his feet even touched the carpet.

'Lord?' I asked.

'I don't often use the title, but it is mine.'

I ate my vegetables. When I had picked the last bit of flesh from my fish I asked, 'So, what were we doing when I was a child?'

'Spycraft,' said my godfather.

'I beg your pardon?'

'Craft for spies. I don't know how I can make it plainer. Your mother worked for me during the Great War. She more or less dragged your father into it too. But he didn't like it much.' He took a sip of his red wine. 'Your mother was a natural. And extremely loyal to me. How about you?'

'Was I doing it?'

'In a rather haphazard sort of way.'

'I did find it exciting,' I said. I took a drink of lemonade. Ladies were not allowed to drink alcohol at the club unless they were married.

'But there are always consequences,' said Uncle Eric. 'You have to live with those. Especially if you have made mistakes.'

'Like the women in Brighton,' I said and sighed.

'I don't think we will ever be sure about them. From what I learned they became quite eager about your little crusade. One of them had been Trask's father's lover when young, I believe? I presume she thought that in very different circumstances she might have married Trask's father, and it gave her some kind of maternal complex. Older spinsters can get the oddest notions. Freud loves them. Not bachelors, of course. We simply mature with age, like fine wine.'

'So, you believe me responsible for their deaths?'

'Hope, it is hardly ever my job to assign blame. More often than not it is to remove it.' My godfather allowed himself a sour smile at that. 'I am not judging you,' he continued. 'Anyway, why should you care what I think?'

A huge weight appeared to be bearing down on my chest. I blinked hard, determined not to cry. 'I do care,' I said. 'I don't want you to think I did a bad job.'

'Is my opinion more important to you than whether you were responsible for their deaths?'

I put down my spoon. My appetite vanished. 'Do you seriously want me to answer?' I said.

Uncle Eric allowed himself an actual smile. 'I think I do. That is, if you know?'

I swallowed hard. His gaze was hardly hostile, but it was level and direct. I did not consider lying. 'Yes,' I said. 'Your opinion is more important to me.' Treacherous tears brimmed on my eyelids. 'Does that make me a terrible person?' I blurted.

Uncle Eric gave a small crack of laughter. 'My dear Hope, I assure you – and your mother would doubtless corroborate the fact – that I am not the sort of person one should ask for a moral judgement.'

I sipped some lemonade and tried to calm my racing heart. 'What do you think did happen to them?' I said.

'Clearly, they didn't kill themselves, but I suspect they got on the wrong side of drug traffickers. As you may know, Brighton is one of their main importing areas. It could have been the fascists, but that's a bit too much of a long shot for me. As we can't ask the ladies themselves, I must assign their deaths to misadventure while snooping beyond their capacities. But, yes, it could still have been your fault, as you engaged them as assets—'

The waiter collected our plates, shortening this part of the conversation. I took the time to reconsider if I felt responsible for the death of the Brighton ladies. 'Their deaths seem somehow unreal,' I said. 'As if they happened far away.'

Uncle Eric nodded. 'You've disassociated yourself from them emotionally. It's a useful skill, but the consequences I have been speaking about can mean not only the deaths of strangers, but even your friends. That takes a lot more getting used to. It is not something everyone can deal with. I wouldn't want to break you, Hope. Your mother would never forgive me, quite apart from the fondness I feel for you.'

'I don't want to get used to losing people,' I said.

Uncle Eric looked at me with the closest expression I have seen him display to pity and said, 'You may have no choice.'

The waiter returned with the final course. I coughed on my first spoonful of trifle. Eric leant over and dipped his unused pudding spoon in my dish. He tasted it. 'I'm glad to see they toned down the sherry on my instruction.'

'Really?' I said, my eyes now watering for real.

227

'No idea how to do sweets here. It's a gentleman's club. Unless you're one of the old codgers who've regressed to the nursery and want sweetened pap.' He shivered. 'I'd rather be dead than a walking corpse.'

'It doesn't seem to bother you, talking about death,' I ventured.

'Well, in these particular circumstances I wasn't at fault, for once,' said Uncle Eric. 'Although I suppose if I had trained you better you would have been more aware of how the situation was escalating out of your control. Though what you would have done if you had realised this, we will never know.'

'What did I miss?' I said.

Uncle Eric patted his mouth with a napkin. 'Well, let's think about this. Kew and his associates were obviously hired thugs. No political affiliations that I can discover. Next, you have a run in with the Blackshirts. How did you think they were involved?'

'At first, I thought perhaps they were kidnapping debs, but it didn't make much sense. Unless they were trying to blackmail a large part of the British aristocracy.'

'Far too big an operation,' said Eric. 'It would have been quickly noticed by my people.'

'So, they were being used by someone?'

'I'm sure they considered themselves under orders. Ask no questions and all that. But even before the Blackshirts there were those shady characters Bernie got involved with.'

'She doesn't always have the best judgement,' I said. I felt bad for this comment, but it was true.

'I think you will find they expended some effort in enticing her into their group. They hoped to discover what the pair of you knew and to divert you from your amateur investigations. They tried to entice you too, but they used the wrong weapons. First edition books would have been more tempting for you than late-night jazz clubs.'

I blushed at the word 'amateur', but didn't feel I could defend myself. Instead I asked, 'And were they under orders too?'

'I expect they received suggestions as to how they could help the cause. A word here. A comment over luncheon there. That sort of thing.'

'So, who was behind it all?' I said.

'Obviously, a foreign power,' said Eric, 'but annoyingly we don't have the king-pin. Yet.'

He turned his attention back to finishing his cheese and said no more. Eventually I broke the silence.

'How is Harvey?' I said.

'He is recuperating in Bournemouth where, I am reliably informed, confidence tricksters are in short supply.' He looked at me. 'I have no problem with you using Harvey as a leg-man, if you excuse the pun, but I don't think we'll be bringing him into the fold just yet. He may have divided loyalties. He's obviously a bit sweet on the pair of you. I doubt he knows which one he likes best yet, but you can work on him.'

I turned scarlet.

'Hope, you will have to learn how to run your assets.'

'What do you mean, divided loyalties? You can't suspect him of being a Blackshirt?'

'No,' said Uncle Eric. 'If anything, he's more of a socialist. No, your Harvey has an aged father and a number of siblings to look after. He's a very dutiful eldest son, by all accounts.'

'I feel bad about his injury. The doctor said he will always limp,' I said.

'He may have cause to thank you for that,' said Uncle Eric and called for the waiter to remove our plates. I had no idea what he meant, but I knew better than to pester him with questions. He only ever told one what he wanted one to hear.

We took coffee in the smaller members' lounge as the main lounge never admitted ladies. We settled into two wingback chairs, with coffee and petits fours before us. 'I think, if you are going to do this, Hope, we should do our best to persuade Bernie to settle with you in a flat in town. Did you mention the idea to her yet?'

'Not yet, but she is keen to avoid going back to the States with her parents.'

'Yes, I hear Amaranth rather over-played her hand. Warning someone against taking the path of vice by mentioning one has experience of it oneself is never effective. At least I haven't found it to be.'

'You, Uncle?'

'I live a colourful life, Hope. Your mother only ever suspected the half of it or she would never have made me your godfather.' He allowed himself a smirk. He looked so smug I almost laughed.

'What was your relationship with my mother? Were you one of her suitors?'

The look my godfather gave me made me feel about two inches high. He paused long enough to ensure I felt extremely uncomfortable and then continued, 'As we were saying, Bernie. Girl has pluck. Smart, but not overly endowed with common sense. And she knows all the right people.'

'She's a great gossip,' I said.

'She can hardly knowingly work for the British government,' said Uncle Eric.

'As long as she has a good time I don't think she will ask any searching questions,' I said. 'What about Saulier?'

'Ah, he's working for us now. By the way, did you discover his mother was French? Both siblings were brought up abroad. Paul Saulier worked to lose his accent, and with a British father, conveniently dead and respected, the F.O. were foolish enough to take him on. So much egg on their faces.' He smiled blissfully. 'They didn't even know his father was half French by birth. Of course, his grandfather changed the name from *De* Saulier. Now, if anyone had had the sense to ask me . . .' He leaned back in his chair and gave a little chuckle. 'That'll show 'em,' he said more to himself than me.

'So he's a fascist?' I said in disbelief.

'Amazing what ideas get into foolish young men's heads when they attend second-class universities. Cambridge, naturally.'

'Oh . . . I take it you're an Oxford man?'

'I certainly wouldn't have let you go anywhere else.'

230

I digested this.

'Back to Saulier,' continued my godfather. 'He's ours now. He's not happy about it, but we gave him no choice.' He offered me one of the petits fours. 'Double agent. Nasty business. Never ends well. I'm not sure what upset him the most – being forcibly recruited by our side, or learning he wasn't as important in the organisation as he thought. Still, a small fish can be used as bait to catch something larger.'

I took it and nibbled on it. 'Mama did this kind of thing? With Papa?'

'Really, Hope, I don't care to repeat myself. If you work for me it will be more of a formal arrangement. Your father was only ever an amateur, although I advise you not to tell him I said so. He very much trained on the job, which in itself was only ever in a semi-official capacity. Your mother did have formal training, of a sort. You, on the other hand, have been groomed for spycraft since you took your first steps.'

'You never let me tell my parents about our little games. Did you get their permission?'

'Not exactly,' said Uncle Eric, not meeting my gaze. 'But they have always trusted me. I suspected your mother thought I might teach you a few tricks if she made me your godfather. Or at least I might use some of my formidable resources to look out for you. As it turns out I hardly think they would be happy if they thought I might be putting you in danger. Of course, I always do my best by my people, but I can't offer guarantees. Not even for you, my dear.'

'Wait a minute,' I said. 'You mean I'd be putting Bernie in danger without her knowing why? And Harvey?'

'Well, from what I understand, you pay Harvey to do dodgy tasks. He's a grown man and has probably taken greater risks than you ever will.' He sipped his coffee. 'Still, I've buried his police record. Clean slate and all that. You'd better warn him not to mess it up in Bournemouth. I'll give you his address.'

'And Bernie?'

'Consequences, Hope. And major ones at that. Her father, even

231

abroad, will carry some weight in political circles. But of course, she can always seek sanctuary at the Embassy.'

'They are sending us another ambassador?'

'I hope so,' said Uncle Eric. 'It may become important to have one on the ground.'

'But what would I be doing? Saulier is dealt with, and I can't imagine the same situation ever arising again.'

My godfather sat back in his chair and crossed his legs. 'My dear Hope, we are on the path to war. I can assure you there will be plenty for you to do.'

'Seriously?' I said.

Uncle Eric nodded. 'By the way, if you do come to work for me, I think we need to drop the Uncle Eric.'

'Just Eric?'

'No, far too familiar. Call me what everyone else in the business does.'

'What's that?'

My godfather gave me his enigmatic half-smile. 'Why, Fitzroy, of course.'